Matthew d'Ancona is Editor of the *Spectator* and writes political columns for the *Sunday Telegraph* and *GQ*. His two previous novels were published to critical acclaim. He has two sons and lives in east London.

Praise for *Going East*:

'From posh balls to seedy lap-dancing clubs, the rich diversity of London's life is brilliantly and exuberantly captured . . . You care what happens to Mia and because you care, you keep on reading.' *Sunday Telegraph*

'An intriguing cocktail of thriller, satire and love story. The book throbs with cleverly plotted tension.' Lucy Beresford, *Literary Review*

D1492961

Also by Matthew d'Ancona

Going East

The Jesus Papyrus
(with Carsten Peter Thiede)
Weidenfeld & Nicolson

The Quest for the True Cross
(with Carsten Peter Thiede)
Weidenfeld & Nicolson

Tabatha's Code

Matthew d'Ancona

Nothing to Fear

HODDER

First published in Great Britain in 2008 by Hodder & Stoughton
An Hachette Livre UK Company

First published in paperback in 2009

1

Copyright © Matthew d'Ancona 2008

A CIP catalogue record for this title is available from the British Library

ISBN 978 0 340 82849 6

Typeset in Monotype Sabon by Ellipsis Books Limited, Glasgow

Printed and bound by CPI Mackays, Chatham ME5 8TD

Hodder & Stoughton policy is to use papers that are natural, renewable
and recyclable products and made from wood grown in sustainable forests.
The logging and manufacturing processes are expected to conform to the
environmental regulations of the country of origin.

Hodder & Stoughton Ltd
338 Euston Road
London NW1 3BH

www.hodder.co.uk

For Teddy,
A great story-teller

The essence of human tragedy is in loneliness, not in conflict, no matter what the arguments of the theatre may assert.

Thomas Wolfe, '*God's Lonely Man*'

And you, most ancient sisters, decayed,
  deserted towers,
Have heard the whispered thoughts of hearts,
  beneath your crumbled bowers,
And beneath your clay lie buried deep, the
  vestiges that remain
Of Britons bold, whose lives were sold to
  make Old England's fame.

Richard S King, '*Herne Bay Humorously
Expressed & Illustrated*' (c 1890)

Part One

Ginny

I

'Well?' he said, calling up to her from the hall. 'What do you think?'

Ginny looked out of the window on the small landing to the garden: a long stretch of unkempt grass, the snaking path barely visible beneath the green tufts. A willow tree squatted lugubriously amid clumps of delphiniums halfway down the lawn. Beyond its moping branches she could see an old shed, its windows smeared and neglected. Nobody had lived here for a while. How different was the carefully-tended phalanx of cypresses looming over the fence on the right. Orderliness reproached the leafy chaos below her.

'Ginny?' Peter called again. She turned round to face him, wondering how he would react to her decision. She made her way down the stairs and touched his sleeve, signalling that she wanted to go outside, away from the estate agent, who shuffled and simpered in the adjoining living room, pretending to inspect the last remaining books on the shelves.

On the pavement, he lit up a cigarette and offered her one. She shook her head.

'I don't know,' he said. 'It's a bit ramshackle, isn't it?'

'It's certainly that,' she replied. 'That's not so important, though.'

'Are you sure? Do you want builders traipsing around for months while you're trying to write? And how much do you think you're looking at to fix it all up?'

She shrugged. The smoke, acrid and pleasant in the cool summer evening, made her want a cigarette, but she resisted. Of the four properties they had seen that afternoon, this was the only one that approached her needs. It was too big, probably, but she liked the idea of unfilled rooms and space in which to pace and breathe. The other houses had been more apparently suitable: two bedrooms, good repair, access to public transport, proximity to the bijou comforts of the literate middle class. They had the aura of respectability, the joists of a stable life ahead, the maturity of fitted kitchens and high-pressure showers that she knew that she ought, responsibly, to choose. She was newly single, a cash buyer, what Luke, the estate agent, called a 'seriously powerful player' – as if she were about to destabilise a national currency or wreck a presidential campaign. The sensible houses beckoned her towards calm, long afternoons at a newly-acquired kitchen table, and the leisurely baths of the liberated. But she did not like them. They exuded pity and a patronizing welcome that made her feel like a victim or a patient.

This house, in contrast, was pleasingly indifferent to her inspections. Tall, almost toppling, it towered above her like a muttering, distracted uncle unmoved by the return of a prodigal niece. What she most liked about it was the way in which it had wrapped itself in vegetation, ivies clambering up the front walls, behind hedges that were taller than Peter. The front garden was old-fashioned and must once have been a fine spread of rose bushes. Now, its minor forestry formed an assault course between the gate and the porch, from which stairs led down to a separate entry to the basement where the kitchen and pantry were. On the ground floor, two rooms had been knocked together and lined with book shelves – more than enough for her library – and on the first, there were three bedrooms. Up a further flight was a bathroom eccentric in its dolls-house scale. The attic had not been converted in spite of Luke's manic insistence that it was ripe for such a transformation – 'kids, and railways, and that' he said, as if she had a brood of children concealed in the car, desperate to know where they were going to put their huge train-set. But this was not a house for kids and railways. It was a house in which to live on one's own and find companionship in the creaking of bare wooden stairs after you have stepped on them; in which to learn not to find the dark frightening any more.

Peter, she could tell, was anxious because it was he who had spotted this particular property on the lists. He did not want his finger-prints smeared messily across a bad decision, or to let down his old friend and late-night telephone confidante. She recognized the fretfulness in his eyes, the furrowing of his brow and the dance of his finger-tips. He had wanted to be helpful. But he did not really want her to like the house, to make him somehow responsible for the next phase of her life and the unfolding of her little drama. Dear, sweet Peter: always there when you needed him, but never for very long.

'Give us a drag on that,' she said, removing the cigarette from his knuckles, drawing in the delicious smoke and letting it suffuse her for a moment. 'Well, I'm going to put in an offer now.'

'Steady on, Gin,' Peter said. 'You've spent less than an hour here. Don't you want to think about it? It's a bit of a wreck compared to the other places.'

'I know,' she said. 'That's one of the reasons I like it. Sort of a project.'

'More of a bloody liability. Let's ask him if there's anything else.' He motioned towards the window of the sitting-room from which Luke looked out, his salesman's rictus tightening as he saw Peter gesturing at him.

She touched his nose with her fingertip in a way she knew both annoyed and reassured him. 'Don't *worry*,' she said. 'It's my choice, not yours. Call it impulse shopping. I'll sign a disclaimer if you like.'

He laughed. 'Well, if you like it that much. But make sure you offer him at least ten thousand less than the asking price. At least. Please? It'll help me sleep at night. Well, sleep a bit, anyway.'

'Sure,' she said. 'Wait here if you like, while I put the wide boy out of his misery.' From the window, Luke grinned, the smell of a sale reaching him even through the glass.

By the time she got to the front door, he was there to open it for her, his clipboard clattering against the jamb as he did his best to conceal his excitement.

'Any thoughts?' he said cheerily. 'What does your partner reckon?'

'Oh, he's not my partner. He's just a friend – helping me house-hunt, you know? I'm no good with these things on my own'.

Luke put up his hands as if to say it was none of his business. 'Fine, fine. Nice to have the company, I guess.' The gel on his hair was unevenly applied, giving the right side of his head the appearance of a water-logged porcupine.

She cleared her throat. 'So. I'm thinking of making an offer.' She could see Luke's toes wiggle inside his loafers with Christmas-morning excitement. Otherwise, he maintained a semblance of cool.

'Great,' he said. 'Great. Finance, of course, is no problem with you. So – have you thought of a figure?'

She named her price. He nodded sagely. 'I know the Whittakers were hoping for the asking price. But I also know they want a quick sale. So I am on the north side of the optimism border. Let's see where we can take this. I'll call them now.'

Ginny wondered how often Luke found himself south of that particular border, trying to cheer himself up at the end of another day of lost sales and irritable clients. Today, however, he was heading north.

'Before you call them – is there anything I should know? Neighbours, and so forth?'

'Uh-huh,' said Luke. 'Well, I believe there's a retired couple on that side – quite pleasant, although I've only spoken to them once. And a young guy lives on his own there—' he pointed towards the house with the cypresses in its garden – 'and the Whittakers said he leads a pretty quiet life, out at work a lot, you know? So I think you'll find life here quite, well, *tranquil*, if you like.' He used the word as if it was an attractive fixture that would come with the property, at no extra cost.

'That would be good,' she said. 'I am planning on doing some writing, you see. It's just me and my cat. So it sounds ideal.'

'Good,' said Luke. He stood to attention. 'Well. Better make that call, eh?'

Half an hour later, she and Peter toasted her new home over lattes in a coffee shop nearby. 'So, Miss Clark. Congratulations on your new purchase, I suppose.'

She clinked her mug against his. 'Thank you. And thank you for helping me look around. It's impossible to do this sort of thing without moral support on tap'.

'You're happy?'

'Yes. Yes, I am. I need this, and the sooner the better.'

He smoothed his trouser seam. 'A room of one's own, eh?'

'Something like that. It's fine at Dad's, of course, but I need my own space. I don't have a prayer of getting on with the book while I'm there. He still treats me like I'm twelve, which is lovely in principle, but pretty gruelling sometimes. Fact is: I'm a homeless divorcee aged thirty-six, no children, one cat, and I can't still be living in the room I occupied when I was twelve. There's a Duran Duran poster on the wall, for Christ's sake.'

'Not your Dad's, I assume?'

'No, you fool. Can you imagine Geoffrey listening to Duran?'

'Planet Earth? Girls on Film? Not easily. Although hasn't he been going to those dance classes since your mum died?'

'Yes,' she said. 'But they're of the Darby and Joan, Strictly Buspass variety. You know – ballroom stuff at arthritic pace. Keeps him happy. No shagging, but the thrill of the chase. Or its distant memory. Something like that.'

'He'll miss you,' said Peter.

'I know,' she said, looking into the muddy surface of her coffee, and running her fingers through her blonde hair to the darker roots. 'And I'll miss him. But, in the end, we're an embarrassment to one another. Neither is quite sure who's meant to be looking after whom. He really tries, he does. But I don't think he finds me and Harry an easy thing to get his head round. He's the last of the Mohicans when it comes to marriage – thick and thin, richer and poorer, all that. I think he sees our generation as unstable serial monogamists who have no idea what's what.'

'Probably right. Speaking of the Prince of Darkness – any word from Harry?' She looked out to the street where a van-driver was engaging in an exchange of awesome verbal violence with a young woman in a hatchback. He spat on her windscreen, got back into his van and slammed the door. 'No,' Ginny replied. 'No. Only the last lawyer's letters.'

This was not strictly true. Harry had called her on her

mobile two days before, ostensibly to check a figure on the final statement of the soon-to-be-defunct joint account. Such exchanges – less frequent now, but no less bitter – followed a pitifully predictable pattern of escalation. With the formal business out of the way, he needled her about her house-hunting and mused on the number of days he must have worked to earn the money, net of tax, that she would be spending on her new home, if and when she found one. She could almost hear the algorithms of resentment fizzing in his brain. When this vicious little calculation was complete, she asked if there was anything else he needed to discuss and exploited a brief pause in his monologue to end the conversation. After that, she had wept only briefly – her tears no longer an expression of livid grief but a reflex triggered by remembered trauma.

From the pulp of a real marriage, most of it mundane, much of it bearable, some of it even enjoyable, the two of them had fashioned a terrible legend. Her life with Harry, all eleven years of it, now struck her as a warning to others, as much as a personal tragedy. A great lighthouse illuminating the sea of human emotion, warning the reckless away from the rocks. More than any relationship she could think of – although she rarely thought of any other – it captured the strange inability of human beings to escape that which makes them desperately unhappy; their delusion that they are performing to some sort of script; and their consequent, dismal limp towards disaster.

*

She and Harry had known each other a little before they started seeing one another: he was the friend of a friend, and an occasional spare male at dinner parties when she was similarly single. She liked him and his barristerial cynicism, suspecting it concealed a warmth that he deployed sparingly. She found him attractive in a distant sort of way, appealing rather than irresistible. When, out of the blue, he called and invited her to the opera – the earthy *Cavalleria rusticana* rather than the cerebral Wagner she might have expected – she accepted without dwelling on the extent of his intentions. And she had been surprised by how much she enjoyed herself, and by the solicitous way in which he asked her over dinner about her researches and the penurious life of a D.Phil student whose university peers were mostly earning decent money and settling down. He told her more about his practice, his chambers and the dysfunctional colleagues who made his working day partly intolerable and partly hilarious. He was not nervously intellectual, like most of the men who pursued her, but robustly clever, at ease with his intelligence and its material rewards. She found herself relaxing in the elegant comfort of his presence, a masculinity that showed no inclination to assert itself unduly. He was tall, unconventionally handsome and dressed with a lack of attention to detail that was endearing. He made her laugh. After dinner, he drove her home, and kissed her on the cheek with no hint of greater expectations. The next day, she called him and asked him to supper at her flat the following Saturday. This time, they were less reserved with one another. They awoke the morning after and realized without ceremony that what had happened was much more than a one-night stand, and could be pursued with pleasure, and perhaps love, on both sides. They were married in six months.

At first, life with Harry was rich. He was an attentive husband, unfailingly generous and often passionate. He did not parade her as a trophy, but he seemed touchingly thrilled by her presence at his side, and the speed with which they were welcomed into the family of established couples. They went on group holidays, some of which she enjoyed more than others, and, as Harry's career progressed and the prospect of taking silk before he was forty became real, they bought a little mews house in Hampstead. She completed her doctorate – a critique of Bettelheim's analysis of fairy tales – and pondered turning it into a book. Harry, of course, encouraged her, but lightly suggested that now might also be a good moment to 'kick-start a family'. And while she baulked at the phrase, which she felt made procreation sound like a business venture, she did want children, acknowledged the logic of Harry's suggestion and stopped taking the pill.

For the first three months, neither of them gave the matter too much thought, aside from the occasional aside about 'the little sod taking its time'. After six months, she became concerned herself and saw her doctor, who told her not to worry and to be patient. When she came back, fragile and uncertain, Harry soothed her and made her laugh. He told her that the doctor was right and that they must not succumb to the easy hysteria of imagined infertility. She kissed him and thanked him: for what Harry had, she realized, was a capacity to soar above the daily path and see the map of life in its entirety. He knew that they would find a way through soon enough, and because he was so certain, so was she.

It was precisely this capacity to think strategically that brought about a sudden change in him after they had been trying for a year. One evening, he sat her down and asked her with a gravity that she did not recognize whether she had considered going back to the doctor. She had, of course, and she did. And so began eighteen gruelling months in which the quest for a child ceased to be a business venture – starting a family – and became a miserable military campaign. Against her temperament, she found herself obsessively reading books on fertility and, at two in the morning, consulting obscure American websites offering miracles. Her academic vocabulary – the vocabulary of Jung and Freud and Zipes – was displaced by the medical lexicon that a woman is handed at the gateway of reproductive despair: luteal phase defect, basal body temperature, hyperprolactinemia, intracytoplasmic sperm injection, amenorrhea, hyperandrogenism. All these terms became familiar to her. She signed up for IVF treatment. She consulted an obstetric acupuncturist. She considered having her amalgam fillings replaced with porcelain, persuaded by a post on a fertility chatroom that this would increase her chances of what she and her fellow yearners in cyberspace called the 'Big Fat Positive'.

Always women, of course. The men – well, where were they? Where was Harry? Dutifully present at the joint consultations when necessary, an uncomplaining participant in tests when so required, a respectful sender of e-mails directing her to one weblink or another. Patient in the waiting rooms. But, in the end, this was not a problem shared. This was, he made clear with every glance, every stilted telephone conversation, every scientific appraisal of the latest odds, her problem, a problem that has linked every patriarchy and every culture in the history of man: the problem of the barren woman. *Barren*. Harry would never have used such a brutal word, perhaps not even have thought it. But the word hung between them like a sullen winged creature, pushing them apart and defining their respective loneliness. Hormones, ovulation, endometriosis: these were to be her department and her responsibility.

As eighteen months turned into two years, she began to feel the strangest sensation: close to bereavement, a sense of sadness for the children she would never have, children she could not even lose. She saw their eyelashes, imagined their tantrums, wondered about the first words they might speak. They clung to her legs and looked up at her insistently, puzzled at her refusal to let them become flesh. Never broody or especially drawn to children in earlier life, she had come to feel like a matricide, like a curse on the source of life. She was disgusted by her own melodrama, but no less disgusted by Harry's refusal to share her emotional spree with her. His recoil from her pain and her shambolic outbursts became less and less concealed as the months passed. What he had initiated as a sensible timetabling measure in their life as a couple had come to dominate and disfigure hers as a woman. And – dismayed at some primordial level by what he evidently saw as her failure – he wanted no part of it. She could see that his original delight in her had mutated into something approaching abhorrence. The problem with Harry was that he had always been too grateful to her for becoming his wife. Too much gratitude, she knew, was usually the precursor to resentment.

One night, he came home unusually early and asked to speak to her with a formality that left her in no doubt of what, in general terms, was coming. He started by saying that the last thing in the world he wanted to do was to hurt her, but that he could not lie to her either. She could see that he was wondering whether or not to take her hand. Having decided not to, he cleared his throat and said his piece. He was, he said, in love with someone else: a much younger woman called Estelle who had recently been offered tenancy at his chambers. Yes, she thought: *Estelle*. Of *course* Estelle. She remembered her from a dinner at Lincoln's Inn: not beautiful, by any means, but vivacious, smart and seductive. Wrapped in tight black dress that could barely contain her luscious femininity. *Fecund*. A balm to Harry's battered virility, no doubt, an easy solution to an elemental problem. Impossible to compete with, really. And as Harry continued his wearying explanation of how it had happened, and how he had cross-examined his feelings as closely as he dared, put himself in the dock, so to speak, she was already forming her plans to escape the dead thing that had once been their marriage. She was both baffled and pleased by her sudden ability to see what was required. All she needed was somewhere to live: let Harry and Estelle earn their money and spend it on themselves and the babies they would have, but let her have a place she might call her own where there were no thermometers, no graphs, no stifled monthly cries of desperation from the bathroom, no talk of consolation and trying again. The bleakness of the moment – all those wasted years! – was crippling. But she realized there and then, on the sofa, that she did not love Harry and had never loved him: not truly. For if she had loved him, she would not want to walk away. She would have stayed and fought. She would have sunk her claws into the rival at her door, invading her hearth. But she did not want to fight. She wanted, at last, to stop fighting.

'You're miles away.'

Peter interrupted her reverie. 'Oh,' she said. 'Yes. Well, it's a big deal, I guess. I've never bought a place on my own before. In fact, I've never really lived on my own. Not since university, anyway, which hardly counts.'

'Well, it loses its appeal after the first fifteen years, I'm afraid. But that's the difference between a bachelor and a divorcee. I don't know that marriage is a bad idea. But you already do.'

'I suppose at this point I'm meant to say that not all marriages are bad, only mine.'

'I believe that is your next line, yes.'

'I think I'll pass. Marriage probably is crap. Anyway, you're married to the newsroom.'

'I am,' he said. 'Saucy minx she is, too. And that reminds me. I have to go and see a man about a god.'

'God?'

'Fabulous voodoo nonsense going on round Vauxhall. Full-on *Angel Heart*, chicken claw stuff. Very nasty. Very good copy. That'll give me a lovely Saturday spread, if I'm lucky.'

'I see. Well, who am I to delay you from serving the public interest? Thank you for your time, Mr Byrne'.

He kissed her on the cheek and hugged her. 'The pleasure was all mine, as ever. Good luck with your new home and your builders.'

She smiled and dismissed him with a loving flick of her fingers.

She ordered another coffee, and surveyed her new neighbourhood. It was far removed, in every sense, from the perfect little village of Hampstead. The area was what Luke had called, with averted eyes, 'mixed': only two streets away from her new home was an estate notorious in London for its gang shootings and spectacular levels of social breakdown. She had seen a documentary on its pathologies and those who occasionally swooped upon it from Whitehall or town hall with this remedy or that gimmick. The house she had just bought was near the front line, in theory at least. Perhaps that was why the previous occupants had swathed it in garlands of greenery, building a fortress of vegetation that might not repel intruders but helped the house to recede from its urban setting, to withdraw into itself. It had stood unoccupied for almost six months, Luke said. It needed the warmth of a new custodian.

She walked back to the street and turned the corner. It wasn't so bad, really. Some children played across the road, shooting back and forth on scooters. A people carrier and a taxi tried to pass one another without grazing each other's wing mirrors, moving with the stop-frame stealth of the practised urban driver. The sun peeked over the roof, dipping towards the estate and the long, unfilled hours of summer evenings of six packs, and dancing, and spliffs on the bench. Looking past the post-box and the skip, towards her new home, she thought she saw a tall figure shutting the gate of the house next door, retreating down the path. It was hard to see in the glare of the sun, and it did not really matter, anyway.

Tonight, she would tell her father the good news and start to pack. There was no reason, Luke had said, why she should not have the keys by the end of the week. No reason at all.

II

'Sugar?' asked Audrey Benson.

Ginny was distracted by the spectacle of Roger Benson mowing the lawn. Raging in his cardigan and sweating profusely, he pushed the machine across the uneven grass with a toddler's lack of rhythm. Fronds of white hair, apparently stuck to his forehead, dislodged themselves at moments of maximum exertion, only to return to their original position at a leisurely pace quite at odds with his general fury. The task was one in which he invested great importance, Audrey said, and which he hated in equal measure. She kept out of his way on lawn-mowing days, knowing that even the completion of the job would not allay his anger and dissatisfaction. When he switched the machine on and pushed it awkwardly around the garden, he seemed to plug into some sort of subterranean river of wrath. In theory, he ought to have been a comical sight, but, in practice, his distress was compelling rather than funny.

'Sugar, dear?' Audrey asked again.

Ginny turned. 'Oh. Oh, no. Thank you. I was just—'

'I know, it's quite a sight, isn't it? Trust Roger to choose the day our new neighbour moves in to attack the garden.

He should be in here, meeting you properly. But he won't be told.' She sipped on her Earl Grey. 'Men are funny, aren't they?'

'Well, yes,' said Ginny. She took her cup and sat down at the long pine table.

'So, are you settling in?'

'Trying . . . I have more stuff than I thought and – well, it's rather difficult after a divorce. You know: boxes here, there and everywhere.'

Audrey frowned, but not, Ginny thought, with disapproval. She was a small, dapper woman with short grey hair, an elegant shawl and an air of precision. Her face bore the worry lines of one charged too often over the years with untangling the dilemmas of others. She did not exude the tiresome aura of sanctity, of a life unblemished. Only the knowledge of how complex the lives of others tended to be, and the burden which that knowledge invariably brings. Her two grown-up children, she had told Ginny with remarkable haste, showed no sign of weaning themselves from their parents' organizational and financial care. Her son, Mark, was in rep for an undistinguished touring company; her daughter, Fiona, a sales manager for an economy airline. Both were single and intermittently broke. Her own investments and Roger's were dwindling fast, as their children bit into the capital.

'Well, it must be hard, I can well imagine,' she said, squinting as though the imaginative effort was, in fact, huge. 'If Roger had left me, it would have taken me a year to clear out this place.'

'How long have you lived here?'

'Oh, more than twenty years,' Audrey said. She shuffled a salt cellar and pepperpot on the surface of the table, as if their respective positions represented a minor infraction of some domestic bye-law. 'I doubt we'll ever move, unless we get too decrepit. Roger would miss the lawn.' The two women laughed in hesitant conspiracy.

Audrey smiled as she finally set the cellar and pepperpot in their designated spaces.

'You were living in Hampstead, before, yes?'

Ginny saw this as her cue to deliver what she called her 'executive summary' of the divorce. This was a five-minute speech that gave friendly strangers or new acquaintances the headline facts and the illusion of intimacy, with none of the emotional truth. She had, she realized, become a master of euphemism, elision and other verbal tricks. She would say that she and Harry had 'drifted apart', agreed to 'try a separation' and that he had now 'found someone else' as if describing a sequence of more-or-less unconnected events and an outcome which, though regrettable, was nonetheless a model of civilized middle-class behaviour. She did not mention the time that, driven to distraction by the distance he was keeping, as he looked out of their bedroom window at a half moon of unusual brilliance, she had called her husband an 'impotent cunt'. Nor did she mention the night when he had drunkenly poured red wine on her desk with a smile of uncommon savagery. The septicemia within her divorce was concealed by her expert verbal bandaging, a skill she had acquired by trial and error and by watching others.

Audrey nodded sagely. 'Well, these things are never easy, I imagine. But it must be nice to be making a fresh start?'

'Yes. Yes, indeed. And meeting new friends.' Ginny raised her cup a little apologetically.

'New friends,' Audrey said. 'Have you met your other neighbours yet?'

'No,' said Ginny. 'Not yet. I don't even know who lives on the other side. At number twenty-six.'

'Oh, that's Sean. Nice young chap. Incredibly polite. Very shy, mind. I've barely spoken to him since he's been there – what, two years? Always about routine stuff, you know, mail, or a local petition, or whatever. Not a gossipy chat. I think he keeps himself to himself, mostly. Certainly won't be any bother, I guarantee that.'

'And across the road?'

Audrey shrugged. 'Mostly young families. Lots of newcomers I don't really know.'

She sniffed. 'But, all in all, it's a nice area. We like it.'

They fell silent. Embarrassment hung in the air for a moment.

'I like your kitchen,' Ginny said, straining for a new topic of conversation. 'Is it new?'

'A year old,' nodded Audrey. 'Very modern, I know. But I love to cook and needed new surfaces. Roger doesn't care and the old fittings somehow looked like they'd born the brunt of two children for too long. So I splashed out.' She beamed. 'Will you be making changes? We rarely saw the Whittakers, but the place has been rented for so long, I'm sure it could do with some work.'

'Well, yes,' said Ginny. 'I'm not sure where to start, really. My study, I suppose. I'm trying to write a book. Or at least that's the idea.'

'Heavens,' said Audrey, brightening. 'A novel? I love a good read.'

'No, sadly . . . Not much of a fiction-writer, myself. No, it's a rather dry book about fairy tales. You know, what they mean – the Brothers Grimm, and Hans Christian Andersen, and so forth.'

Audrey frowned once more, as if the intrusion of the academic to their conversation was vaguely improper. 'Good heavens. That sounds very impressive. What are you going to say?'

Ginny laughed. 'Well, I wish I knew. I have written about the subject before – for university work, and so on. But now I want to join the dots a bit more, try and work out what these stories really are.'

'Hansel and Gretel and Rumpelstiltskin, and all that.'

'Yes, exactly. All those stories we grew up with. Actually, I'm not sure children grow up with them so much any more. But for a long time, they did.'

'Oh, yes, well, I remember reading an article in the newspaper a while ago – what was it? Well, anyhow the idea was that fairy tales are really all about—' she whispered – 'you know, *sex*.'

Ginny nodded. 'Lots of people think that. I suppose there's something in it, although the people who say that tend to be the people who say everything is about sex. You know, this table, the kettle, the way people say "good morning". I'm not sure it's really as simple as that.'

'Oh,' said Audrey, a little deflated. 'I see. Well, then. What do you think they're all about? Or is it a big secret between you and your publishers?'

Ginny shook her head. 'Oh, no. No. What do I think they're about? Well, I'm not sure, really.' She nodded, as if in private dialogue with herself. 'Fear, mostly.'

There were thirty-five boxes in all, stacked in what would become the living room and she had opened only four. With Harry's grudging agreement, she had taken a few items of furniture from Hampstead – a Louis XV carved sofa, a bed from the spare room, her writing desk, kitchen table and chairs – but she craved space in the new house. It seemed irrational and pathetic to move from one home stuffed full of marital bric-a-brac, and to recreate the milieu – or half of it – in her new one. The point was to pull the guillotine down on that part of her life and celebrate the different character of the next chapter – whatever it might prove to be. From her parents' house, she had taken some of her mother's line drawings, and an oil painting of her paternal grandfather, resplendent in his mess kit.

There was a black and white photograph of herself and her parents, taken in the Dordogne when she was three. They formed a happy trio, the chiaroscuro of the fading summer light lending glamour to the youthful faces of her mother and father and the gleam of her smile. What, she wondered, had they been saying to one another as a friend took that picture? Was that a moment when, as in the negative and the surviving print, time had stood still, and the future had been kept at bay by the impregnable pleasure they took in one another and in their surroundings? Now her mother was gone and she and her father lived alone. If time stood still that amazing, sun-blasted day, it did not stay still for long.

Winston clambered on to a large trunk beside her, licking his lips after his late tea. He surveyed her benignly over his whiskers: a black and white king, blinking as if to signal his feline approval of his new domain. She stroked his brow, and he arched his head into her palm. He had spent most of the day sniffing and scrutinizing, padding from floor to floor, following her and then vanishing to explore some unknown crevice of the house. Winston had never liked Harry. Nor was he truly content at her father's house, jealous of the rival patriarch and claimant upon her attention. But he sensed at once that their new home was truly his own kingdom, and during the afternoon she occasionally saw the bushy pipe cleaner of tail disappear into the undergrowth as he pursued some imagined sprite, before emerging both scandalized and hugely pleased with himself. He found a dead mouse and presented it to her on the doormat, before she shooed him away, sending him scampering gleefully towards the fence. Now he purred in satisfaction at a good day's work and – by implication – a fine choice of home.

Unpacking the books filled her with a childish greed to reclaim what was hers. This was her real life story, from the battered Molesworth and child detective books via the novels of her teens, the showily modern fiction of university, to the more obscure literary theory texts of her research. There were junk books, picture books, oversized art books. Each was a fragment of her biography, a present, an indulgence, a long-awaited delicacy. There were plenty of mistakes in her library, of course: books un-read and half-read, books bought out of sentimentality, or on a whim at a station in a hurry. But they were important, too, mementoes of small failure and of caprice, of her dialogue with books over decades and her longing to keep them beside her, even the strays who sat awkwardly alongside the highly-strung thoroughbreds from the university presses.

From a volume of M.R. James fell a postcard from Harry: it was a familiar Klimt – even now, she did her best not to scorn the cliché of his choice – and the message read: 'I love you, H.' True? So hard to say. Still hard. Did he mean it at the time, as he wrote those words in his efficient, compressed hand, the calligraphy of the lawyer used to making notes in the margins of a brief? Well, once, perhaps, he had meant it. But, before long, what he – and she – had really meant by those words was: 'I love you, because I had a good evening'. Or: 'I love you, because you are so much less glib than the colleague's wife whom I had to listen to over dinner'. Or: 'I love you, because this white wine is perfect.' Or: 'I love you, because to say otherwise would be such a vulgar admission of defeat.' That fatal 'because'. When did Harry write those words on the card? In the kitchen after a row, or before one, or on a train exhausted from a case, or as he wrapped a birthday present for his wife at his chambers, his mind already dwelling on the long legs of his mistress in the room next door and the next hotel tryst, his heart pumping out the treachery as it prepared to move on.

Ginny knew that the shelves in the large ground floor room needed to be repainted, but she did not want to wait. For four hours she unpacked the book boxes and began, brick by brick, to rebuild the fortress of her inner life. It was a stockade whose structure only she understood, and that made her feel even more safe within it. There would be – had been – so many who said her life was in ruins, that she was gasping, airless, on the ground, a desperate woman fit only to be pampered and pitied. Poor Ginny! Dumped by Harry, and all for . . . well, you *know*. And how much more they would say that, when Estelle announced, as she surely would, that she was expecting Harry's baby. How grave they would all be as they considered the wretchedness that consumed their friend.

But Ginny's life was not in ruins. Already, under a naked light bulb, she was proving them wrong, restoring herself book by book, text by text. Soon, she thought, she would unpack her reading light, and her sound system, and she would play her music – hers, not his – and smoke an illicit cigarette. She would flick through the weekend supplements and contemplate a light supper and, eventually, go up to bed: the bed of an adult woman, not a child's bed, or a marital bed full of pain. Perhaps, she thought, in this new routine could be discovered the beginnings of a small triumph. Better, by far, to be alone than lonely.

She was summoned back from this inner audit by her mobile trilling. She answered it.

'Ginny?'

'Dad.'

'How are you, love?'

'Oh, fine. Shattered, actually. I've pretty much done all the books.'

'All of them? The ones from storage?'

'Yes, well. I thought, you know, why not?'

'Well, I admire your energy.' He paused. 'Everything all right?'

'Fine, Dad. It's a terrific place. I met some of the neighbours earlier.' She told him about the Bensons and embellished the story of Roger's grappling with the lawn mower for his entertainment.

'Your Mum was always one for talking to the neighbours,' he said. 'Never seen the point myself. I've always found it depresses me that I have ended up living where those sorts of people live, too. If you see what I mean. But I suppose that says more about me than them. Doubtless they feel exactly the same. *Mary* and *Michael* and their *fascinating cruise holidays*.'

Ginny laughed at his outburst of sarcasm. 'Well, she seemed fine. Audrey, I mean. I have to make a bit of an effort. Quite apart from anything else I need to butter up someone nearby in case Winston needs feeding one day and I'm not there.'

'How is the old bastard?'

'Fine. He sends his love, too.'

'Furry little brute. Never took to me.'

'Can't imagine why, Dad.'

'Cats have no sense of respect, you see.'

'Well, that's the point. Mum was right: freehold on dogs, leasehold on cats.'

'Yes, yes. I remember.'

'So. I'll give her a key soon.'

'Who?' At such moments, her father sounded like a baffled retired major propping up the bar at the golf club, rather than a university librarian of national renown who still worked part-time because his college had begged him to do so.

'Audrey, Dad. My neighbour.'

'Oh, the *neighbour*. Well, yes.'

'And Dad?'

'Yes?'

'How are you doing?' She realized even as she said it that the 'doing' was wrong, investing the question with too much emotional weight, making him sound like someone who had been recently bereaved.

'*Doing*? Oh. Well, you know, much as ever. Shame not to have you round the house, my love, but you are a big girl and all that.'

'I wish,' she said, softly. 'Love you, Dad.' In this case, there was no unspoken 'because'.

Ginny awoke early – Winston, usually up before her, stretched and muttered on top of the duvet – and walked over to the window to look at the street. It was too early for the kids to be leaving for school, but there were already some adults on their way to work, glazed eyes and hunched shoulders betraying the limbo which they still stalked, not quite asleep, but not yet alive to the perils of the day. Most wore headphones, an unambiguous signal that they did not want to speak or be spoken to. It was a five minute walk to the Tube, and the nearest bus stop was just round the corner. Like a herd of half-dead livestock, blinking in the unforgiving light of the early summer morning, they slouched towards the point where they would be picked up and carted off to unhappy destinations. A young man with dreadlocks dragged an old pram full of newspapers, delivering them from door to door, cursing softly to himself. An Asian man in a fleece jacket passed by with his daughter skipping ahead of him in her red school uniform. Cyclists in Lycra cruised past from time to time, a few with laptops strapped to their backs. For a while, Ginny watched the bad-tempered, high-tech human traffic and was glad that her days did not begin in this way. Winston rubbed at her legs. She bent down to pick him up, and he chirruped in pleasure. 'Silly old cat,' she whispered into his ear. She decided to make some tea, and get down to some reading then remembered that she had no milk.

She pulled on a T-shirt, sweatpants and baseball shoes, brushed her hair and put on her glasses. At the bottom of the stairs she looked up and saw Winston on the landing, preposterously haloed by the celestial light pouring through the tall window. He miaowed indignantly.

'You look daft, Winny,' she said. 'I'll be back in a moment.'

She stepped out, shut the door behind her and walked down the path to the street. It was still mild, but the promise of summer was vivid in the breeze and the clearing sky. It made her tremble a little, not from fear, but with anticipation. She felt as she had on summer mornings at home, when school and exams were past, and weeks of freedom stretched ahead towards a horizon so distant that it was impossible to believe that leaves would fall again, she would go back to the classroom, and the garden of childhood would become, with each passing year, smaller and smaller until one day she would find the gate locked. Now, for a moment, as a white van drove past her new home, she remembered those days and wondered if she might feel free in that way for a while, before autumn came again, as it always did.

In the corner shop she bought some milk and bread and a newspaper, resisted the strong temptation to get more cigarettes and asked if they could order the literary weeklies for her. The shopkeeper was amused by the request, but since his shelves included American *Vogue* and *Wallpaper*, alongside rows of celebrity and lads' magazines, she guessed she was not the first customer to make a peculiar demand of this sort. 'Whatever you like, miss,' he said with an air of mildly salacious conspiracy. 'Is no problem.'

Heading back, she wondered how many words she should set herself to write each day, or whether that was a foolish approach for a scholarly enterprise. No – the first thing to do was to settle her rattled brain, to find her intellectual moorings once more, and then to start at the beginning. She must first read, and then plan, and only then start to write, with no targets or false quotas. Her deadline was comfortably far-off, and her finances adequate for the time being. There was, for the first time in a very long while, no pressure upon her to perform. She could, at last, find out what it was like to live without the frictions and snares and lesions of another life alongside her own.

As she walked up the path she could hear Winston complaining at the door, and she smiled at his easily triggered grouchiness. She treated him like a kitten, but he was, in truth, a sturdy ten-year-old street cat, rescued from an abandoned box a few days after his birth and passed on to Ginny, a creature who loved only her and expected her company and attention at all times.

As she approached the porch, the door to Number 26 opened. The hallway within looked sepulchral in its gloom, although she caught only the briefest of glimpses before a young man shut the door behind him and ventured out into the light.

He was one of the most striking individuals she had ever seen. There was no single reason for this. But it was true, nonetheless. Most striking of all was his hair, black, cut short round the sides and fashioned into an old-style quiff, as if trimmed that very morning by a barber who had not changed his ways since the 1950s. His features were fine, and he wore large, black-rimmed national health spectacles which could not conceal the shyness of his brown eyes, lonely in a face of astonishing paleness. He was tall, and, beneath his old sports jacket, looked as if he might be powerfully built. But, as he locked the door behind him – three separate locks, each methodically attended to – she saw that there was no swagger about him, no physical confidence. Quite the opposite: if a back could communicate embarrassment and anxiety, his did. He was visibly agonized to be scrutinised while carrying out this private ritual, inspected by a newcomer, and she felt suddenly like an intruder. Flustered, he dropped his keys and then bent slowly to pick them up, his satchel almost reaching to the ground. He wore black jeans that had seen better days and a pair of old brogues. Even though it was warm, and likely to be hot by mid-morning, there was a pullover under his jacket, on top of a white shirt. He looked like a man who spent most of his time alone, inside the house. He looked as if he had been plucked from another decade and left heartlessly beached in the 21st century.

'Hello,' she said, finally. 'I'm Ginny Clark. I've just moved in.'

He edged towards her outstretched hand as if it might conceal a toxin that would consume his flesh. She had never encountered someone so slow to respond to such a straightforward introduction.

He slipped his grip into hers and – with a hint of controlled strength – shook her hand briefly and lightly. He smiled, but barely. His expression was one of kindly mystification, as if he had stumbled across a new species in the space between his front door and the gate.

She returned his smile, waiting for him to introduce himself. He did not do so, but seemed no more able to end the encounter. He was, she realized, awaiting her permission to hurry off as he evidently longed to do.

'I met Audrey yesterday,' Ginny said, finally. 'You must be Sean.'

'Yes,' he said, very quietly. 'Yes, I'm Sean.'

Faltering, unnerved by his presence but sorry for him, too, she heard herself begin to gabble. 'Please don't let me hold you up. I only wanted to say hallo . . . and it really is lovely to be here. A lovely area. It's just me and my cat. Winston. I think you'll find we don't disturb you very much. I'm writing a book, so . . . Well, as you can imagine, I'll be keeping myself to myself. You'll barely notice us.' Finally, she dried up again.

'Yes, I see,' he said. 'Please excuse me. I have to get to work now.'

'Of course,' she said, laughing. 'Of course, I'm sorry.'

He smiled again, more warmly this time – grateful, she presumed, to be liberated from an excruciating encounter – and loped off towards the gate.

'Nice to meet you,' she said to his retreating back. Then, more quietly: 'Oh, God. Why am I such a bloody idiot?'

III

It was a long bus journey to the cemetery, longer than when she had lived in Hampstead. But she did not like to leave too long between her little pilgrimages to the plot. When her mother was dying, of the cancer that her doctors had been convinced she had defeated eight years before, she instructed her daughter not to make a fetish of such visits.

'When I'm gone, I'm gone,' she said. 'Don't go trooping to a spot in the graveyard out of some mad sense of duty, because I won't be there, and it's not what I want. A cemetery is a place to put dead bodies, and that's all there is to it.'

Felicity Clark's hair was gone now, but it had once been a splendid mane of auburn, some of the original colour surviving even her first bout of illness. She wore an Aztec hat, given to her by one of the nurses who had taken a shine to her, and who enjoyed her robust sense of humour. She was determined, Ginny knew, that her daughter should not let her vivid imagination confuse her when it came to the matter of death. Felicity did not want to die, and made that very clear. But – if she had to die, as it seemed she did – she reserved the right to issue orders about how the whole thing was to be handled by her family.

'You should be thinking of Dad,' she warned, propped

up in bed on a mountain of pillows. 'He'll fall to pieces, but he'll tell nobody. Your big job, darling – your *only* job, apart from taking care of yourself – is to let him do so in his own good time, and then do your best to pick up the pieces. And, for God's sake, make sure he gets himself a fancy woman. Geoffrey's so bloody old-fashioned that I know he'll never get married again, silly fool. But I want him to have companionship, a bit of fun. Make him go on dates. Fix him up with your friends. Hire a buxom escort. *Anything*, darling. Just don't let him turn into a crappy widower. I would find that *very* embarrassing looking down from the Pearly Gates.'

Such conversations made Ginny weep and laugh simultaneously. She marvelled at her mother's clarity, knew that it masked deep fear, and loved her all the more for her capacity to put her loved ones first, even at the last. She herself was a long way from accepting what her mother had realised for a while: that time was short, and that all she could do was to fortify the love that she would leave behind. The manner of her exit, she said, was a matter of profound indifference: she would be, she very much hoped, 'doped up to the eyeballs' and had already identified a handsome young Asian doctor who, she said, was more generous with the morphine than were his colleagues. By the time she died, she said, pain relief would be her only concern, and anyone who tried to complicate the matter could go to hell. So it was important *now* to ready her husband and Ginny for what was coming, while they were all sitting in the departure lounge waiting for her flight to be called.

When that call came, she was asleep, and neither Ginny nor Geoffrey was at the hospital. Her 'turn for the worse' – what a stupid euphemism, Ginny thought – had taken them all by surprise. She would have felt no pain. She would have been completely unaware of what was happening. Ah, thought Ginny, the necessary lies of the medical profession: how could the doctors and nurses possibly know any of that?

How could they know what, if any, agonies Felicity Clark felt as she drew her last breath? How could they possibly tell whether she had been aware of her extinction? What enabled them to say, with such soothing confidence, that the switch of life had simply been turned off, that her mother had not been catapulted into some metaphysical realm quite unknown to science? Were there demons and angels quarrelling beside every deathbed, the smell of sulphur and incense at war as the portals of other worlds opened briefly to snatch a soul, or only the ticking of a clock, the scent of fading flowers, and the slow night-time groan of the other patients, as they shuffled up one place closer to the front of the queue?

Five years on, she had half-kept her promises to her mother. She had not yielded to the absolute despair that she felt was both inevitable and decorous: the thought that she would never again kiss, or be kissed by her mother was enough to trigger something that felt like dizziness and nausea. The notion that she would never share a triumph or a failure with Felicity seemed to bring to an end the meaning of her own story: for what was a story without an audience? Who would be her interpreter? That, in Ginny's eyes, was the true meaning of death: life ended when the listening ended, when the teller told her story only to a blank wall behind which lay a void without limit. The appropriate response, she felt, was to give up the ghost herself, to hide away in some hidden corner and wait to be swept away.

But that is not what she had sworn to her mother that she would do. By an extraordinary effort of will – by acting out a part she considered deeply fraudulent – she held herself more or less together and tended to her father, whose pride could not conceal the absolute devastation within. Rarely able to give voice to his profound love for Felicity, even when she was alive, he teetered on the brink of irreversible emotional aphasia. But Ginny, drawing on reserves she did not know she possessed, hauled him away from the edge. She knew that there was no point in confronting his pain explicitly. He could only be coaxed back to something approaching normality, shuffling awkwardly, sometimes retreating, but almost always responding, in the end, to his daughter's invitation. She saw him every day to start with, then two or three times a week, for many months. They went on drives, had pub lunches, tried out plays and films, laughed at the sharks in the London Aquarium. Some outings were more successful than others. But all this activity distracted Geoffrey from the inertia that suddenly came so naturally to him. It forced him to respond and to offer judgments, however glib. One day, as they ate Chinese food by the river, and discussed a future jaunt to Bath when Harry was busy with a huge case, she realised that she had found herself, accidentally, in the role of parent. She had been forced by circumstances to rescue her father from the infantilism of overwhelming grief. And so, unexpectedly, at the behest of her mother, she had become, if only for a while, something like a mother herself.

But she had not respected her mother's ban on visits to the grave. This, she felt, was still a matter for her. For all her rationalist certainty, Felicity was no better equipped than the doctors to know what survived of her, and where. And while Ginny did not imagine that some spirit-version of her mother hovered above the plot, swathed in white robes and celestial light, she believed in the symbolism of her visits and thought that it helped to formalise her remembrance of the person she had loved, and still loved, most. As the seasons changed, as she herself grew older, she could come here and feel security in her sadness, reassured that her mother's life and death had not been meaningless and that her visits showed that the bonds between people could, after all, survive mortality. On the stone were the words of Thornton Wilder that Felicity, in spite of herself, had given Ginny permission to use on her inscription: 'There is a land of the living and a land of the dead and the bridge is love, the only survival, the only meaning.'

She laid the tulips, a spray of yellow and white, on the grave, and stood back. The cemetery was quiet, a few elderly men and women making their slow observances in the morning sun. She looked at her mother's dates and wondered, as always, why it had not been possible for her to live another five years, ten, a hundred. She wondered about the capriciousness of disease and fate and pain. And then, to her shame, she felt glad, as she so often had, that her mother had not lived to be told that she would never be a grandmother.

It was, Ginny knew, a monstrous injustice to Felicity that she felt this way. Nobody would have been more supportive of her trials than her mother. She would have been the first to uncork a bottle of wine, say that children were a nightmare and congratulate her daughter on her splendid good fortune. She could imagine Felicity – never quite sure of Harry, it must be said – tearing him to pieces if she had detected even a hint of the misery to which he had subjected her daughter.

All that was true. But still Ginny was pleased that her mother had not had to deal with what she herself saw as a great lacking, a deficit and an unforgivable incapacity. As generous as she knew Felicity would have been, she was glad to have been spared that conversation. She had not had to say: I shall never be to anyone what you are to me. I shall never know how you feel, and have felt. I shall never travel down that road. Sorry, Mum: the chain of life ends with me, in my body, in my dying cells and disposable genes. The busy little chromosomes have hit a wall, and will die with me. My flesh is deaf to their story.

She sat down on a bench near the grave in the shade of

a tall oak and watched the leaves shiver in the whispering breeze. It was getting hot, and soon the graveyard would resound to the cries of kids taking the short cut to the shops during their lunch break. They would come back, laden with junk, and yell at one another, ticked off occasionally by a park attendant or a bereaved relative. As a lorry rumbled behind her, Ginny wondered idly what her mother would have made of her new neighbours, of the Bensons and of Sean: the pale young man who could hardly bring himself to say hello. She stood up and mouthed a silent farewell before setting off to the bus stop.

It was a matter of great, if illogical, irritation when she arrived home that the parcel was where she had left it in the hallway. Heavy and squat, it admonished her each time she walked past it. Winston's nose twitched with suspicion as he smelt it yet again. On the side, there was a large 'Handle with Care' sticker and another addressed in ugly felt-tip to 'Mr Sean R. Meadows'. It had arrived that morning and the delivery man had left her with no option but to take it. She tried to explain that Mr Meadows would much prefer to receive the goods himself, whatever they were, and that it would be quite inappropriate for her, as a very new neighbour, to take them.

What if they were valuable or needed urgently? No, it was quite out of the question.

The delivery man stood in his shorts brandishing an electronic box for her signature. He sighed in deep frustration.

'Then, man, he has to go to the sorting office to get it. You take it now, he gets it tonight. Crazy otherwise. If you aks me. Which you probably ain't.'

Ginny felt herself redden. 'I – it's just that I know he would prefer to get it himself. He is particular.'

'Listen, love, whatever,' said the man, mopping his brow. 'But if I was him, I would be seriously pissed off to find out that my neighbour wouldn't take my package, and then I had to go down special to the sorting office and queue, innit. I would say to myself: blood, that was an *unnecessary* journey. But that's only if you aks my opinion.' He smiled the smile of the pitiless logician.

Ginny felt sure that there was a good riposte, but could not think of it. She relented:

'Oh. Well, all right. I suppose—'

'Sign.' The box was pressed under her nose. She took it and scrawled a messy electronic signature. The man snatched the device back, and was gone before she could thank him, his heavily-loaded van careering down the street towards his next ill-tempered encounter.

So now the box was hers, until she could hand it to Sean. And what would normally be a simple transaction had made her feel uneasy and preoccupied. Twice she had thought he was in, plucked up the necessary courage, and knocked on the door to no avail. A day had passed, and the box remained in her keeping. She blamed herself for – for what? For looking after a parcel? No, for not trying hard enough. For being mortally embarrassed by their first meeting, his awkwardness and her flustered stream of consciousness. Shyness could be intimidating, and she realised that she did not want to expend too much energy on his apparent difficulty with human contact. Worse, he – or rather his pathology – was oddly intriguing in a way she would not have wished for: a dysfunctional neighbour was a distraction she did not need. Bland couples like the Bensons were ideal. She wished, in short, that he had been in when the delivery man had come, and that she had not been dragged into the whole wretched business. But he had not been in, and so his package was still reproachfully in her care, a reminder of how badly she had handled their introduction to one another.

The package was still in the hallway at six when Julie arrived. Her best friend was less concerned by its contents than by its rightful owner.

'Is he fit?' she asked.

'What?' Ginny said. 'God – certainly not conventionally so. I mean, he can barely talk.'

'Irrelevant,' said Julie, pouring herself a glass of wine. 'Men are better when they can't talk. Those that can, talk rubbish most of the time.'

'Yes. Well, he looks like – I don't know, a youthful Morrissey or something. Like he's stuck in the Fifties. Very strange. As if he's in black and white, somehow, rather than colour, if you see what I mean. In costume. I half expect him to start talking about VE Day or John Osborne, or something. Probably harmless, but – I don't know. A bit odd.'

'He sounds good enough. And young. What are you waiting for?'

'Oh, shut up,' Ginny laughed. 'What are you doing here, anyway?'

'I am paying homage to my newly-single friend's newly-opened and very impressive love-shack.' They clinked glasses. 'May it see more action than a bad night in Baghdad.'

Julie, as Harry had remarked, with increasing sourness over the years, was a non-negotiable part of Ginny. They had met in their first week at university and discovered instantly how little they had in common. Ginny was academic by inclination, born into a house where the *TLS* and *The New York Review of Books* lay on the table and expectations were high. She was inexperienced with men, a few unremarkable fumblings aside, and had yet to shed her earnestness. She still dressed with reserve, as if on a school trip. Julie had grown up in Hastings, prospered unexpectedly at sixth form college and got the A levels she needed to move up and on. When they first ran into one another at a seminar on *Beowulf*, she was in the process of dumping her boyfriend – not her first serious relationship, it transpired – who also happened to be ten years older, married and the father of a young child. Ginny found this entanglement and the contempt with which Julie was ending it extraordinary, scandalous and intoxicating. Julie, meanwhile, saw that Ginny was clever and warm, and might be an excellent companion if she could learn to relax. The differences remained, but a friendship of great resilience was forged in a matter of days, a splicing of two lives that seemed perfectly natural and perhaps pre-destined.

Eighteen years on, they were sisters in all but name, their love for one another punctuated by ferocious rows and occasional sulks, but as simple and strong as either could possibly hope as their lives grew ever more complex and precarious. At college, they had been inseparable, and had remained flatmates for a long while afterwards. As the years passed, they had grown into adulthood very differently: Ginny pursuing her academic path uncertainly and then firmly in Harry's shadow. Julie had trained as a solicitor – somehow, amid her weekend parties and multiple affairs – and eventually found work in the music industry, a berth that provided her with precisely the balance she craved between occasional excess and essential stability. She claimed, implausibly, to have made the intimate acquaintance of a very famous boyband member in the back of a taxi on the way home from the Met Bar: a story that became more lurid and hilarious every time it was told. This alleged encounter with 'Mr Download' and a string of other episodes – real or fabricated – had added lustre to Julie's legend and delighted nobody more than her best friend, who relished these despatches from another, demented planet, and the arch philosophy Julie had woven from her experiences.

'Anyway, I'm in such a *rush*,' she said, kicking off her high heels and tucking her legs beneath herself on the sofa. 'Supposed to meet Stephen in half an hour before dinner with the horrible Elliots, whom I wish would *die* slowly, but have to see once every two months. Supposedly because they're "really nice", but self-evidently because Stephen finds Sam Elliot *unbelievably* sexy, and wants to stock up on a few mental images of her cleavage so he can go and engage in bouts of furious self-abuse until the next ghastly dinner.'

Ginny sniggered at her friend's unapologetic crudeness. 'Wow. That seems a bit harsh. Stephen never struck me as the wandering type.'

'Trust me, love. There is no "wandering type". There's just the "male type". What happened to you is, I fear, what will happen to all of us, sooner or later, in one shape or form. In a way, you got lucky because you're still young and gorgeous, and have that recent divorcee tragic allure thing going that men go mad for.'

'Don't see many men going mad for it right now,' said Ginny

'Oh, shut up. Ah – I knew there was something I had forgotten to tell you. You know who was going on about you at Shoreditch House the other night, like a love struck teenager?'

'Who?'

'Kit Car Keith.'

Ginny laughed. 'Oh, terrific.'

'Don't forget, you *did* snog him twelve years ago. And for men, that's practically getting engaged. Oh – they say that they're sowing their wild oats, and shagging everything that moves, but the truth is that the minute a guy gets his tongue in your mouth, there is part of his brain that is athletically vaulting over the first shag, meeting the parents, the first row and that tense three-month anniversary, to marriage, children and affairs.' Julie drained her glass.

'You see, you can't *have* an affair unless you're married. Not a real one, that people will gossip about in a seriously nasty way. It's a logical necessity, you see. Men *have* to get married, so they can have affairs. It's the Nuptial Paradox.'

'So what you're actually saying – let me get this right – is that Kit Car Keith wants to marry me so that he can shag someone else.'

'In essence, yes.'

'Well, then, wouldn't it be more exciting to *be* the someone else? In general, I mean. Not with specific reference to Kit Car Keith. Who, incidentally, drools when he snogs. I remember that, even after twelve years.'

'How vile. And the answer is "no". The only thing worse than being a wife is being a mistress. Men make their mistresses feel special, but in the end they'll always go crawling back home: "I love them bairns, I do, let us in, please, I swear I'll never do it again" – you know. It's the way they're programmed. Harry is exceptional in this respect. Sorry to point this out, but it's true.'

'Oh, thanks a lot. And I still think you're being harsh on Stephen. You're not even married to him. Which suggests, according to your crazy thinking, that he is, in fact, completely honourable.'

Julie pointed at her, admiring her implacable logic. 'That *is* true, technically. Well done. But we're as good as married, really. It's been so long, he's probably forgotten we're not.'

After Julie left, Ginny decided to leave a note for Sean. Buoyed by her friend's presence, and several glasses of

Cepage Sauvignon, she scribbled a few lines, folded the paper over and, grabbing her keys, went outside. The evening was warm and it was still light, allowing a group of children to chase a football up and down the pavement on the opposite side of the road. They screamed obscenities at one another with an innocence that was almost poignant: they were raiding the verbal armoury of adulthood without the slightest idea how much damage they would one day do to one another with such words. The children piped down briefly as an elderly woman walked by.

She wondered if Julie would really hate her dinner party as much as she claimed or whether, once she arrived at the Elliots' house and got her jealousy of Sam Elliot under control, she would enjoy every minute of it, performing and charming her way through the evening until she and Stephen got a cab home much too late and fell asleep in one another's arms. Would it be like that? Was Julie's vision of couples in infernal captivity – cheating, lying, bored – an accurate one, or a creation of her vivid mind conjured up to make Ginny feel better about her solitude?

She made the detour to the end of the path and round into Sean's front garden. The flower beds were neatly tended, rose bushes clipped and cared for. For the first time, she noticed the riot of colour and fragrance, pinks and yellows and reds ablaze before the drawn curtains. There were orderly rows of potted plants and a small sculpture of a dove by the windows. She wondered who looked after the garden for him: it was hard to imagine him scurrying from his lair with a trowel and a watering can on a Sunday, risking the cheery hellos of passers-by and the banal chatter of his neighbours. No, somebody did this for him. Somebody who loved him, or felt sorry for him, or both.

She walked towards the porch and pushed the note through the letterbox. Then she spun on her heel, her conscience salved, and headed back towards the pavement. She had done her bit. He could pick up his mysterious package when it suited him – as she said in her note, she was usually in, and she left a phone number just in case he wanted to call before coming round. She, meanwhile, could wash her hands of a task that was in danger of becoming a serious irritant.

'Miss Clark?'

The soft voice was barely audible, little more than a whisper. She wondered if she had imagined it, but when she turned around to check he was standing at the open door, his face both appalled and beseeching. The uniform was unchanged, although his sleeveless jumper was now grey, rather than black.

'Miss Clark?' he said again, this time a little louder. 'I just got your note.' He waved it feebly. 'Thank you. Thank you very much. May I come round now and pick the package up?'

She sighed with relief. He had managed to speak more than ten words to her without running away. 'Of course. And please – do call me Ginny.'

This time his smile was broad and real. 'Yes, of course. Thank you – Ginny.'

He shut the door behind him, and laboriously repeated

the triple locking procedure. When he saw her face, he evidently guessed what she was thinking. 'Oh, I know, three locks. Well, I am a bit security-conscious I suppose. Sorry for the delay.'

He followed her around, and once more she was struck by his lope, the deliberation of his movement, as if he were thinking through each flex of muscle, sinew and bone. There was something compelling in his oddness. She sensed that it indicated, not a deficit of thought and feeling, but a surplus. He had the brittle countenance of a man who thought and felt too much for his own liking.

'It arrived yesterday,' she said as they made their way round to her house. 'I tried a couple of times – you must have been out.'

'Oh, yes. I was. Sorry to have inconvenienced you.'

His voice and manners were unplaceably English: they had been scrubbed clean by institutions – private school, she imagined from the accent – so his origin and character were that much harder to guess. It was a good camouflage. You could, she thought, hide anyone inside an Englishman.

'Here we go,' she said, opening the door. 'Only one lock. Not as careful as you. Perhaps I should be, these days.'

Her cat stood like a baleful sentry in front of the hall radiator. She expected him to miaow but he looked at them with deep disapproval.

'Don't mind Winston,' she said. 'He's a bad-tempered old man, but sweet underneath.'

Sean chuckled for the first time. 'I had a cat once. That was a very long time ago.'

'Oh, really?' she said. 'What sort?'

'Just a cat that used to come searching for scraps at my house.' He paused. 'I grew up by the sea.'

She tried to fathom this non sequitur, but thought it best not to press him on the matter. 'Look, there it is.' She pointed at the parcel.

'Oh, wonderful,' he said. 'At last. I've been waiting for these to arrive for a while.'

'Oh, I see,' she said. 'Do you mind me asking—'

'Oh, of course not. No, it's my painting supplies. I have a particular shop I like to use and they send me things when I need them. It takes a while, but it's worth it.'

'Are you a painter?'

He let out a shrill laugh that was laced with something that sounded like bitterness, as if she would somehow understand why that was a funny thing to ask him. 'Oh, no. Me? No. No. I am not a painter. No. It's something I do in my spare time, for pleasure.'

'That's very impressive. What sort of things do you paint?'

He recoiled a little, bathed in the half-light of the porch. 'Oh, it wouldn't interest you, Miss – I mean, Ginny. Nothing to speak of.'

'No, really,' she said. 'I'd love to see your work. It's something I wish I could do. Paint, I mean.'

He laughed again, this time more quietly. 'Oh, no. You're very kind, but really it's just something I do on my own, for my own satisfaction. I don't think they'd really stand up to much scrutiny.'

'Shame. My mother used to say that a work of art doesn't

begin to exist until somebody looks at it, or reads it, or hears it. Until that, it's a dead thing.'

'These aren't works of art,' he said, as if distinguishing one illness from another. 'They're paintings.'

'I see,' she said. 'Well, I'm glad you have your stuff now.' She paused, dwelt on her options. 'Would you like to have a cup of tea, or a glass of wine? The house is a tip of course, but you'd be very welcome—'

'Oh, no. No, thank you. That's very kind. But I – I have things to do, I'm afraid. And then another very early start for work.'

'Really? What sort of work do you do?'

He relaxed a little. 'Probably the most boring job in the world. It's computers and so on, and the hours are unpredictable. But it's only me next door, so I suppose it doesn't really matter when I come and go.'

'Yes,' she said. 'Well, I'm just getting used to that myself.' She noticed his puzzlement. 'Oh, I was married before, you see. But not any more.'

He frowned – at what, she was not sure – and then brightened again. 'Well, thank you so much for taking the trouble.'

She smiled. 'Not at all. My pleasure. Sorry you can't stay.'

'Yes. Yes,' he said. 'Well, goodbye, then.'

'Bye for now.'

Winston set off in suspicious pursuit of this unwelcome man, grumbling in furry displeasure, and she hustled the cat back into the hall. As she turned to shut the door, she looked out to see Sean halfway down the path, deep in thought, devoting every ounce of his energy to some inner task. Finally, he looked back. His face was like ivory in the fiery red of the fading sun.

'Thanks again. Well, I mean . . . What I was thinking was, perhaps I could come round for a cup of tea tomorrow?'

She smiled, nodded and closed the door.

IV

Once again, she was trembling: but this time it was shock, not the infinite possibilities of a summer morning, that sent ripples coursing through her body, her skin, her hair. It was the cluster of fears and the absence of language that follows an exchange of unambiguous brutality. It was Harry.

He called at seven, as she was preparing her supper: a tuna steak – with scraps for Winston – and a salad. She had poured a glass of wine, and lit a candle. Bach's Toccata in C minor followed her like a melodic spirit round the kitchen as she performed little tasks and bathed in the satisfaction of a good day's work. She had mastered a highly demanding offprint article, written in laborious academic prose by a psychoanalyst from Toronto, and distilled from it a comprehensible argument about the meaning of Red Riding Hood with which she now proposed to take issue. Beneath the cod-Freudian jargon lurked a wearyingly familiar claim about the wolf as sexual predator and the red as the blood of the violated virgin. It was all too simple, too pat. It projected adult concepts of sexuality on to children, which was half the story at best. It dutifully reproduced the arrogant assumption of a bearded man in early twentieth century Vienna that the sexual neuroses of his patients could explain all human history and myth. What it failed to do was to explore children's own perception of danger and fear, and their own capacity to strike back. This is what she would write in the morning: a thousand words, perhaps, around which, in time, much else might orbit.

Her mind was starting to fire with pleasing reliability. As she read, she no longer felt overwhelmed or merely supine: she wanted to challenge her precursors, to write something that was new and provocative, if not definitive. Her scholarly ambition was starting to stir – there were traces of vanity there, if she was honest – and she began to feel that the book, when and if it was finished, might say something that nobody had ever said before in quite the same way. For the first time in her life, she felt the incomparable intellectual thrill, often delusory but still overpowering, that she was entering *terra incognita*. The offprint had filled her with hope: it was the leaden product of a leaden conference, written by a man in an office churning out work to justify his university job. With such opposition, how could she fail?

Harry would see to that, if he could. When she picked up the phone, her stomach turned and her limbs stiffened as he announced himself. But, no, she thought, they would be civil, they must be civil. This need not be an ordeal, it was a necessary inconvenience, a procedure they had to complete. There was no need for rancour.

But Harry did not see it like that. He began by chastising her for failing to fill in some form or other, connected with one of their accounts. He said that she was – 'as *usual*' – putting herself first and, as well as taking him to the cleaners, making it impossible for him to get his own life in order. He asked how much longer she intended to 'torment' him and how much pleasure 'exactly' she was deriving from it. His tone was not one she recognised. It bore the strain of desperation, of self-loathing, and of a desire, still astonishing to her, to cause his ex-wife pain. He had called, not to resolve a dispute or to tidy up the last embarrassing trivia of a ruined marriage, but to dump his affliction on her, to see that she got her fair share. After a while, she fell silent: a woman standing on her own in a kitchen in need of decoration, with a cat at her ankles. Harry said that, however much she felt she had 'beaten' him, the fact would always remain that *he* had been the one to escape, to start a new life, and that he was determined to have that life, however hard she tried to thwart him. Was it worth saying that she did not want to stop him doing anything, that she wished only that he would leave her alone, and that the idea that she had 'beaten' anyone was pitiful? Was it worth rising to his challenge, and besting him with calmness and rationality? Perhaps she would think so at three in the morning, when she woke up full of rage and righteousness. But – at that moment, in the basement of her new home – she barely had the strength to stand, startled as she still was by the enervation that consumes two people when love ends, when their bond is disfigured into a rusty chain of dismay and resentment. She did not have the energy to speak the truth to Harry, or to speak at all. After a while, scornful and rambling, he hung up. She sat down at the table.

After a while, she was able to stand and began to pace the room. Five, ten, fifteen paces, don't stand on the cracks, the bogeyman is coming for you. Three, four, lock the door. No, this would not do. She needed air and company and irony. Winston looked up at her, solicitous and confused. She called Peter on his mobile and arranged to meet him at a pub a short walk from her house which, by coincidence, they had been to before, and she knew that he liked.

'Christ, what a day,' he said, dumping his briefcase and laptop on the stained table. 'Bloody hell, you look terrible, Gin. Sorry – I mean, but you do.'

She stood up and held him tight. He patted her on the back and said 'there, there', with the charm of a man whose very incompetence in such situations is accidentally soothing. She tried not to cry and – mindful of the other punters staring at her over their pints – pulled herself together and sat down.

She blew her nose. 'Bloody hell. He's *such* a sod. I don't know what to do. The problem is that, even now, he knows which buttons to press. It's infuriating. You can't live that long with someone and not be vulnerable to them.'

'And he to you, of course,' said Peter, draining half of the pint she had already bought for him. 'Wow. Needed that.'

'Yes, but the point is, I don't want to play mind games with him any more. I've got the new place, work, all that stuff. I just want to get on with things, you know? It's as if he wants to haunt me, or something.'

'Possibly. My guess, for what it's worth, is that all is not well. As a jaundiced observer of the human condition.'

'What do you mean?' she said, trying not to sound too obviously pleased.

Peter drained his drink and licked his lips with deep satisfaction. 'Well, look. I mean, I know Harry only through you, of course, and I don't know his temporary bit of stuff, but I've known you on and off a very long time, and it's profoundly obvious that he's full of regret and, more to the point, that things aren't working out with, er—'

'Estelle.'

'Estelle. I was going to say Esther. Same concept, really. Yes, I mean, Estelle fulfilled a certain, shall we say, function, but, frankly, the idea of the two of them in any long term arrangement is patently hilarious.'

'Why? Isn't she what he wanted all along? Young, obedient, presumably fertile.' Peter laughed. His temples, greying now, twitched when he was amused. Though his suit was shabby as always, he retained a certain poise that somehow survived his shambolic choice of clothing. Slender, with craggy, weather-beaten features, he had never wanted for female company, but had always crept away from anything that had the whiff of commitment. He loved his job, life on the road, and the reporting role that he refused to give up, in spite of many invitations to become an executive on rival papers. He had written books on the stories he covered, ghost-written others for his contacts, and made a name as one of the foremost journalists of his generation. He was, she thought, one of the few people she had ever met who might claim, reasonably, to be happy.

Peter, like Winston, was a stray who had slipped into her life and never left. She met him through a friend of Julie's at a party and they had talked long into the night. To her surprise, neither was particularly attracted to the other, and, apart from a goodnight kiss that went slightly wrong early in their acquaintance, neither had made anything approaching a pass. Julie said that Peter's lack of interest in her was a profound insult, and that she should have nothing more to do with him unless he could provide documentary evidence that he was gay, and could help her choose shoes. Since he had recently split up with a Czech model of great beauty, this seemed unlikely. And, in any case, Ginny was not drawn to Peter as a potential lover. He was too obviously wayward in matters of the heart, and did nothing to disguise this. But she found his company hugely congenial and the chance to confide in a man who led a life so different from her own both exciting and comforting. After a while, Ginny realised that Julie's hostility was that of a challenged sibling who feared that she was about to be supplanted. Peter did indeed become like a brother, but was no threat to Julie. And in a splendid, quasi-incestuous twist, Julie and Peter had a very drunken one night stand after a New Year's Party thrown by Harry and Ginny: an incident that neither was inclined to repeat, but that neither seemed to regret, either. From Ginny's point of view, it was an ideal outcome: having spent a night of passion together – or whatever it was – her two best friends felt they could never moan to her about one another. Thereafter, Peter and Julie maintained a respectful distance at social events, nodding like war veterans across the crowded sofas and forests of bottles.

Peter continued: 'If I know Harry, he'll want more. I mean, he's a walking mid-life crisis. Part of him will want you back.'

'*Never*,' she hissed.

'Of course, you won't take him. But that won't stop him brooding on it. And part of him will be bored with Esther already.'

'Estelle.'

'Exactly my point. Even her name is forgettable. It blurs in the brain. You can't read it. The letters melt into one another. It won't do.'

She laughed and fetched more drinks.

'How was your day?' she said as she set his second pint in front of him and sipped her vodka and tonic.

'Madness. A murder trial is starting next week and, if the defendant goes down, we want the wife to tell the true story of her life of hell. But the solicitor isn't letting me get near enough.'

'What did he do?'

'Oh, he's what my Mum used to call a proper caution. The Bexhill Beast. Broke into a house in Battle, and sliced up a whole family for no reason at all. Pure psychosis. Stopped taking his medication, slipped through the bureaucratic net. It'll be a huge scandal.'

'Bloody hell. How grim is that.'

'Grim. The forensics are not pretty.'

'And how do you get your hands on those, pray?'

'Ways and means, ways and means.'

'And how do you sleep at night?'

He laughed, and raised his glass. 'Chin chin.'

She savoured her drink as he knocked back his. 'Anyway, Pete. I think one of my neighbours is a loony.'

He wiped his lips and set his glass down. 'Oh, really? I thought that spiv estate agent said they were very quiet.'

'Oh, he's quiet all right. The bloke at number twenty-six. Sort of old-fashioned looking. Quite young. Tall.'

Peter shook his head. His eye wandered to the bar where a young blonde woman was drinking alone. 'I didn't see him.'

'Honestly, Pete. Will you pay attention?'

'Sorry. Yes. Bloke next door. Possibly mad. Very quiet.'

'Well, not necessarily *mad*. Just a little bit – well, *other*. As if he were acting out a part rather than a real person.'

'Intriguing. Do you like him?'

'Bit hard to say. I mean, I suppose he is a mystery, which has a charm of sorts. He is threatening to come round tomorrow for a cup of tea, so all may be revealed.'

'And so far?'

'Only weird little scraps. He likes to paint, but won't show anyone his work. He says he used to live by the sea, but won't elaborate. Oh, and he used to have a cat. He ran a mile the first time I spoke to him.'

'Sounds like care in the community to me.'

'In a house like that? Give me a break. No, he has a job.'

'He paints mugs at the day centre and sings Kum Ba Ya after lunch with a care worker called Trevor who has a stutter.'

'Don't be so nasty. No, he's in computers, whatever that means.'

'Anything from Steve Jobs to a brainless operator, I would imagine.'

'He talks very properly. Can't quite work him out. Winston can't stand him.'

'Spooky. Well, report back. Nice to know that you have a new project.'

She examined her drink, the fingerprints left on the glass. 'Is that what it is? God, I do hope not.'

By noon the following day, she had completed 1,000 words undermining the glib assertions of Professor Toronto. Her prose, she realised, was still too breathless and self-satisfied: she needed to cultivate the laconic style of the true academic assassin. But that would come in time. On the screen were the first fruits of her labours and of her independence. If she had had champagne in the house, she would have cracked it open and toasted her achievement. Instead, she sat in the garden with a mug of tea and Winston on her knee, surveying the willow. Harry's phone call now seemed a distant, if still unpleasant memory, the wound cauterised by Peter's company and his refusal to see his friend traumatised any further. It was odd that an unkempt journalist celebrating the approach of middle age with an extra pint a night should have become so talismanic, such a reassurance against the gales of fortune: but so it was proving. Julie's unlikely pearls of wisdom kept her from taking herself too seriously. But it was Peter who protected her against the demons, who seemed able to dismiss them with a shrug of his shoulders. For all his apparent haplessness, he possessed a powerful spirit, and one upon which she had come to depend. He would drift in and out of her life, as he always had, but when the darkness fell, she could rely on him to keep it at bay.

She dozed on the little patio, allowing the sun to lift her up and away. Dreams came and went. She saw Harry's face, first that of the young and solicitous groom, then a caricature of what he had become, hirsute and snarling. It was as though all pity had been blasted from his soul, and had left him in a desert of rage and bitterness. She saw Audrey Benson's features, her nod and her bland smile and the comic anger of her husband. Her father drifted in and out, sad now and troubled – troubled, he said, without his lips moving, by yet another desertion, by the disappearance of mother and daughter, and the recognition that he would live out the rest of his years alone, knowing that he was about to die because he would suddenly be surrounded by people once again. Then, briefly, Sean, pale beyond life, pale beyond death, the eyes of someone forever hunted, unable to speak the truth.

When she awoke, it was already three. A distant siren declared the city's thousand-year insomnia, its defiance of sleep, day or night. Somewhere, perhaps not so far away, something bad had happened, something for Peter to write about, for Harry to take to court, for Julie to dismiss with the bravado of the citizen-soldier who toasts the savagery of London every day. It was a mercilessly hot afternoon. The trees in her garden seemed to stoop under the oppressive sun, as though they were on the verge of desiccated collapse into a million dry shards. Plants wilted in their pots: she must, she thought, give them water in the evening when it was cooler and she could face the effort. Slow and slothful, she went inside and took a shower, her second of the day. The cold water brought her body back to life, restoring the energy that the sun had extracted from her pores as she slumbered. Braced and revived, she went upstairs and changed into a loose red cotton dress. The air was fragrant with the perfumes of the flowers from below: roses, mingled with the sharper scents of the blossoms in the Bensons' garden.

He arrived just after four. The air was still thick with summer heat, and, in spite of the hour, teatime seemed a long way off. But there he was, on the porch, in shirt and jeans – no pullover this time – blinking, it seemed, at his own impertinence.

'Oh, hello, Sean,' she said.

He started to apologise at once. 'I'm sorry. This is probably a bad time, I'm sure you're busy. I—'

'Of course not. I've stopped work for the day. Come on in.'

He crossed the threshold as if entering another world,

looking up and around at every detail. His thumbs were hooked awkwardly into the pockets of his jeans.

'Did you ever see the house when the Whittakers owned it?' she asked.

He was distracted. 'The Whittakers?'

'The last owners.'

'Oh, no. They had tenants, of course, a family with two small children. They were always very busy. Once, I think, they asked me to let the gasman in. And their children trick or treated me at Hallowe'en.' He smiled. 'But that was it. They moved on and the place has been empty for six months.'

She beckoned him downstairs into the kitchen. His nerves seemed a little more under control. The fearful, asocial man she had first met was now merely blinking like a boy sent next door on a forbidding errand. She was determined to put him at his ease, to find out what his anxious reticence concealed.

'Tea?' she said.

'Oh – please.'

'I've only got builder's tea. Nothing more fancy, I'm afraid. Hope that's okay.' She waited for the kettle and put biscuits on a plate as he looked around, examining the few possessions and keepsakes she had put up: framed pictures of holidays, a snap of Winston taken by Julie, a wedding picture of her parents: handsome, groomed and serious, stiff with ceremonial propriety.

They sat down awkwardly, she with her legs stretched out and her bare feet on a chair, he more formal with both hands on the table, facing one another.

'So, Sean. How come you're home from work so early?'

'Oh, like I said, my hours are pretty flexible. I mean, I can't exactly come and go as I please, but they – my bosses, that is – don't hold me to strict hours.'

'Why not? Isn't that inconvenient if you're running a business?'

'Yes, but what I do is quite technical. I write software, and so I really have very little to do with other people at the firm.' He smiled, and she noticed that his teeth were near-perfect, as if they had been tended by an expensive cosmetic dentist. 'Well, I'm not the most sociable person in the world as you've probably gathered, so they're not missing out on anything much.'

'I see. So where is your office?'

'Near Chancery Lane. I like it because I can get there by bus, and the service runs round the clock. I sometimes go in at three in the morning if I can't sleep and I just blitz my next project.'

'Does it get lonely?'

He considered this. 'Not the work, no. It's solitary by definition. The less interruption, the more exciting it is. When I'm here at home, I tend to do my own thing: painting or reading. Some people find that odd.'

'Well, I suppose the world pretty much divides into those who can stand their own company, and those who can't.'

'I read somewhere,' he said, 'that the world divides into people who divide the world into two kinds of people, and those who don't.'

'Very clever. Who was that? The Dalai Lama?'

'No, Stephen Fry, I think.'

For the first time, they laughed together. He made a little more sense now, this curious recluse in her kitchen. His oddity, she guessed, was an oddity of intellect, of a mind coursing with thoughts and always in need of serious occupation. She could imagine him sitting alone in a cubicle at his workplace, brow furrowed, charting the digital world for hours on end, a pioneer in cyberspace scouting out terrain for the untalented and mediocre millions who would follow and think themselves clever as they used his programmes. Sean was the 21st century counterpart of the medieval illuminator, hunched over his parchment, working his magic until the candle flickered out and he was called to vespers. He lacked only the tonsure of the modern monk, working in the holy ether of data clouds and wi-fi.

For the first time, as she considered the shape of her own days, she wondered whether Sean looked at her, and thought her no less an oddball. A divorcee with only a cat for company, working at home, and as nervously garrulous as he was nervously tongue-tied. What right did she, of all people, have to look into the mirror and say 'normal'?

Winston crept into the room, scrutinising Sean with the deepest scepticism, slinking alongside the cupboards with melodramatic caution. 'What do you do?' he asked. 'For work, I mean.'

She explained the ideas she was pursuing, and her plans for the book. She even told him a little of her one-woman conquest of Toronto that morning. Like a marionette brought suddenly to life, he became animated and engrossed; it was as though her revelation of a cerebral life had liberated him, and made him feel safe. She was touched by his absorption, by the brightening of his eyes, and by the flick of his dark hair.

'But that's so interesting,' he said. 'You really are at the coal face, aren't you?'

'How so?'

'Well, a fairy story is more than just a story, isn't it? I mean, it comes from deep within the human psyche. It must tell us something about what we all share and fear. Although I've no idea what.'

'That's very *Jungian*. The collective unconscious, you mean?' She felt like a flirt as soon as she had spoken: he would think her too arch, too much of an intellectual floozy.

'Well, I don't know that I'm qualified to use that label,' he said. 'Jung, Freud . . . that's more your field. But there's obviously something in the idea that these tales flow from a common source.'

'Yes,' she said, reassured by his response. 'More tea?'

He nodded.

'But what is the common source?' she said. 'That's what interests me.'

'What do you mean?'

'Well, the assumption is that fairy tales are essentially lessons in life devised by adults. A means of conveying a fundamental moral or psychological truth to children by repetition and fantastic imagery. And that may be part of it.'

'But?'

'But – well, what if at least a part of the fairy tale tradition reflected psychological traffic going the *other* way? What children dreaded or dreamt of, what *they* told their parents, rather than the other way round.'

'Why would that be important?'

'Because if the stories came *from* children, at least in part, they tell us something about what it is like to *be* a child. Not just what it is like to be a son or daughter, and subjected to ritual education in life by your parents through an inherited narrative. But some of the things that children actually fear in the world, the things they see, the conclusions they draw. Things we adults have forgotten about, or chosen to forget about.'

'Give me an example,' he said.

'Well, take Little Red Riding Hood. Now, for ages, everyone has bought into the idea of the story as a coming-of-age warning to young girls: keep away from the wolf, or lose your chastity. The blood of the hymen, all that.'

'Yes, I've read that.'

'It's pretty orthodox. Not to say boringly salacious. But what if the story conveys a much more basic, savage truth: the way children see the dangers of the world, and the treachery of adults. Or The Three Little Pigs: it has a happy ending, sure. That was the adult contribution, no doubt, the working out of the problem. But the core image is still that of the weak always facing attack from the strong. I find that just as compelling an explanation.'

Sean warmed to her theme. 'So – if you're right – these

aren't just messages from adults to children. They're warnings from children to children.'

'Precisely.'

He sat back, and mused on this. 'An alarm bell from an ancient nursery. A distress signal from the cot.'

'Yes, exactly,' she said, delighted by his enthusiasm. 'Sent down through the centuries, countless generations, collected in books, and still used now. You know, Lewis Carroll said that a fairy story was a "love-gift". But I don't think that's all they are.'

He took off his glasses and breathed on the lenses. Without them, he looked even younger, though his features were stronger than she had first thought. 'So how are you going to prove all this?'

She smiled. 'I have no idea, Sean. But it's worth a try, isn't it?'

He nodded and returned her smile.

They sat in companionable silence. After a while, she said: 'Look, are you hungry?' He leaped to his feet as though she had uttered an obscenity. His face was suddenly stricken, the face of the inconsolable child confronting the intolerable. His shoulders heaved in a spasm of misery. 'Oh, God,' he whispered. 'I'm late. I can hear . . .'

'Oh, sorry. I didn't mean—'

'I must go, I must go.'

'Of course. I'm so—'

He looked at her, abject in his suffering. 'I must go.' He turned on his heel, clattering awkwardly against the chair, and strode frantically from the room, up the stairs, and out of the house. She heard him shouting apologies as he ran down the path, absolute, unconditional expressions of sorrow to someone else unseen. She heard another voice – the voice of a woman – and then the groan of the gate. Ginny walked to the window and strained to see who had spoken to Sean, what he was late for, what had shattered their conversation so completely. She wanted to know who the woman was and why, at that moment, when he had seemed so engaged and articulate, he had become so agitated that he could not even say goodbye to her. But, through the shutters, in the late afternoon sun, all she could see were his disembodied white knuckles gripping the door as it closed, as though he had been dragged into a house of gingerbread under a witch's cowl.

V

As she wiped the blood from the wall, she realised that it was a full week since Sean had bolted from her house. Seven otherwise normal days, with moments of terror as their book-ends.

The day after he fled she went to Oxford for a seminar on Spenser, and stayed overnight in a friend's house so that she could work in the Bodleian the next day. Her books took a while to find their way up from the stack, and she dawdled in Blackwell's across the street and then ate a pub lunch in the King's Arms. Killing time, she wandered around Radcliffe Square, and watched the students shoot past on their bikes, bumping along on the cobbles, mobile phones pressed to their ears. They gathered in gaggles on the steps of the Radcliffe Camera. The sound of laughter echoed across the walls of Brasenose, and cigarette smoke filled the air. She did not remember it being so easy. Perhaps it only looked easy now. Perhaps her memory was correct and the apparent innocence of these young people – my God, so young! – masked the turmoil and equivocation within.

Her books did not arrive till late afternoon, and so she ended up staying three nights on her friend Abigail's couch.

In the evenings, they walked arm in arm into town and ate at a converted bank on the High Street which was now a busy restaurant. They toasted Ginny's independence, and giggled over red wine as they recalled ancient escapades involving men and drink. Abigail was now a tutorial fellow at Keble, an early modern historian who was earning plaudits for her articles and her yet-to-be published thesis on religion and the English gentry. Uninterested in her own appearance, and a little gone to seed, she was still recognisably the feisty redhead of their undergraduate days. She had recently turned her back on men altogether and taken up with a dour Portuguese postgraduate called Anna. Ginny envied Abigail's application and her sense of purpose. As much as her old friend rained down encouragement upon her, the contrast between her grounded academic ambition and Ginny's fledgling project could not have been more stark. Abigail was set on a course now that would probably lead her to a chair in a provincial university, too many committees, and a measure of academic acclaim. Her home in middle age, wherever it was, would be a tumbledown sanctuary full of cook books and candles and godchildren. She and Anna – or more likely, one of Anna's successors – would lead a contented life, thanks, Ginny believed, to Abigail's fearless navigation in these perilous years. On the last morning, Abigail drove her to the station. They parted company tenderly, and agreed that the girls should come down when term was over for a London break and take advantage of Ginny's spare room. Even as they made this pledge, Ginny knew from Abigail's smile that she would not keep her promise.

Julie called that afternoon, as she was taking desultory notes on a scholarly edition of Hans Christian Andersen, and Winston was starting to forgive her for the outrage of her absence and Audrey Benson's fumbling attempts to befriend him on her twice-daily feeding visits.

'I'm bored,' said Julie. 'Nothing ever happens.'

'I thought you were constantly fending off pop stars and living a life of shameless excess.'

'That's what you all think. All of you out there in the crowd. But, let me tell you, showbusiness is a cruel trade. Ninety-nine per cent of our lives is hard work. Ask Madonna or Justin.'

'You're such a tart.'

'You're such a bluestocking.'

'Will there be anything else?' asked Ginny. 'Or shall I just get room service to send up Brad Pitt with your usual medication?'

'If you would.'

'It's done.'

'Much obliged,' said Julie. 'How's your life?'

'My brain hurts. Been in Oxford swotting and listening to a pair of dykes talk about organic food and sustainable energy. All this academia is too demanding. I need to get out more. Experience life. Mind you, my mystery neighbour provided some top psychological material before I left.' She brought her friend up to date.

'So,' Julie said triumphantly. 'The loony clearly has a crush on you.'

'I wouldn't go that far.'

'Such a revealing response. You bat back my claim, because you do not want to discuss it, yet you do not deny it because, secretly, you want it to be true.'

'You're mad.'

'Again, a non-denial. Another tell-tale sign. You like him. Oh, yes, indeed.'

'I don't think so.'

'Fascinating. *So* ambivalent. I will have to come round and inspect him soon.'

'He'd run a mile from you, you gin-soaked harlot,' Ginny laughed.

'Better and better. You won't even let your considerably more attractive, liberated friend near him, lest, bowled over by her model's legs and bee-stung lips, he ask for her phone number and attempts desperately to seduce her. You fear that, only a week from now, he and I will be enjoying a mad lunchtime session in a West End boutique hotel. So am I not good enough for – what's his name?'

'Sean,' she said. 'Now, would you mind fucking off and letting me get on with my work?'

'Not at all. It's been a pleasure. Goodbye – and good luck.'

Distracted, she could no longer face the annotated Andersen and its dense references to Italian and German monographs. She picked up a random volume from the pile of story collections on her desk: *Our Favourite Nursery Tales*, a 1930s treasury of indifferent design and painfully bowdlerised prose. Flicking through the pages, she wondered whether the child who had first listened to these stories was still alive, elderly now. Would that frail man or woman remember the tale of Cinderella and the 'proud, ill-tempered women' who made her life a misery? In the dim light of home, or a home, would that person recall Jack dyeing his hair and disguising himself before he boldly clambered up the bean-stalk?

Here, in a wood-carved illustration, was Merlin, surrounded by amulets and globes and books of magic, conjuring up Tom Thumb, who wore 'a shirt of spider's web and a doublet and hose of thistle-down'. Here was Puss in Boots bowing before the King and Queen, graciously attended by page boys before a long velvet arras. Here, the mother and father of Hop O'My Thumb, desolate in prison before their rescue. Each picture must have been pointed at a thousand times, excited little fingers guided by adult hands: crowns, giants, spells, creatures, witches, princes and princesses. Children, whose parents had known the strictures of the Victorian and Edwardian age, now exploring a world of danger, cunning and magic, before themselves growing into an age of fear and global war. What consolation or warnings had they drawn from these little stories, the bequest of more than twenty centuries and the remembered fears of a species?

She heard the clattering of the letter box, and ambled downstairs from her study to the hall where a folded piece of paper lay. Written in the quaintly elegant hand of another era, it was addressed to 'Miss Ginny Clark' and read:

Dear Ginny

This is a note to apologise for my abrupt departure the other day. I am very embarrassed – it was a private matter, the details of which I would not dream of inflicting upon you. Suffice it to say that I feel terrible about behaving so badly, and would like to make it up to you. I so enjoyed our conversation. I wondered if you might like to come to supper one night soon? I am no cook, but it would be a pleasure to welcome you to the neighbourhood properly and to atone for my rudeness.

Yours

Sean

On the back of the note, she quickly wrote: 'Yes, please – Monday? Will assume fine unless I hear otherwise. G'. She folded the paper again, walked round to his front door and pushed it through his letter box. There was something innocent in the ritual exchange of messages, a slow and courtly means of achieving a straightforward objective that she would normally have found silly. But, increasingly, she found his earnestness touching rather than bizarre. In his clumsiness was something approaching chivalry: something, she reflected, that she had never really experienced before.

The weekend passed like a languorous dream, the heat draining her of all energy and desire to work. Winston slept with a depth that resembled hibernation, loose-limbed and unresponsive on the sofa. She tried to take notes on a less demanding text, but found that the words drugged her, urging her towards slumber. She napped in the afternoons and was delighted to find after one such sleep that she had missed a call from Harry who left a clipped message of unconsummated fury.

As an experiment, she invited Julie and her father to supper on Sunday night. The experiment was not in the chemistry of personalities since her best friend and Dad knew each other well, and enjoyed a teasing relationship based on the pretence that Julie found him wildly attractive and that he disapproved of her entirely, while knowing that she was one of the foundation stones of his daughter's life. Julie had – naturally – put her shoulder to the wheel after Felicity died, even forcing Geoffrey to chaperone her to a movie premiere. He had put up a fight, declaring the whole idea 'effing ridiculous', but had yielded in the end, put on black tie, and enjoyed himself more than he would have thought possible, pointing out celebrities on the red carpet in Leicester Square. In his own guarded way, he loved Julie as a second, surrogate daughter, though one whose behaviour completely baffled him.

The experiment was culinary and psychological: to see if she herself could pull off a supper party, however small, without Harry to assist, check the wine, make the salad dressing and cook the asparagus perfectly. Of course, there was nothing very demanding about a spinach salad followed by a pasta bake and a few bottles of Geoffrey's Sancerre. But she felt a quiet sense of achievement, adulthood even, that she had christened the new house as a place where she could welcome family and friends, and fashion a life of her own.

'So, Geoffrey,' said Julie, drawing on her cigarette over the coffee. 'You never write, you never call.'

'That's right, my girl. I am a respectable retired librarian. I have seen how you showbiz people live with your strange substances and expensive air tickets. I keep well away. Well away.'

'Truth is, you keep away only because you know how much you *love* it. I saw you staring at the super-models. Filthy sod. You were supposed to be staring at me.'

'That would be quite wrong,' interjected Ginny. 'He used to drive you back to university. He could be your father.'

'So?' Julie said. 'That was some years ago, university, you know. Oh, I *forgot*. You're still writing essays aren't you? Well, the rest of us have soiled ourselves in the garden of life, Gin. I am merely demanding that your Dad treat me as a woman, and not as a girl.'

'You are shocking, Julie,' said Geoffrey, trying to suppress a laugh. 'Quite shocking.'

'You are, you know,' said Ginny.

'Shocking? I'll tell you what's shocking, Geoff. Your daughter here, most fancied girl in her year, hiding away, aged thirty-six, still writing about Snow White when she should be up in town every night at the clubs picking up rough-hewn actors and demanding their favours. Instead of getting loads and having the time of her life she's looking for deep meaning in bloody Puss in Boots. Now, if you ask me – which of course you don't, because you think I'm a dreadful boozy old slapper – *that's* shocking.'

Geoffrey bowed his head and considered this outburst.

He looked old for a moment, but only a moment. 'Actually,' he said with a sly smile. 'She's right you know, Ginny.'

'Oh . . .' said his daughter, throwing a tea towel at Julie, amid the laughter. 'Sod off, the pair of you.'

'And what about the bloke next door?' said her friend.

'What bloke next door?' asked her father.

'Sod off again,' Ginny said, but this time more quietly.

The heat subsided a little on Monday and she wrote a chapter plan on the interpretation of Rapunzel and compiled a preliminary bibliography for this section of her book, trying not to spend too much time thinking about what she would wear to supper with Sean and what time it would be appropriate to go round to his house. In principle, she did not wanted to be diverted from her task, which had become so symbolic in her mind of liberation from the past. And yet it was pleasurable to be thus distracted, to spend time dwelling on something small and harmless such as a dinner with her neighbour. After the colossal emotions of divorce and its poisonous aftermath, she was delighted by the prospect of something gentle and simple. She would take a good bottle of wine – one of Geoffrey's – and befriend him properly. Therein lay the chance to put down some tentative roots, to till the shallow soil of her new life and wait to see what might flourish if tended carefully. Next door was as good a place to start as any.

At eight o'clock, she knocked on his door. The street was deserted, cool shadows stretching its length and breadth and a hint of honeysuckle sweetening the breeze. She waited for some response – the sound of hasty footsteps within – but the house loomed silent and disapproving above her. She smoothed the front of her floral wrap dress: a simple choice, she thought, pretty without being coquettish, a message that was reinforced by her flat sandals. No jewellery, other than a silver chain her mother had given her. She did not want him to think her forward, or vampish.

The door opened without warning, as though he had glided through the hall. He peered out, a little flustered, she could see, and wearing a white chef's apron.

'Oh,' he said. 'It's you.'

'Who else were you expecting?'

'Oh, no – I mean, hello.' He smiled. 'Come in, please.'

She handed him a bottle of white wine. 'Oh, you shouldn't . . . Thanks . . . Goodness, that's very kind of you.'

'Something smells nice,' she said.

'Oh, it's nothing. Just some langoustines. I hope you don't mind seafood?'

'No, it sounds wonderful.'

'Great. Well, if you'll excuse me, I'll get you a drink. White wine?' She nodded.

Only as he scurried back downstairs to the kitchen did she start to absorb the world into which she had walked. The hallway, unlike her own, was painted a deep red that seemed the colour of winter. Once the door was closed there was no hint of summer, only the flickering light of the candles that, to her amazement, lined the walls in hooded black sconces leading to the staircase. Between them hung prints, at least a dozen of them: not, as far as she could see, an orderly series, but an eccentric mix of engravings and paintings that made the corridor look like an antiquarian shop. Ginny peered at one of the pictures. It was a Constable mezzotint of a seascape: beneath a turbulent sky, the waves crashed against a dilapidated sea-wall. The masts and sails in the middle ground dwarfed the solitary figure of a mariner on the sands. The print was stained and there were indecipherable pencil scrawlings at its edges. Was it a family heirloom, or something he had bought on a whim to add to his strange little collection?

'There you go.' Sean had reappeared at her side, no longer wearing his apron. He handed her a glass. 'Come through to the drawing room.'

'Don't you have electricity then, Sean?'

He laughed. 'What, the candles, you mean?'

'Yes, very atmospheric.'

'Oh, it's just the way I like things. Things I've *always* liked, or come to like over the years. It's an advantage of living on one's own.'

'How long have you lived on your own?'

She caught his frown in the tell-tale light. He paused. 'Let's go through.'

She had expected grim austerity or white minimalism to match his high-tech profession. But the house was like the inside of a mind, the maze of a life and its disorderly accretions. The drawing room was less the living space of a man in his twenties than the study of a bachelor-don. It was dominated by a decrepit leather sofa that sagged in the middle, its antiquity barely concealed by a throw. There was a mahogany coffee table on which art books old and new lay open, as though Sean had been examining them for inspiration before her arrival. There was an armchair and a scattering of glass-fronted book-cases. A tapestry of Japanese characters hung from one wall, incongruous opposite an oil painting that showed a man in a cape apparently snatching a small child and spiriting her away from her garden. On the frame itself, in a hasty black brush-stroke was the title: *Grand Meaulnes, 1954*. Below the painting was a cluster of house plants and a black sculpture of Shiva that came up to her knee, a tutelary deity hiding in the greenery.

Wherever she looked there was eccentric clutter: pictures, clocks, a Mexican *danse macabre* with tiny skeletons in costume, a model vintage car, a pile of old map books, sheet music strewn across one corner of the room, dried flowers in an ornate chinoiserie vase. There was a small porcelain chest, with a key in its lock, a one-armed bandit, a bust of some august statesman or other, and a pile of vinyl records, some out of their sleeves. The only nod to modernity was a battered sound system that looked as if it had been bought in a charity shop. Against one wall was a row of what looked like stamp albums.

But, as in the hallway, it was the light, or the lack of it, that struck her most. The room was too busy with objects and life to be dingy or drab: the dance of the candlelight with the shadows was, it seemed, deliberate, the way her host liked to live. It suggested enchantment rather than the sadness she had half-expected. Neither the tomb of a lost soul, nor the hermitage of a recluse, this was the den of a brilliant boy who loved his own company and his curiosity shop of the mind. She sat on the sofa, as intrigued as she was on edge and waited for him to return. On the table in front of her was an open volume of Aubrey Beardsley's illustrations of Salome, evidently a welcome distraction from the technical software manual at its side. She could not decide if the fruit in the bowl – apples, oranges and pears – was real.

'This room is – interesting,' she said.

'I suppose so. It's just me, really. All the things I've picked up over the years. I tend to hoard. And I can live as I please.' He took a sip from his own glass. 'So I do.'

'It's very nice of you to invite me round. You needn't have gone to so much trouble.'

'Oh, it's no trouble. No trouble at all. And I felt bad about leaving so abruptly the other day. Couldn't be helped.'

She shifted in her seat and smoothed her dress. 'You had a visitor?'

He paused. 'Yes. Yes, I did.'

'A lady, I think?' She worried suddenly that he would think that she had been spying on him after he had left.

'Yes,' he said. 'That's right.' It was obvious that he had no desire whatsoever to elaborate. 'Excuse me, again.'

He went downstairs and returned after a few minutes with a tray. There were two dishes, a basket of crusty bread, butter, the wine and a pot of langoustines, smelling briney and delicious.

'I thought we could eat in here,' he said. 'If that's okay?'

'Fine, of course,' Ginny replied. 'It smells fantastic.'

'Easy to do, and I cook them for myself quite often. Here, try the chilli mayonnaise.'

She did. 'That's really good. Coriander?'

He nodded. 'A bit of lime, garlic, pepper. Really easy.'

She peeled one of the crustaceans. 'Do you like to cook?'

'Yes. Though I'm not very practised at having guests. Well, as you can see. I really should have cleared up.'

'Not at all,' she laughed. 'I'm honoured to be one of the chosen few.'

'Well, I would have felt awkward not returning your hospitality. You did your best to make me feel welcome. Not everybody does.'

'In what way?'

'Oh, I don't know. I live unconventionally, I suppose. Well, definitely. And I think most people find that a bit weird, in all honesty.'

She put down her plate. 'Well – can I be frank?'

'Please,' he said. She could see he was already wincing.

'Not many men of your age – mid-twenties, I guess? – not many of them live a life like this. And people are very attached to the predictable. Things that break the pattern make them feel uneasy.'

He nodded, apparently relieved that her judgment had not been more harsh. 'Yes, I suppose so. Although I would have thought people would be happy to have someone around who gets on with his life, and keeps himself to himself. I know I would.'

'And then you end up with a nosey neighbour, poking around in your house.'

Sean smiled again. 'Yes, but you're obviously – different.'

'*Different*? You mean: mad as a snake?'

'No, I'm sure you're very sane indeed. No, I meant that you obviously want people to feel at ease. Which is a great gift – to other people, I mean.'

'I'm not sure about that,' Ginny said. 'I'm just coming down to earth after a divorce, so I don't feel in much of a position to judge anybody.'

Unbidden, she told him a little of her story, and he nodded with what she took to be confused compassion. He did not look as if the thickets of adultery, infertility and divorce were familiar to him, even at second hand, and his rapt attention suggested astonishment as much as empathy. She felt like a weary traveller who had returned from the darker shores of adulthood with a terrible tale to tell. She sensed that his innocence ran deeper than mere shyness. His eyes widened, and she noticed again that he had long eyelashes. It made her trust him.

'That is a lot to go through,' he said, finally.

'Yes,' she said. 'It wasn't much fun. But it's over now. All over. At least I hope so. Moving here has been a big step, an important step.'

'Yes, I have liked living here, on the whole.'

'How long has it been?'

'A couple of years.'

'Where were you before?'

Sean blushed. 'Somewhere else. It doesn't matter. It isn't that interesting.'

'Oh,' she said, embarrassed to have broached an unexpectedly sensitive subject. She tried to recover: 'Tell me more about your painting.'

He sprung into life. 'Do you know, I was thinking about you this afternoon?'

'Really?' she said. 'Whatever made you do that?'

'Wait here,' he said and dashed out of the room.

While he was gone, she looked at the mirror above the fireplace, its etched gilt frame tarnished and old. She wondered if Sean ever had cause to look in it at this time of night, when he was on his own, vaguely aware of the noise outside, and she wondered what he saw and what he thought, and whether he was lonely.

'Look, look,' he said. He sat beside her and presented her with a book. 'I hadn't looked at this in years. It was in a box. But – well, I thought it might interest you.' The volume, she saw immediately, was a fairly early edition of Perrault's Fairy Tales, illustrated by Gustave Dore, leather-bound, and, according to a bookplate within, a school prize awarded to a child in 1923. The inscription read: 'St George's School. To: John Fairley. For: Outstanding drawing and reading in the Michaelmas Term.' The plate was signed illegibly, but clearly dated 'December 15, 1923'.

'This is quite something,' she said. 'Where did you get this?'

'Oh, no idea,' Sean said. 'It was in my family, I think. I certainly don't remember buying it.'

'It's in terrific condition,' she said, her fingers caressing the cover and the spine. 'The first English edition with Dore was published – 1920, or thereabouts, I think. But this is a beauty.'

'I thought you'd like it.' As he sat delightedly beside her, she could feel, for the first time, the warmth of his body.

The book was, indeed, a treasure, especially when she compared it to the battered 1930s collection she had been examining so recently. Even in the flickering candlelight of Sean's drawing room, she could see the magic of Dore's illustrations, as if the power of the etchings was itself somehow luminous. She loved the exquisite line of these images, the shadows and the astonishing detail. The cobwebs in the castle of Sleeping Beauty; the bulging eyes of Blue Beard and the ring upon his chubby finger; the mouse hanging from the belt of Puss in Boots; the succulent scraps of pumpkin on the floor of the kitchen, scooped out by the gnarled hands of Cinderella's godmother. But what most struck Ginny was the sheer horror that Dore had captured on these pages. Babies on a dish beside the ogre's throne; the giant, crazed and unstoppable, about to slash the throats of his seven sleeping daughters; most of all, on the last page, the terror in the eyes of a child sitting on the knee of an old woman, surrounded by her siblings, listening to a story read from an open book. In those eyes was the fear that Ginny was trying to write about herself, the terrible warnings passed down from generation to generation. The artist had understood that the soul of man was dark and treacherous, and that the magic did not always travel in the right direction.

'It's remarkable,' she said. 'I haven't seen a better copy.'

'It's yours,' he said.

She looked at him. 'No, no, Sean. I couldn't possibly. Really—'

'I insist. It was sitting in a box. What use is that? No, much better that it finds a home where it will be read and looked after.'

She saw from his expression that he was not only serious but had planned this as the centrepiece of the evening. 'Well, that's incredibly kind.' She closed the book.

'Listen, I'll make a deal with you. I'll borrow it, all right? And you can renew the loan while I'm using it.'

'It's a permanent loan. Go on, take it.'

She smiled. 'Thank you. Thank you very much.'

She sensed in his shyness, the flush of his cheeks, a first intimacy that she did not find unwelcome or awkward. For all his evasions and eccentricities, he meant well, and, against what were obviously his deepest instincts, he wanted to be a friend to her.

As Sean reached for the wine, she heard the pounding. It sounded subterranean at first, the sound of fury from some unimaginable dungeon beneath them. It was speeding up, becoming more insistent.

'Christ,' she said. 'What's that?'

Sean stood up. 'I have no idea. Where is it coming from? Over the road?' He walked towards the drawn curtains.

As she heard her name called out, she realised what had

happened, was happening, was about to happen. It was the voice she least wanted to hear, and the only voice that could ruin – as it already had, in a few seconds – her pleasure in the evening and in the gift. It was a voice that had once represented reassurance to her, but now signalled the opposite. She did not know why Harry was outside her home, shouting for her, but she knew that she would have to go and find out.

'Oh, God,' she said. 'I am sorry. It's my ex-husband. I had no idea—'

'What does he want?'

'Who knows? I am so sorry.'

'Please, don't be. Will he go away?'

'I doubt it. I don't know. He's been—'

The pounding on her front door resumed, faster this time.

'God – I *wish* this was not happening.' She choked back tears. 'He is determined to prevent me having the *slightest* peace of mind.'

Sean sat down beside her again and placed an arm tentatively around her shoulder.

'Listen. There's no reason why you should have to put up with this. None at all. Can't you just ignore it?'

'No – I – and then what? He'll only come back. No, I have to deal with him.'

'Well, why don't we go round together, and—'

'No.' She put up her hand, and then wiped her eye. 'Sorry, Sean. I appreciate your offer, I really do. I have to sort this out on my own.'

She heard Harry call out her name again, his lawyer's baritone now streaked with hysteria. 'Oh, Christ. Look – I hate leaving like this,' she said. Sean opened his mouth to speak, and then thought better of it. He seemed to acknowledge that he was not equal to the moment, and that she was right to exclude him.

'To be continued, okay?' Ginny said. Then she fled the room, through the hall and out into the cooling night.

She marched down the path, determined not to look to her side where her ex-husband was waiting. Even as she turned the corner and made her way towards her own front door, rummaging in her bag for her keys, she kept her gaze fixed on the red and black tiles. Only when Harry spoke did she look up.

'So you were next door all along?' he said.

She faced him. He was unshaven, and she could smell the booze on his breath. His clothes were crumpled, and he twitched with a fury that seemed aimed not just at her but at the whole world.

She tried to compose herself. 'Harry. Why are you here?'

His face softened: he looked suddenly lachrymose. 'I – I wanted to speak with you.' He surveyed her. 'All dressed up, I see. Been out on a date?' He wobbled a little.

'Why didn't you call first? I was out. What was the point in raising hell outside my house?'

His features twisted. 'Oh, yes, of course, *your* house. I forgot. The one you worked so *fucking* hard to buy. Your house.'

'Harry. Please. I don't want to have a fight with you. What is it?'

'What is it? Am I supposed to discuss my life with you out here?'

'Well, you can't come in. You're in a state.'

'What's that supposed to mean?'

'It means you're drunk and you should be at home yourself, drinking coffee. Where's Estelle?'

He swatted away the question with his hand. 'Gone. She's gone, hasn't she?'

'What do you mean?'

'Fucked off. Yesterday. Said it wasn't working. Said I'm—' he gestured madly with his arms '—*suffocating*. Suffocating? I wasn't suffocating when she was after tenancy. I wasn't suffocating when she moved into my house. When I signed the divorce papers.' He mumbled to himself. 'Bitch. I hate her.'

Ginny found that she was shocked rather than thrilled. 'I thought everything was fine.'

He pushed his face into hers: 'So. Did. I.'

Ginny began to steel herself. 'Listen, Harry. I'm sorry you're having problems. But they're not my problems. They're just not. Okay? We're way past that now.' She watched him as he blinked, a scowling caricature of the man she had married. 'Go home, all right? Wait out here, and I'll call you a cab.'

So diminished himself, he now seemed to resort easily to scornful impersonation. '*Wait out here?*' The voice was a whining parody of her own, a terrible insight into how he now saw her, the woman he had once cherished. 'Why should I wait outside my own fucking house?' He raised his eyebrows with the impatience of a judge.

'It *isn't* your house,' she said. 'It's *mine*. I'll call you a cab, Harry. Take it, or leave it.'

'No!' Now he was shouting again, and, she feared, out of control. 'Let me in *now*.'

'No.' She walked past him, put the key into the lock and was starting to turn it, when she felt the rough force of his hand on her arm. She wrenched it away and watched as he stumbled against the porch. He cursed to himself, as she finally opened the door and tried to get into the house, while keeping him out. His body was at first a dead weight against the frosted panes, and then became sinewy and mean once more. He pushed, first clumsily and then with sheer brutality, driving her back into the hall.

Breathing hard, he wiped the back of his hand against his brow. He reached out, found the light switch and turned it on.

'Harry—'

The force of his hand against her chest interrupted her viciously, and sent her crumpling to the ground. She was badly winded, and began to weep silently as she struggled to recover her breath. She felt a twinge of pain in her ankle, as if she had twisted it as she went down.

She looked up to see Harry advance towards her. Through the tears, she could only make out his silhouette. His head was bowed, as if he were dwelling upon the next outrage to inflict upon her. There was nothing about him to suggest shock or remorse. Only the indecision of a man who has crossed a line for the first time, and wonders what to do next. It seemed to her that he was contemplating – no, could this be so? – a further blow, this time to her head. Yes: that was what he was considering. No more words, no more calling out her name. The unambiguous slap or punch to punish her for everything he held against her.

And then all was a blur as she saw another figure loom behind Harry and a hand grab his collar and something smash into his back with such power that he was driven hard into the wall with a single blow. She expected him to cry out in fury or pain, but he was silent. Then he let out a gurgling whimper, stunned, disoriented, and slumped against the wall. The same hand kept a grip on his collar and smashed Harry's head against the wall once more, this time with finality. The blow was not enough to kill him, she thought: but one more just might. One more such savage collision and his bleeding head would surely give way and she would hear the unthinkable cracking of bone against brick. Harry's life was at the mercy of the hand that held onto his jacket. She watched, aghast, as the grip loosened and her ex-husband fell unconscious to the floor. She could make out a patch of blood on the wall where his head had split open. Dazed and muddled, she wondered how she would clean it off.

The second figure turned and crouched before her. A hand reached out to touch her face.

'My God,' whispered Sean. 'Are you okay?'

VI

'The tricky truth, my dear,' Julie said, chewing gleefully on a leaf of rocket, 'is that you rather miss him.'

'Do not,' said Ginny with a speed that she knew her friend would not let pass.

'Do too,' she continued. 'Again, the psychology would be well within the grasp of an amateur, let alone a brilliant legal mind such as mine. Really, love. You, with your Freud and your Jung and your Bettelheim.'

'I'm not a Freudian. As well you know.'

'Whatever. It is revealing, not to say entertaining, that his absence is what triggered this lunch.'

This was technically accurate. Sean's rapid departure – for 'a few days' break by the sea' in the words of his note – had thrown her, if only because she had not had the chance to speak to him properly before he left. So, in a sisterly reflex, she had called Julie and asked her out. The two of them sat in a chic basement restaurant, one of Julie's favourites, near to the Royal Opera House. Their two o'clock reservation – determined by a long morning meeting with a client in Kensington – meant that the room had already drained of most of the chattering ad men, suits and media hangers-on by the time their main courses arrived. The pine tables, with their bowls of oil and sea salt, and baskets of ciabatta, were deserted. A bottle of Cava had already come and gone, and Julie poured her friend a second glass of Pinot Grigio.

'This is nice,' Ginny said, pointing at the glass. 'Don't you have a job to go to?'

'Don't you? No, I forgot. You don't. Actually, I have a clear diary now, and I intend to take full advantage of it, having already nabbed a few hundred grands' worth of work for the firm this morning, thank you very much. *That* case will run and run, God bless it. I feel no guilt.'

This, Ginny thought, was the absolute truth behind her friend's pleasing patter. And it was what separated the two of them, just as kindness guaranteed their bond. Julie was instinctively suspicious of the promptings of guilt, and needed much persuading that it was an emotion to which one should ever yield. She believed that most social crimes were, in fact, victimless and that most convention was simply the imposition of somebody's authority, however remote. She conformed because it was in her interests to do so. But she believed that generosity and tolerance were all you really needed to get through life well, and that the rest was a sack of old bricks you could quite happily dump at the roadside. John Calvin, she said, was not a great Protestant superman and historical figure to be admired, but a 'total tosser' whose sole achievement of any note was to have inspired half a designer's name. Ginny, with her shame and her guilt and her introspection, often looked on with envy and admiration at her friend's simple formula for a life well lived.

'Anyway – is that olive oil? Great, thanks – anyway, to return to Mr White Knight, you do *so* miss him.'

'I wouldn't describe what happened as the action of a White Knight. He gave Harry the kicking of his life, and – why are you laughing?'

'Because,' Julie said, trying to compose herself, 'if anyone on the planet has been asking for a kicking in the last few years it is Harry Rowlands. All that barrister charm turned into vicious bastardry against you. All the bullying and lies and the rest of it.'

She was serious now. 'And you still don't know how far he would have gone if Sean hadn't marched in. Do you?'

'I can't – I won't – believe that Harry would ever really hurt me. Physically, I mean.'

'That is so naïve. Listen to you. He'd already manhandled you. He was pissed out of his brains. How can you be so sure? The man's got nothing to lose now that Big Tits has walked out on him.'

Ginny allowed herself a snort of contempt. 'Well, that's certainly true.'

'So I wouldn't be so sure that you would have been okay. Come on, you know the figures on domestics and violence against women – no, this isn't going to be one of my lectures. All I'm saying is that precisely because you don't believe in your heart that Harry is capable of hurting you, he knew, somewhere in that pissed-up brain of his, that he could – and maybe even get away with it.'

'He'll be back. Not sure how, though. I thought he might

call the police first of all, but I suppose it would have looked so terrible for him.'

'Christ, yes. He'd risk being disbarred if you took him on.'

'But – no, it's something else, really.'

'What?'

Ginny brushed a strand of hair away from her forehead. 'Well – it's as if all of Harry's layers have finally been removed, and left this furious, lumbering creature looking for something to hit and hurt. I mean, he was out of his head, for sure. But the look in his eyes – it was new. Desperate, of course, but I've seen that many times before. But this was as if all the restraining bolts had just sprung out. You know – just utterly destructive.'

Julie sipped her wine. 'It sounds like you should get a restraining order to keep him away from you. I'm serious.'

'Actually, it crossed my mind. But I don't think this is about consequences or rational stuff anymore. I think he's at the edge of some sort of precipice in his life and he basically doesn't give a fuck what happens next. That's what I think. And I think he'll find a way of coming back to hurt me, even if it's not what I expect.' Her eyes filled. Her friend reached over and touched her hand. 'He'll have to get past me first,' she said. 'And he doesn't scare me, I can tell you. Harry Rowlands? I could have him any day. Manolo to groin, mace in face, mobile to my friend Jimmy the cop, who would certainly write in his report that the assailant broke four fingers when falling to the curb shortly after being thrown there by Jimmy. Oh, yes. Most appealing. Harry won't hurt you.'

'I hope you're right,' Ginny said, shaking her head and wiping the tears away with her napkin. 'Would Jimmy the cop really do that for you?'

'And much more. My bondsman, and one of many. Now – enough of this battered ex-wife talk. I want to talk about Sir Lancelot Morrissey and his exciting defence of the damsel in distress.'

Ginny frowned. 'But it wasn't exciting.'

'Not even a little bit?'

'I – well, it was all a bit of a blur. But, you know, he sort of beat Harry at his own game.'

'Two brutes, you mean?'

'Yes. Except that Harry was this great sad ape and Sean was so much more in control. He just came in and did what he did without any warning. Absolute focus and no – well – no compunction, I suppose. He's such a hesitant, mild creature. One minute he's worrying about his langoustines being properly cooked, the next he's trying to break another bloke's skull. I can't relate one to the other. It scared me.'

'I wouldn't be scared if I were you. Look, what was he supposed to? He sees someone he likes being attacked in her hallway. Now, he could go all Neighbourhood Watch and sound the alarm, call the police, blow a whistle, or whatever. Or he could do what had to be done. Which—' she filled up their glasses '—is precisely what he did, thank Christ. And if you can't handle washing a bit of blood off your walls, just be glad it was Harry's and not yours.'

Ginny nodded and pushed her fork and knife together, no longer enthused by her sole.

'Anyway, when is he back? Sean, I mean?'

'Oh, I don't know. There's this old woman who comes to see him, his mum I suppose. He said they were going off for a few days. He doesn't talk about her. Or much else, for that matter.'

'Well, so what? He gave you a lovely book. He cooked you dinner. You know what he does for a living and that he's solvent. He beats up drunken assailants with a lack of hesitation that I find sexy, even if you don't. Who cares about his mum and their holidays together? Scarcely the most important question, is it?'

'And what's that, then?'

'Send him round to my place, and I'll let you know.'

She looked at her giggling friend and refilled her glass.

Ginny pressed Delete and began the paragraph for the third time:

The rise of right-side brain neurology has drawn much-needed attention to the role of empathy in cognitive response. Insufficient work has been completed on the role of the right hemisphere in narrative development and the interaction between fear-based creativity and the left-side sequential form of conventional story-telling.

What she meant to say was that fairy tales rose from the yeast of childhood fear as much as the moral structure of adult stories. But somehow, when she thought of the academic community by whom her monograph would be read – those merciless reviewers practising their dark arts in the quarterly journals – she could not help but smother the thought with showy references to other disciplines and the obscure language in which scholars choose to talk to one another.

Clarity, clarity, clarity: this had been one of her tutor's mantras when she had read out her essays to him. He'd warned her that convoluted prose was not only risky: nobody would understand and care to read on. It was also dishonest: it tried to impress the reader with obfuscation and fake complexity. Only stupid readers would fall for this, he'd said. True complexity could be conveyed only by simple language. This was the lesson from the ancients, from myth and folklore. She liked him enormously, not least because, with his pipe, he conformed to Stephen Leacock's definition of Oxford teaching as 'smoking at your pupils for three years'. It was only much later, when she read his own work on the philosophy of literature that she realised, with sadness, that he had really been admonishing himself. She remembered the first sentence: 'The heuristic dilemma of narratological counter-valence is not easily resolved, even by the critical apparatus of the "hedonic" school proposed by Schneider.' If this meant anything at all, it was that her teacher had had nothing to say, other than to warn his students in private not to make the same mistake. And here she was, doing just that.

It was late. The candle she had bought in Covent Garden flickered on the table next to her desk, creating a strange parallax in the bottle of mineral water. In the pile of books she saw a thriller that she wanted to read, and wondered at what point she could declare her day's work complete. She clicked on word count: 150. Not good. Not a good haul even for a woman who had grandly declared that there would be no daily work quotas in her new scriptorium. She was blocked, the claims of the inner life trumped by the interventions of the outer. Her longing for a cool life free of emotion had already been thwarted. To be desireless, to be without fear: these were the conditions of a truly intellectual life. She wanted to be a scholar, not a poet. But the sea kept hurling her against the rocks.

The door-bell rang, and then again: this time insistently. She flinched. Her desk chair had been chosen precisely because it allowed her to curl up, and she realised that she had instinctively withdrawn into its deepest leather-bound recesses, trying to make herself small and invisible like a creature under attack. She felt pathetic even as she acknowledged her anxiety. The curtains were not drawn and she wanted to shuffle over to the window and look out, to find out who it was, to see whether Harry was pacing drunkenly up and down the path, preparing his next diatribe, his next incursion into her soul. But she did not want to see him. She did not want to guess how many stitches he had needed, how much the wound still hurt, how much angrier he was than last time. Did he know that Sean was away? Had he waited until her protector left before resuming his attack? He was more than capable of such surveillance, of such forethought. He might be disbarred. But so what? He had lost a wife, another woman he hoped to marry, his dignity, his self-control: all had gone in the space of a few years, the edifice of smooth excellence that had once been Harry Rowlands now just another ruin. He would expect his career to be next, and she could imagine that his chambers would already be alive with stories of his slow demise: he would be taking fewer instructions, drawing up fewer opinions, losing his reputation as a pupil-master. Word would have got out in the bars of Fleet Street and Chancery Lane that it was all up for Harry. So why should he not resume their earlier confrontation – this time, without the interruption of a neighbour? Knowing his mind, she realised that such a return made perfect sense. He hated the incomplete, the untidy: he was back to finish what he had started.

Peter had been no less strict than Julie about how to handle her ex-husband.

'Don't take any chances, Gin,' he'd said, when she'd recounted the incident over the phone. 'This is no longer play time. Do you want to stay at mine for a bit – just until Harry cools down?'

'No, no. Thank you. Really kind of you, Pete. But I'll be okay.'

'Yes, but this neighbour of yours – Sean?'

'Sean.'

'I hope you're not relying on him. From what you say, he sounds a bit – well, a bit of a wild one, frankly. I mean, did you have any idea he could be so – you know, *physical*?'

'No,' Ginny had said. 'But it was a such a weird, horrible

moment. I don't know what to make of how Sean reacted, really. It looked like instinct to me.'

'Well, it sounds odd to me, if I'm honest. I don't know him, and I am sure he meant well. Keep me in the loop about both of them. Okay? Promise?'

'Promise,' she'd said and rung off.

Now, alone, she faced fresh confrontation. The bell rang a third time. She expected Harry to shout her name, but he did not, probably determined not to create a scene as he had last time. He would ring the bell until she went down and then try to talk his way into the house, apologising profusely for what had happened, calling upon her sense of mercy, asking her only, out of respect for what they had once had, to hear him out. What was there to say? Nothing, and everything. They could, indeed, revisit their failure a thousandth time, replay the film and freeze-frame on the ending to see if it might be different on this viewing. Of course, it would not. Their relationship had passed beyond mere lifelessness to become something much worse: a succubus that drained hope and energy from both of them, that perched on their shoulders and cackled at their folly. Her attempted escape was a flight from the thing itself, the winged demon, as much as from Harry. She did not want to go down.

But now the bell rang a fourth time, because he guessed that she was in, and he would not go until she gave him what he wanted. And that part of her which was still in hock to Harry, that deep, inoperable part, responded as she knew it would. It was not petrified obedience, but something worse: a fear that he was right, that she could never be entirely free of him. Trembling and shuffling like a child, she went downstairs into the hallway. She turned on the light. The bell rang once more.

She cleared her throat. 'Harry. What do you want, Harry?'

'Open the door, please!' The voice was not Harry's,

'Who's there?'

'Oh for God's sake . . . It's Mr Benson. Roger Benson. From next door. Kindly let me in, Miss Clark! I really do . . . Oh, bloody hell—'

She rushed to the door, undid the newly-installed chain and opened up, to see the flushed features of her neighbour and the appalled saucer eyes of Winston who was struggling furiously in his arms. Seizing his chance, the cat sprang free and scampered muttering into the house.

'Christ!' said Roger Benson. 'That *bloody* cat! Why didn't you answer the door? Little vermin!'

So relieved was Ginny that she found herself both speechless and having to stifle laughter. In his frayed lumberjack shirt and cardigan, he was sweating even more heavily than the day she had seen him mowing the lawn, the odour of late middle aged exertion now pungent in the evening air. The lenses of his glasses magnified the outrage in his eyes. He mopped his brow: it had clearly been quite a wrestling match, and she saw that his hand was bleeding from scratches. Quickly, her amusement turned to pity and embarrassment.

'God, would you like to come in? I am so dreadfully sorry. What happened, exactly?'

'Come in? You must be joking. I have no intention of going anywhere near that mad creature ever again.'

'Sorry, I don't follow—'

'I just caught him in my garden. He had already destroyed one of my rose bushes and was digging away at another, you see. Vandalism, pure and simple. Now, before you make excuses, I realise that my affection for my garden may seem eccentric, quaint even, to you metropolitan types and I dare say Audrey thinks I am over-protective. But it's my garden. And I won't have twenty years' work destroyed by some – by some bloody cat!'

'Please, Mr Benson. Do come in. Look, your hand is bleeding. I can put it under a tap and clean it up with some antiseptic. I'm sorry. Winston is a little sod, he really is. It's very good of you to bring him back. And, please – let me reimburse you for the damage done to the roses.'

'Good God, I wouldn't take your money. What do you take me for? This isn't about *money*. It's about common decency and neighbourly conduct.'

'Oh dear.' Ginny was not remotely prepared for this sort of row, having expected something much worse. Her regret at Winston's transgression was fast turning into irritation at Roger Benson's self-indulgence.

'What I want to know is this: are you going to keep that little beast under control, or not?'

'Mr Benson, it's a cat we're talking about, not a labrador. I don't keep him on a leash.'

'Well, perhaps you should.'

'I don't think it would work somehow.'

'That's your opinion. But may I remind you that the law is on my side if your cat causes damage on my property again.'

'Meaning what?'

'Meaning – how can I put this delicately? – that next time I shall not bring him back and risk having my hands shredded in the process. Let him take his chances.'

'Mr Benson, be reasonable—'

'I *am* being reasonable young lady. An unreasonable man would not have brought your cat back to you. He would have defended his garden immediately, by force if necessary. But no – I am, I hope, a fair-minded person, and I do not wish there to be hostility between us. And I know you have had very pleasant conversations with Audrey.'

'Yes, very pleasant. In fact—'

'But there are limits, Miss Clark. Limits that make good relations possible. And when they are crossed, too often, someone has to act. Please make sure that that someone is not me.'

She felt a wave of fatigue overwhelm her. Roger Benson was enjoying every tiresome moment of their exchange, relishing what she imagined was a rare opportunity to make full use of his talent for bombast. He was the sort of man who went through a life full of comfort, and free from want, persuaded nonetheless that he was being cheated by someone, somewhere. He would be the first to sign a petition against new accommodation for refugees in the area, an expert spotter of 'welfare scroungers', a zealous defender of the spirit of world wars he had not fought in.

He would hate Old Labour for its honesty and New Labour for its duplicity. He would identify 'political correctness' everywhere: in supermarkets, on television, at schools with which he had no connection, at the surgery when he was waiting for his repeat prescription. He would probably refer pointedly to 'Rhodesia' and 'Peking', even though these places meant nothing to him. He would lament the passing of the hereditary peers, though he could not name one, or what they had done. But that would not silence him. She could see Audrey reining him in at social functions, at the supermarket, in the car: a lifetime of soothing and calming, a child-man who longed only for the chance to be righteous.

'Look,' she said, sighing and folding her arms. 'I can only say I am sorry. Can't I? I'll do my best to keep him out of your garden, and if he plays up again, call me, and I'll come and get him straight away. Audrey has my number.'

'Well, we shall see. I realise that to someone of your generation, I may appear unnecessarily severe. But I do believe in certain things – things that seem to have been forgotten and ignored as this country has become . . . has changed. But *I* haven't changed. Well, tough on everyone else. So there it is. I have said my piece. I hope we understand each other.'

'Perfectly well.' Her tone was brusque now. She wanted this ridiculous man off her porch and back in his kitchen, where he could bore his wife with the injustices of modern life.

'Good night, then.'

'Good night.' She closed the door and went inside to

phone Peter, who she knew would love the story of Roger Benson's nocturnal clash with Winston more than anyone else.

Sean liked it, too. He laughed in her kitchen as she made tea and recounted the bathos of the conversation. His cheeks showed an unusual blush of colour from, he said, walks by the sea. She wanted to cross-examine him about the location of the beach, his mother, and what they had talked about. But he recoiled when she made even the most tentative inquiries, with a smile that signalled his readiness to shut up for good if she pursued the matter. And it did not seem important enough to risk the gentle connection they had somehow forged. She found his company both baffling and pleasing. He allowed her to be herself, and was not afraid of companionable silence. Indeed, it seemed to suit him. What she could not yet do was to reconcile this benign presence with the man who had smashed Harry against a wall with such primordial ease. And this tension did need to be confronted somehow if they were to remain friends.

'He really was quite absurd.'

'Sounds it,' he said. 'I've never really spoken to him. But he just *looks* so angry. Unlike her – Audrey. I imagine she has to hoover up most of it.'

'Of course,' she said, sitting down at the table, and moving aside a pile of newspaper supplements, 'I *did* think it was Harry. And it occurred to me that Harry might have worked out that you were away.'

'Away,' said Sean. The echo was an obstruction rather than a warm confirmation.

'So I was worried that – you know.' She stirred her tea. 'That he might think it was okay to come back for a second round because you wouldn't be able to – well, to step in and help me. What do you think?'

He was silent. Was that the hint of a smile curling at the edges of his lips? A whisper of self-congratulation? No, she was imagining it; she must be. His face was, as so often, the face of someone apparently perplexed by the very fact of the question: troubled that it should be asked at all. It was as if she had breached some taboo obvious to all in the tribe, and had thus marked herself out as a stranger. Or that the question was simply beyond his capabilities to answer, and that he was humiliated by this incapacity. She wanted to help. But she also felt her gorge rise with the first intimations of impatience. Why could he not give her a straight answer?

'You see,' she said, trying once more, speaking softly. 'It was quite odd to see you do that. To see you *able* to do that, if I'm honest. Can you understand how odd that was for me?'

The air was heavy and a drowsy fly stumbled across a plate in front of her. Finally, he shrugged, the first time she had seen him express anything approaching frustration.

'Do you want me to leave, Ginny?'

No, no, you fool, I want you stay. I want you to help me so that I can let you stay.

'Because I'll go if you want.'

Don't do it, Sean. Don't blow this at the very start.

She drew herself up. 'I don't want you to go. I just want you to answer my question.'

'Which one?'

'You know what I mean. God, don't be difficult, please. Here you are, one sort of person. You welcome me, you cook for me. The sort of person I think I might be able to trust. And, believe me, Sean, trust is not something I'm doling out very much these days. And then – from somewhere, God knows where – you summon up another person altogether, who leaves blood on the walls of my hallway. Now, don't think for a minute that I'm not grateful. I have no idea what Harry would have done if you hadn't turned up. He was – well, he was out of control.'

'I wasn't out of control.'

She reflected. *No. That's exactly it. That's why I ask.* 'I didn't say you were. I just – I was surprised that your talents extended to physical violence. I had you down as the brainy type, frankly.'

He stood up so sharply that she thought he might be about to make good his implied threat, and march out. She had gone too far this time, accused this gentle, chivalrous man of nursing a secret gift for brutality. What did she expect? Of course he would leave immediately. But he walked instead over to the door at the back, looking out into the garden. His face had resumed its unearthly pallor and his back was as straight as if he were standing to attention. She could see that he was suffering, rather than angry, desperate to give her an answer, but struggling to do so.

'I'm sorry – look, take your time,' she said. 'I'm not trying to make you feel uncomfortable. Can't you see that it matters to me what you're really like? Doesn't that matter to you?'

He turned back, his features smooth and pale like porcelain. A word out of place and he might shatter into a thousand pieces. He drew breath and she could see that he was about to tell the truth. Not all of it, perhaps, but enough. Summoning up a great effort of will to reveal something of his innermost self, and whatever conflict there was within.

And then, as quickly as the opportunity arose, it passed. It was as if a great oak door had opened, a sliver of light offering hope, and then slammed shut. He relaxed and shrugged once more. She knew he was going to say something trite and obvious now, and she was disappointed. 'Look,' he said. 'I can see how weird it must have been. The whole thing. But, really, I just did what I had to do. Didn't think much about it – quite surprised myself, if I'm honest. But he obviously meant you serious harm so I had to do something quickly, and, I guess, something pretty decisive. I don't know. What if he had been carrying a knife?'

She relented, unwilling to challenge him. 'That's true, I suppose.'

'Look at it from my point of view. You left my house in a state, and then I heard him shouting, and when I came round you were already on the ground. And – Christ, Ginny, the look on your face. I could see how *terrified* you were. I didn't know what to do – I – what would you have done?'

She looked at him. 'I don't know. The same, I suppose – in your shoes, I mean.'

He held her gaze. 'And, please, Ginny. And I really mean this. *Don't ever, ever think that I enjoyed it.*'

Christ, she thought, is that what he believes I think? Have I become so wary that I treat new friends like psychopaths? 'God. Sean. Is that how it seemed? I would never think that.'

He said nothing.

'I was just confused. I didn't mean to imply . . . I didn't mean that you did anything wrong. I was just – Oh, shut up, Ginny!' She laughed and, without thinking, walked towards Sean and embraced him, held him close to her.

He was profoundly uneasy, unused, it was clear, to such spontaneous displays of affection. Perhaps unused to such contact at all. But as she held on to him longer than she had originally intended, relaxing into his chest, and closing her eyes, enjoying the pulsing warmth of another human body, she felt him letting himself go a little, too. His frame – robust, as she had first thought – became more yielding, allowing her to nuzzle him. She sighed involuntarily with something approaching contentment. She had not got the answer she was seeking. But that did not stop him smelling good, or the sensation of his heartbeat reassuring her. Slowly, his arms gathered her in to himself. His touch was gentle. There was not the merest whisper of menace or anger she had feared might be bottled up within. Only a transparent concern for her, and the early intimations of something more. His left hand moved up her body to her head, and he stroked her hair. She murmured into his chest, startled at the easiness of the situation in which they found themselves, how safe she felt in his arms, and by the exhaustion that was seeping through her. It seemed possible that she might drift off to sleep, cradled and soothed as she had not been for a very long time. She could sense the beginnings of his arousal, too, but that did not matter, nothing mattered, because he was not acting indecorously, even when he put his hands to her brow and kissed her forehead.

To her dismay, he pulled away. 'Don't go anywhere,' he whispered. He ran up the stairs and out of the door – but did not close it. She stood, waiting for him, and realised she was swaying a little, recovering from her moment of abandon. She had enjoyed it. She was confused and uncertain, but she wanted him to be back in the room with her.

When he reappeared after a few minutes he was as excited as a schoolboy, clutching a frame. 'There,' he said, presenting the picture to her. 'The frame was just one that was lying around, but it isn't a bad fit. I put it in last night when I got back.' He was breathless with excitement.

She smiled. 'What is it?'

'I drew it by the sea.'

Under the glass was a pencil drawing of a woman reading, one hand under her chin, absorbed by her book and deep in thought. It was a study, not a finished work, but that was its charm. The draftsman was talented, of that there was no doubt: his line was sure and practised, the result of long hours of trial and error rather than teaching, she thought. His subject was beautiful, but not idealistically so. It was the beauty of lopsided life. Her hair was in a bunch and she toyed with a pair of glasses, as if she was not sure whether she needed them to read or not. She was distracted. It was Ginny.

She looked at him again, and smiled. 'Thank you,' she said. She returned his earlier kiss, but, not being able to reach his forehead, settled for his lips.

VII

When Ginny Clark was five, her mother took her to a shopping centre that she wanted to try out. It was half an hour's drive from their home, and Felicity decided to give the trip the status of an expedition. She talked to Ginny at bedtime about how exciting it would be, and told her that they were going to buy some important things for the house, a present for Daddy's birthday and – who could say? – perhaps, if she was lucky, a toy for her. They would have lunch there, too, and enjoy one another's company. Ginny was easily persuaded that their trip would indeed be a fine one, and she could barely sleep the night before.

On the allotted morning, she kissed Geoffrey goodbye, a little gravely, expressing sorrow that her father should be excluded from the fun, but promising to come back soon with Mummy. In years to come, Ginny would be amazed at her precise recall of the day and its every detail. She remembered her mother's hair being up, the tone of her mascara, her fawn coat and red woollen scarf. She remembered her own patterned dress, sandals and duffel coat. She remembered the Dr Seuss book she was reading in the back, and her questions to Felicity about the provenance and powers of the Cat in the Hat: she could already read well, well enough for her teachers to urge her parents, with forlorn resignation, to remove her from her class and send her to the local prep school. This, Felicity was still resisting, though with fading determination. Her daughter kept up the conversation and critical inquiries – 'But how does the Cat fit two Things in his Hat, Mummy?' – all the way to their destination. Many years later, Ginny could still recall the people she saw from the window: the Caribbean street stalls; the pensioners in their head-scarves towing their carts; the mothers out shopping with their buggies, flustered and perplexed; the skinheads in their green bomber jackets, red braces and boots prancing outside the pubs, flicking beer at each other. She could remember the stained concrete of the car park, the cans of beer by the pillars and the stench of urine. All this was very clear to her, like some archive of another London preserved arbitrarily in her mind. She did not remember many other days in this way.

The shopping centre was what, in the mid Seventies, passed for middle-class abundance, choice and total convenience. It formed a large T-shape, one end of which was mostly consumed by a large Sainsbury's, flanked by Top Shop, Radio Rentals, Miss Chelsea, Timothy Whites and twenty other stores. There was an Allders at the other end of the T, four floors of clothes on racks, bathroom essentials, fabrics and a coffee shop at which you could buy damp white-bread sandwiches and a slice of gateau. But it was to Currys that Felicity headed, firmly grasping Ginny's hand.

In the electronics shop, Ginny let her mother talk to the man as she inspected the astonishing devices on sale. A game that let you play tennis on a television screen. Machines that made the tea in the mornings. A box with a green screen on top called a computer that let you do clever stuff. Electric typewriters. Calculators with their flickering red numbers so you never had to do sums again. And rows and rows of televisions – black and white and colour, with their huge olive curved screens, set on trolleys. It was like the inside of a space ship.

Outside, she saw a little boy playing with a football. His hair was cropped, his chubby features freckled. She smiled at him, and he smiled back. She looked back at her mother who was deep in conversation with a man in a short-sleeve shirt that was stained by many pens. The boy kicked the ball gently over to her, and she went out to kick it back. He laughed, and she gave chase, laughing too. He wore a red anorak, so he was easy to spot as he wove in and out of the grown-ups and their prams and shopping bags, dribbling the ball in front of him, always a few paces ahead of her as she squealed at him to stop so she could play. Then she could no longer see him, and his laughter was suddenly more distant. She thought she could hear the sharp voice of an adult and then the laughter stopped altogether. The boy and the ball were gone.

Where was she? She looked around, breathless, still excited by the curtailed game. She did not recognise the shops on either side, or the yellow door in front of her.

Perhaps that was where the boy had gone. He would help her find her way back. Yes, that was best. She ran toward the door and, pushing hard, found herself in the car-park. The area was not enclosed, and the wind took her by surprise after the recycled air of the centre. Above the walls, she had a clear view of the tower blocks and the gas towers. She could hear the traffic from below, and the sound of road works.

The pillars that separated the parking bays were like concrete trees. Perhaps the little boy was playing hide and seek now; perhaps that was why he had led her into this gloomy grey forest. She looked behind five of them, still giggling, though now with a trace of apprehension. 'Where are you, where are you? Come out.' But she could hear nothing other than the sound of cars above and below her. If the boy was there, he was better at hiding than she would have been. Where was that bright red coat? Not a peep, not a suppressed snigger. He must have been keeping perfectly still. 'Hey!' Ginny shouted indignantly. 'That's not fair. Where are you?'

She walked further down, towards the turning up to the next storey. She wondered where their own car was, and whether she should find it and wait there for her Mum. There was a ledge beside the lane leading up, and she hopped along it, trying to avoid the cracks in the paving stones, humming as she performed her little dance.

The next floor up was darker, the openings to the outside world narrower. There were more cars parked as far as she could see, but no sign of her playmate. She felt cold, and wished she had not been so diligent in looking for him. She should have waited. Those were the rules: always wait for Mummy, no matter what. Now she might not even get her toy. She wanted Felicity at once. Where was she? She felt the sudden airlessness of panic, the goose bumps and giddiness that accompany such paralysis. Flee? Yes, she wanted to flee. But where? All around was the same monochrome grey. No shortage of doors, all marked 'Exit' or 'Fire Exit', but nothing to tell her which way to head back to safety. She knew she would be in trouble, but she would welcome a scolding if it meant she could be back in her mother's arms.

At first, she thought it was just a tarpaulin covering something: a sign or an upended table. Part of the grey bric-a-brac of the car-park. But then she saw it stir, flex and stretch its wings, the tarpaulin suddenly becoming a cowl. Where had it come from? The figure, dark in every detail – every fibre dark – turned and confronted her. It must have been a hundred paces or more away, but the connection between them, child and monster, was instant, and beyond any sensation she had ever experienced. The beast surveyed her, tilting its gnarled head from side to side. She thought she heard a snort. There was no face to be seen beneath its hood, not even the red pebble eyes of the other-worldly. Only an unspeakable void threatening, even at this distance, to engulf and imprison her.

This is what the world is really like. If we stray only a few paces off the map of safety, there are horrors beyond imagination. She wanted to cry out, to scream, but could only whimper, her tears now graduating to shuddering sobs. The creature – seven foot tall, eight? – was now confident of its terrain, and set upon its prey. It began its march towards her, except that the march was less a march than the beginnings of a flight, as its black wings spread pitilessly, like a giant moth's. What she could not see, she imagined: rows of razor teeth, hidden in the folds and jowls of a mossy black face, ravenous and enraged. Deathly tendrils sprouting from who knows where, seeking her out, to take her to its nest in Hell, to wrap her in a web, to make her flesh ready for the feast. *Sugar and spice and all things nice.*

At last Ginny found her scream and, with it, the ability to move. She bolted back towards the kerb up which she had come, stumbling along the way, looking back to see the creature bristle in fury, its wings spread behind it as it picked up speed. *If only she could make it to the door. It was not so far. The door.* One, two, three . . . twenty more paces, maybe a few more, and she would be back in the neon-soaked safety of the mall, where there would be adults, phones, sleeves to pull on so she could ask for help, anybody's help. If only she could reach that yellow door, and save herself, she would never make such a foolish mistake again. Childish prayers coursed through her heart: to her parents, to the baby Jesus, to the benign faces in story books, to all of them. All she needed was their intervention for a few seconds more – only a few seconds – and she would be free from the monster, the flapping of wings and the whiff of sulphur.

She broke through the door and into her mother's arms. Felicity's face was streaked with criss-cross tears, her make-up a mess. Ginny had never seen her mother so frantic, or so angry. She shook her daughter sharply by the shoulders and then, to their mutual shock, slapped her once across the face.

'Don't you *ever* do that again!' Her mother's voice was unrecognisable, shrill, demented. She was, almost literally, not herself, having visited, for a few minutes her own parallel Hell, darker still and more epic in its horizons than that into which her daughter had stumbled. She clutched her as if she might never let her go.

And now, at last, Ginny was crying the normal tears of a child, angry, repentant, consolable. Her mother's fury, though astonishing, was a small price to pay for these comforts. She would be contrite, as contrite as Felicity demanded. Only let her not be parted from her mother again.

'My God, Ginny. My love. Where did you go? Where? You know you're not supposed to wander off. *Anything* could have happened. In a place this big? I was worried *sick*. I didn't have the first idea where to look.'

'I – I,' she tried to collect herself. 'I saw this boy, and we played, and I lost him, and then—'

'Hush, hush. Never mind. It's okay now, it's okay. I'm sorry. As long as you're okay.'

'I'm sorry. Mum. I'm sorry. Sorry. Sorry.'

'Don't, now. Hmmm?' Felicity wiped away Ginny's tears, and her own. 'We were lucky, weren't we? Lucky that Rose here found you? What a nice lady. Shall we say thank you to Rose?'

'Scared as a little mouse, she was, poor love.' Ginny wondered where the kindly voice came from, and looked up. She screwed her eyes, sure she was mistaken. But no – no, the treachery of it! There, framed by the bright overhead lighting, much closer this time, but unmistakable, was the monster. An elderly woman in a black poncho, with a badge that said 'Shopping Centre Staff'.

The monster spoke again, shaking its wings as it did. 'I didn't mean to scare you, lovey. We get lots of kids getting lost, running around. Well, it's no surprise, bless them, they're excited. And what with us only being open these six months. I'm glad I found you before you ran around too much with all those cars. Sorry if I frightened you.' She smiled again, a smile of lopsided, grey teeth.

The cunning of the beast! To transform itself, so quickly! To bewitch her poor mother! Ginny withdrew from her embrace and stepped back: once, twice, not far enough.

'What's the matter, darling?' said Felicity.

'Now, then, dear,' said the monster, 'Rose ain't going to hurt you.'

Ginny screamed again, and this time, she did not stop.

This was one of many stories Ginny told Sean in the days that followed his presentation of the drawing. It mattered to her more than most of them because the feelings were still so livid, the sense of order underpinned by menace so fresh. Even across the decades, she could understand the reaction of the five-year-old child. Even now, with all the accrued rationality of adulthood and logic stuffed retrospectively into such memories, she still took the side of her younger, afflicted self against the treachery of Nature. Nothing could explain away that terror, or vanquish it. The cowled figure had been real enough.

He listened intently, lying on his back on a blanket in her garden, a paperback resting on his chest. From time to time, their fingers entwined. He let her speak, unconnectedly, openly, as if he were hearing her confession. She disclosed more than she would have guessed possible about herself, about her life with Harry and what was left of herself now. He offered no judgment on her past or her present hopes, but let her know with the simplest of gestures that he understood what she was trying to say.

In return, he offered her not stories but images: visual scraps from his past. She asked him tentatively about the sea, and why he liked it, and he closed his eyes. 'There was a beach, a small one, I used to love going to. It was quiet, if you knew the right times to go there. Beautiful colours, all the rocks and clumps of seaweed. And they had such brilliant names, the different kinds – of seaweed, I mean – bladderwrack, dulse, and laver. Sometimes, the fishermen would cook them up with their catch over driftwood fires. The cliffs went up 100 feet and, if you stood on the shingle, you could see all the layers, the different strata. I remember the sand martins swooping over me and then taking off over the horizon. And the fossils – there were fossils of shark and fish if you looked. I'd take them home.' He paused, lost in memory. 'It was a place you could go and feel peaceful, watch the sea rolling in and out, and nothing to worry about. And at sunset there was this amazing ruin above – Roman, maybe – and it looked like two incredible black pillars stretching all the way up to the sky. I think that was a place where I was happy.'

'Where was it?' Ginny asked.

He did not answer her question, but continued. 'I think that's where I'd go if something bad happened. Everyone should have a place like that.' She saw from his distant expression that she should pursue it no further.

Sean built his work around their afternoons together, leaving in the early evening to busy himself at his screen. She read when he was gone and rose early to write. The words began to flow once more: still too stilted for her taste, but words all the same, there to be edited and improved. A germ of optimism took root in her intellect. She believed again that she might, eventually, produce something worth reading.

Ginny went to stay with her father for the weekend – she feared he was lonely – and shopped and cooked for him. She noticed that the house was beginning to look the worse for wear, his touching attempts at housework no match even for the limited mess created by a widower. After a brief struggle, Geoffrey acceded to her demand that she arrange for a cleaner to come twice a week to do the house and to iron the shirts he wore when he went into the library. She found a pleasant young Pole called Greta who advertised at the nearest newsagent and said that she could start the following Wednesday. And though her father pretended to be grumpy and to resent the invasion, she could see in his eyes a new kind of gratitude. For – a difficult truth for her to absorb – this lion of a man, her constant companion and hero, was drifting very slowly towards that 'second childishness' of which Shakespeare's Fool warned. Her father would need her more and more, and she was determined not to let him down. As mystified as he was by the shambles of his daughter's life, Geoffrey had never once made her feel like a failure: she had done that work herself. And now, as his need became imperceptibly greater, week by week, month by month, until the traffic of support would all be one way, she would honour his trust.

When she returned, there was a note pushed through her door, as she had hoped there might be. It invited her to a 'second attempt at dinner – in the hope that this time, there shall be no interruptions, interventions, or even assaults!' She smiled, glad now that he was making light of it all and glad, too, for the opportunity to finish the dinner that Harry had ruined. And, while out shopping for her father, she had bought a dress, hoping that this moment would come. It was a simple white summer slip that showed off the beginnings of a tan, and looked right with sandals and a cascade seashell necklace. She bathed and shaved her legs, chose a perfume, applied just enough make-up, and took out a bottle of Meursault Le Limozin from the fridge. She checked herself in the mirror, ran her hands through her hair and went next door.

This time, he was not wearing an apron. She was pleased to see that he been through his own parallel preparations, though more self-consciously and with much less guile, she was sure. One thing could be said of Sean with complete certainty: he never dwelt upon, or was even aware of, his *effect*. She wondered, indeed, if he had ever had a proper girlfriend. His knowledge of relationships seemed as rudimentary as his kindness was instinctive. But while she brought with her a toxic history, he bore no obvious romantic scars. Indeed, his innocence and his reticence were touching. Not once had he tried to initiate anything more than the lightest kiss or the most gentle touch of the hand. He awaited her lead, permission which most men would have taken for granted long before. But this evening, for the first time, he had dressed for her. He wore freshly laundered jeans and a lilac shirt that suited his complexion. It looked new. So he too had been shopping. It amused her to imagine him in a shop off Chancery Lane not quite knowing what to ask for, thinking of making a run for it but staying the course and leaving, bag in hand, with a fresh-minted sense of triumph. She smiled and kissed him on the cheek.

'I am starving. I hope you cooked a whale or something.'

'Bouillabasse. Could chuck some whale in if you want. Drink?'

She handed him the wine. 'Open this. Whatever you've got open, this is better. Trust me. I requisitioned a few of these from Geoffrey's cellar as commission for fixing him up with a cleaner and her down payment for a fortnight. Actually, I was still robbing him blind. But he says he doesn't drink much these days. So I feel no guilt. Go on, get busy.'

He took the bottle downstairs and returned with a cooler and two glasses. She took hers and raised it. 'Here's to Geoffrey.' He clinked his glass with hers. 'Geoffrey.' They savoured the wine, subtle, light and chilled perfectly. 'Christ,' he said. 'That is amazing.'

'Told you,' she said. 'Always raid other people's booze. It's so much cheaper.' She sat down. 'You look nice.' He blushed, but was clearly pleased. 'What have you been doing?'

'I worked twenty hours yesterday,' he said.

'You're mad.'

'I wasn't planning on it. I just started something, and lost track of time. It happens a lot if you live alone. I find, anyway. If there's nothing to make you get up in the morning, or come home at night, why should you?'

'I suppose. What about your sultry next door neighbour?' She flicked her hair theatrically.

Sean laughed. 'Oh, yes, of course. With the exception of that. But sometimes I get lost in what I'm doing, and the next thing I know the security guy is tapping on my cubicle, and I ask him if he's closing up, and he tells me he's opening the building because it's six in the morning. He thinks I'm mad. But my employers are always happy because when they give me something to do, it usually just gets done, quite quickly. I don't have kids to pick up from school, or anyone waiting up for me.'

'What about the things you like, though? Painting and stuff.'

'Yes!' It was as if she had inadvertently spoken a password. 'Yes. That's *exactly* what I wanted to show you before supper.'

'What?'

'My paintings. You said you wanted to see them. And I've been thinking about it. And I thought, well, since you seemed to like the drawing, why not? Come on.' He took her by the hand, led her through the candle-lit hall, past the engravings and prints, and up the stairs to the first floor. There were two doors, one open, one not. He took her into the first room.

'What do you think?'

'My God. Sean.' Astonishment was not something that came often to Ginny, but at that moment she could only marvel at what she beheld. The room was not a studio, or even a small gallery. It was a more like the visual catalogue of a life: a riot of paintings, drawings, in oils, water colours, pencil, crayon, charcoal. Every inch of the walls was hung with his work. The quality was variable, the themes jumbled. But the degree of commitment that the room declared was extraordinary.

On the bare planks of the floor there were piles of surplus frames and large folders, each meticulously dated. Still lifes, landscapes, modernist experimentation, flowers, seascapes, faces, studies, half-finished works, abstracts. There was no order to the sequence, no dominant style or aesthetic. Just a private carnival of creativity, all hidden and squandered in this lonely room. It suddenly made her sad.

'Sean. This is all by you?'

'Oh, yes, of course. I don't work in here – I use a room upstairs. *That*'s a complete tip. But this is where I put the ones I want to keep. It's nice to come and look at them when I'm bored, or down.'

'I don't know what to say.'

'Well, take a look. See what you think.' He was nervous, but also thrilled to be sharing his creations with her. How many people had seen these works, ever, she wondered.

She stepped over a pile of framed drawings and looked more closely at the nearest wall. The most striking image was a very simple line drawing of a young man – possibly a self portrait – in the style of Matisse. Beside it was a fair watercolour copy of a Turner fishing-boat on choppy waters, blending into the churning blues and greys of the sky. To the side was a painting of one of the tables in Sean's sitting room, executed in the manner of Van Gogh. And below that was a rather less successful attempt to emulate a Lucian Freud nude, the greens and yellow oils not quite achieving the impression of mass and earthiness that was sought. But the standard was generally high and – more curiously – the range of styles breathtaking and bewildering. He had not tried to teach himself to be an artist, but to be every artist, to see through their eyes and to feel with their hearts. Of course, in each case the simulacrum fell short of its model. What did she expect? He was not a professional. But his range was remarkable, his ambitions apparently without limit. The awkwardness he felt in dealing with people disappeared when he held a brush or a pencil. Only when she looked up did she see that the ceiling itself was painted, a minor domestic Sistine, with kitsch cherubs, gods and goddesses, and countless animals.

'The ceiling was just for fun. I couldn't help myself.'

'Why – how do you do all this? When?'

He shrugged. 'I don't know. It gives me pleasure. I love to copy the great works, or paint something in the style of a master. Everyone has a hobby, don't they? It's fun.'

'Don't you ever want to paint just for yourself? In your own style?'

'Oh, yes.' He seemed less sure. 'But it's more difficult, in a way. To develop your very own style, I mean. I like the challenge of trying to match a blueprint. You never do, of course. It's like sitting at a piano and thinking you can write a Mozart symphony off the top of your head. But it's fun having a go. I've been doing it for years, experimenting like this – and well, here we are.'

'How many people have seen this?'

'Oh, not many. Here. Look at this one. I did this last summer. It's my feeble attempt at Goya. You know, the dark paintings in the Prado?'

The canvas was the most disturbing in the room. It was Sean's facsimile of the Spanish painter's *Saturn*, the ghastly maddened eyes of the old, naked god looking away from the young body he is devouring, the scarlet of the blood lurid amid the ochres and the streaks of white and the all-consuming dark. 'That's horribly good,' she said. 'Did it take you long to get it right?'

'Oh, sure,' Sean said. 'But it was worth it. Imagine what

it must have cost old Francisco to do the original. They say he had gone mad with yellow fever, or unrequited love, or Alzheimer's, or something. I don't know. All those witches and ghouls and crazy faces he painted. You just wonder what takes a man to the point where he paints something like that. It intrigues me. I love that – well, that inner speculation, I suppose, when you copy something. It draws you as close as you can get, I think. Close, but not close enough. You never get there.' He smiled and looked around. 'Come on, let's get something to eat.'

They sat in the kitchen this time, and feasted on the bouillabaisse which did not have whale in it, but everything else: prawns, mussels, John Dory, and monkfish, seasoned with parsley and saffron. They finished the Meursault and moved on to a lesser white that still complemented the seafood well. She looked at him across the bowl of bread and watched him eat, the lines in his face in sharp relief in the candle-light.

'What's in the other room, then?' she said.

'What other room?' He did not look up, soaking up the juices in his bowl with a piece of bread.

'The room next to your personal Prado.'

'Upstairs?'

'Yes.'

He hesitated, stiffened a little. 'Oh, there's nothing to see in there. I keep it locked up.'

'So it's empty?'

'No. What's the big mystery?'

'Don't know. It's intriguing. Everything about you is

intriguing. Your jumpers are intriguing. Your weird ancient music centre is intriguing.' They were both laughing now.

'Weird?' he said, feigning outrage.

'Yes. Weird. Why don't you buy a bloody iPod dock like everyone else?'

'I don't know. You and your questions – incredibly nosey. God, it's a wonder I have you round here.'

She caught his eye. 'Yes, but you do. Don't you. *Intriguing*.'

'Intriguing? You can talk. At least I don't have madmen coming after me in the middle of the night.'

'*Touché.*'

'Now,' he said. 'We need cheese. And grapes. Yes. Excuse me for a minute. They're in the pantry. Do you want some red with them? There's some claret, I think. If it's of sufficient quality for mademoiselle's palate, that is.'

The wine was doing its work. She felt warm and alive, and happy to be with him. She waved her glass. 'Why not? Eat drink and be merry. A little wine for thy health. And other such nonsense.'

'Back in a moment. Don't run away, now.' For the first time, he was truly playful.

She stood up and told him she was going to the loo.

Ginny climbed the three flights of stairs back to the landing that led to the gallery room. She was emboldened now, by the wine and by his mood, and wanted to seize the moment to discover all she could. The door to the other room surely wasn't locked. Was it? That would be absurd.

She reached out for the door handle, hoping he would

not hear. Before she could grasp it, she felt a hand on her shoulder.

'Don't try to go in there. It's locked. Please.' She turned round. He was close to her now, looking down, a little more imperious than before.

She backed against the door. 'Why on earth not?'

'Because I asked you not to.'

'What are you hiding?'

He dipped his head so his mouth was next to her ear. She could smell his musky cologne. '*Nothing.* I just don't want you to go in there.' He waited. 'Can't you just, for *once*, do as you're told, Ginny Clark?'

She whispered back. 'What do you want me to do?'

'Nothing. Nothing at all.'

And then his mouth was hard against hers, and his hands on her shoulders, and her arms around his neck, and she felt him lift up her dress, and she was pulling hard at his jeans, and grabbing him, and caressing him, and he groaned with pleasure, and the sudden urgency that had possessed them took her breath away. He lifted her up with one hand and pushed her knickers down with the other, and entered her sharply, and she cried out his name, and then, 'God, yes,' as he pushed her against the wall, and there was nothing standing between them any more, no words or pretence or courtesies, and she took his face in her hands this time and kissed him hard and fast, their tongues darting in and out of each other's mouth, as she stroked his cheeks. And then as he began to speed up, she thought he might push her into the wall itself, but she didn't want him to stop, not just yet, and she let herself go, completely, with no fear or hesitation, and then he came, too, and she felt the warmth crawling down her thigh, and the sweat on her brow, and his frantic kisses on her neck. And now it was done, and there was no more tension, and she stroked his face again because, at that moment, she felt so strongly for him, and she told him that, yes, it had been good, that it was what she had *wanted*. And he nodded, breathless and clutching at her as if he never wanted to leave her embrace.

She awoke in Sean's arms. It was only a quarter to seven but the summer light was blazing into the bedroom through the cracks in the curtains. She reached for the bottle of mineral water and drank lustily from it. He stirred and she kissed him. 'Don't get up. Don't. I'll get us breakfast in bed.'

She picked up her dress and pulled it over her head. Then she went downstairs. She would make him something good, like French toast or go out and get some croissants. Yes, that was it. Some fresh croissants from the corner shop, and a newspaper for them to read together and to each other. She put on her shoes, which she found under the kitchen table, dug some money out of her bag in the sitting room, and tied her hair back. She opened the door and went down the path, wishing she had brought her sunglasses with her the night before. She was too hungover and too sleepy to cope with this much brightness.

As she passed her own gate heading towards the shop, she glanced down and kept walking, not absorbing what she thought she had seen, but could not possibly have seen.

She stopped, and felt her stomach turn over. No, no. That was not what she had seen. Her early-morning mind, still intoxicated by last night's love-making, was playing tricks with her. She stepped back a few paces and looked down at her path.

The noise she made, she would later learn, had awoken at least four people in the street, including Sean, who had drifted back into slumber but dashed down immediately, pulling on T-shirt and shorts as he ran. It was the voice of absolute, unvarnished horror from the depths of her soul and it was quite involuntary. There was no act of will required. Which was more than could be said of what she had to do next: to pick up the bloody, furry little corpse of Winston, and fall to her knees as, weeping uncontrollably, she cradled the remains of her beloved cat in her arms.

VIII

Lili Marlene, Glenfiddich, Iceberg, Elizabeth of Glamis, Blueberry Hill: she made sure, as she carved and hacked, that she knew the names of everything that she was destroying, taking careful note of the tiny black calligraphy on the white labels around the stems. The thorns were taking their toll on her hands, but this made no difference to her. A patch of the cat's dried blood formed its own terrible rose on her dress. Her own scars were of no account. What mattered was to complete this work quickly and comprehensively. If she took too long, she would be apprehended and the point of the exercise would be lost.

While it is true that, in law, a cat is a free roaming animal and not considered to be trespassing when it is on land other than its owner's, Ginny knew that Roger Benson would have done his homework. As she rocked back and forth on the pavement with Winston's remains in her arms, she had already dismissed the idea of telling the police or the RSPCA what had happened. How could she prove that the beating Winston had received before he expired, probably of shock, or perhaps from internal injury, had been administered by the portly man next door? Their earlier confrontation would be of only circumstantial relevance. And most people, looking at Roger, would not think him capable of such savagery. But she had seen the look in his eye and the deep longing for release that lurked within. To mark all his frustrations, all his failures, all his ludicrous anger with the world, Roger Benson did indeed want to hurt something. But that something could scarcely be human: he was too much of a coward, too frightened of other people. In an ageing, mischievous cat, he had found the victim he had long been looking for.

When had he committed his foul little atrocity? At night, no doubt: waiting, ludicrously, in the dark, with a torch and perhaps even binoculars, half-longing for, half-dreading the cat's return that would force him to act. Spying Winston, trembling, and then, when the cat was cornered somewhere, or preoccupied by a scent or a marking – giving chase and grabbing him by the tail. A struggle, more vicious than the last, and Roger Benson finally unleashing all that pent-up fury, all that starchy, sexless violence he had nurtured for God knows how many years, smashing and pummelling away at the feline intruder until he could smash no more. Then creeping out of the alley and dumping the corpse on her path with a shaky flourish of disgust before returning to his house to clean himself up and be sick. His sleeping wife need never know. He would deny everything, of course, accuse Ginny of hysteria. As long as he was not detected in the act, his plan was sure to succeed.

So she must escalate. That was what she must do, all she could do. As she clung to Winston, and rocked back and forth in the street, and Sean tried to comfort her, to usher her back into his house, she decided upon a course of action.

'I'm going inside,' she said quietly, gesturing towards her own front door. 'I'm going to put him in a pillow case from my bed and bury him.' Her words competed with the sobs of pure affliction. Snot dripped from her nose.

'I am so, so sorry,' he said, trying to wipe the tears from her face with his thumb, and then a tissue dug out of his pocket. 'I don't know what to say. So awful. Poor little thing – who could do this? It's the work of a madman. Disgusting. I don't understand how—'

'I know who did it.' She looked towards the Bensons' house.

'Oh, now – you don't really think . . . ? I mean, this looks more like kids playing sick games and goading each other on. You know how horrible they can be. Surely – I mean, Roger was just trying to put the wind up you, wasn't he?' He paused. 'What about – you know, your ex-husband?'

She shook her head. 'It was Benson. I know it was him.'

'Will you say that to him?'

She did her best to conceal the delicious icy resolve within her broken exterior. 'I don't know. What's the point? He'll only say I'm mad, where's my evidence . . . I think I would find it even more upsetting.'

Sean started to say something, and then thought better of it. 'Look,' he said. 'You must be feeling awful. Let me help you. I can maybe dig a hole in your garden while you take a bath. And then you can give him a proper burial.'

She touched his face. 'You're sweet. But no – if you don't

mind, I'd rather do this myself. Me and Winston – well, he's part of my past. I need to do this alone. I just feel more comfortable that way. Do you understand?'

He smiled gently as if to say that he didn't really, but would not press the point since it obviously mattered to her. 'Well, look,' he said. 'I'll go back and head off to work. Will you come and see me later?'

She nodded.

'And you're ok?'

She nodded again. He leant down and kissed her on the lips. 'Okay. I'll get something nice for you to eat tonight.' And then he left her.

The burial of Winston would have to wait. She took him into the cool of the kitchen and wrapped him in a towel. Then, stroking his matted forehead for the last time, she slipped the bag of fur and bones – so very dead – into a pillow case and tied it tightly with string. The hole would need to be deep, in case the foxes came digging. But that task would fill the latter part of the morning. For now, there was more urgent work.

She laid out her tools like a surgeon on the kitchen table. A carving knife, a pair of secateurs from the bottom drawer, and old shears. She would need them all. And she must act immediately. At the very bottom of her garden, the fence was waist high: it looked as though the builders had run out of lap panels and had to resort to a length of trellis. She had watched Winston hop over it many times, and it was not difficult for her to clamber into the Bensons' back garden behind Roger's shed.

The main rose bed was on the other side, behind a tacky gazebo swing that Roger doubtless considered the height of elegance. She looked up at the house and saw that the curtains were still drawn. The Bensons did not arise especially early, or, if they did, they were still fussing upstairs over their ablutions, creams and pills. Still, there must come a moment before too long when Roger would twitch the curtain aside and look out with pride upon the flowers that the murdered cat would never again desecrate. However nervous he was about Ginny's reaction, he would, she was sure, allow himself that moment of uncomplicated triumph, a dwarf king surveying his wretched realm.

She wasted no time, approaching the floribundas and the climbers with her makeshift scythes. She was as clinical and controlled as she could be, aware that anyone who saw her, with her bloodied smock, would think her a madwoman. But she did not care. The speed with which the petals fell pleased her greatly. Rich salmon, amber yellow, pure white, dusky scarlet: the work of months and years was quickly the confetti of the dead, fluttering hopelessly to the soil. Then, she began to hack at the stems, harder than the sprays to cut through, but still a straightforward task with the shears. Snap, snap, snap: the devastation of the flower bed was all over in less than ten minutes. She kicked hard at the roots, and dislodged a few of the bushes completely. There must be nothing left to salvage, only a mosaic of destruction and multi-coloured vengeance. Unless she was seen – and she looked up from time to time –

Roger Benson would be no better placed to accuse her than she was to confront him with Winston's death. But he would know. Oh yes, he would know. He would run out into his garden, arms flailing, and cry out in despair, knowing that his savagery had been topped, that he had been bested. She was glad that he would suffer.

The slaughter complete, she gathered her tools, sucked absent-mindedly on her itching scratches and climbed back into her own garden. She would get something to eat and then set about the time-consuming work of burying Winston. She knew that her grief as she performed that task would be agonising – her love for the cat was much deeper than the mere sentimentality others assumed it to be – but she would carry it out with a clear heart, knowing that her little companion would go to the grave properly avenged.

It was Audrey who called first, not long after lunch. 'Oh, hello, dear,' she said. 'I'm sorry to bother you. Only I heard from Number forty-five that you found – that your cat had died.'

'Yes.'

'I'm very sorry, dear. How awful for you. In the road, was it?'

'On my path, actually.' Ginny wondered how glacial she should be with the wife of her enemy. Then it occurred to her that Audrey might just be calling in good faith.

'I know Roger had a run in with the poor thing the other night. I do hope he wasn't – you know, *excitable* with you. You know how he gets. But I just wanted to say how sorry we are. *Really*.'

She wondered what the force of the final word was. 'That's kind. I am upset. He was a lovely old cat, Winny.'

'I can well imagine how sad you must be,' said Audrey. 'One gets so attached. Mind you, you're not the only one. Roger's beside himself.'

Ginny did her best to feign ignorance. 'Why?'

'Someone vandalised the garden last night. Tore his flowerbed to shreds. *Unbelievable*. Years of work gone.'

Ginny paused. 'Oh, no. And – how did that happen?'

'Well,' said Audrey. 'Roger thinks . . . Well, he thinks it must be some of those, you know, *youths* from the estate. It wouldn't be the first time. They come into decent people's houses and properties round here, and they just cause havoc, destroy things for no reason.' Audrey was on the verge of tears.

'I see,' said Ginny. 'Well, that's awful.'

'Yes, well, Roger thinks it's no coincidence that your poor cat was killed on the same night. He was up for telling the police. But now he's saying they probably wouldn't send anybody round, anyway, they're so busy fining motorists and filling in forms, and whatnot. So he says he might go round the estates tonight himself and get some answers.'

Ginny savoured this image of Roger Benson making a final kamikaze flight into the modern world. 'Well, I'm not sure. Do you really think they're connected?'

Audrey volunteered no personal opinion. 'Roger's *sure* of it, dear. Mind you, I've not seen much of him today. He takes these things very . . . well, hard. I think he's upstairs in his study just now.'

Was this how it would end, Ginny wondered. Roger upstairs, pacing up and down, arguing with a bottle of scotch, Audrey downstairs on the phone to a neighbour, hopelessly adrift, in search of moorings. But, today at any rate, she was looking in the wrong place. 'Listen, Audrey, is it all right if we speak properly a bit later? Only, I'm still – you know, a bit sad myself.'

'Oh, of course, of course, dear. Here's me going on about our flowerbed. I'm so sorry. Well, look – we'll speak tomorrow. Yes. Bye for now.'

Peter phoned shortly after Ginny had replaced the receiver, and she was delighted by his timing. As mournful as she was, her limbs lazy with grief, she did indeed want to share the story of her revenge with someone, and was not yet ready to tell Sean, worried that he might be put off by her reckless behaviour. Peter, on the other hand, knew her all too well, and would take her side on principle. But there was something in his voice that made her hesitate before embarking on their usual banter.

'It's me,' he said.

'Hello, you. So nice to hear your voice. Been a hell of a day already, I can't tell you.'

'Why?'

'Winston died.' There was a long pause. She thought they might have been cut off.

'Hello? Peter.'

'Winston. No. My God, I'm so sorry, Ginny. Hit by a car?'

'No, much worse. Someone just beat him to a pulp. Vicious bastard. And I know who, too.'

'You do? How?'

'Well, don't you remember? I told you about that arsehole from next door who came round the other night—'

'Oh, yes, of course. Listen, I need to talk to you—'

'So talk.'

'No, I'd rather do it face to face.'

'That's very mysterious. Are you okay?'

'Oh, yes, I'm absolutely fine,' he said. 'It's probably nothing. Just – look, can we meet at that pub near your place that we went to? Say, in an hour?'

'Yes – but don't you have to work?'

'Nothing that can't wait. This can't, really.'

She had experienced Peter's tendency to be annoyingly cryptic before, especially when he was working on a big story. But this time she could detect a genuine note of concern in his voice, too. There were gaps in his usual nonchalance.

By the time he arrived, she was halfway through her glass of wine, her hangover now pleasantly despatched and her sadness pushed to one side, at least for the moment. His face was paler than usual and he blinked nervously. Without speaking, he pointed to her glass, and she nodded. He returned with what looked like a large gin and tonic and her drink.

'So,' he said. 'Not a good day in the Clark house. Poor Winston.'

'No, bloody awful. But I have already taken my revenge.'

She described her raid on the flowerbed early that morning with relish and drama, and expected Peter to laugh or at least to smile the lopsided smile that showed he was absorbing and enjoying a story. Instead, he nodded politely and smiled, but without engagement, the fidgeting of his legs betraying deep agitation.

Finally, she lost patience. 'Excuse me,' she said. 'But are you actually listening to a bloody word I'm saying? I mean, I have had a bit of a day of it, and if you're thinking of some serial killer at the Crown Court or another naughty teacher then why don't you sod off back to the office?'

'Oh – well, no.' he said, declining to meet her eye. 'Look, I'm distracted because I'm embarrassed, and because I think you're going to be cross with me. In fact, I know you will.'

'Why?'

'I've been making a few – well, you know – inquiries.'

'What sort of inquiries?'

'You know, the sort I make for a living.'

'About what?'

'About your neighbour.'

'Roger Benson? You're kidding me.'

'No, no, not him. The other one. The one who smashed up Harry.'

She was sharp this time. 'Sean?'

'Yes. Sean.'

'What the hell are you doing nosing around Sean?'

'Now, listen, hear me out before you go ballistic.'

'I'm not one of your trial stories, you know. This is *my* life, Peter. This is my *private* life.'

He frowned. 'Oh dear. It's like that, is it?'

'Fuck off, Peter. That's none of your business. Look, I am about to get up and walk out, so you'd better apologise quickly and explain yourself, because I am in no mood for any games, today of all days. I've been scrubbing Winny's blood off my hands.'

'Okay, okay. I'm sorry. Look, this is just . . . a nagging worry. That's all. Probably nothing. Bad timing, I'm sorry. But I found out something that concerns me. Forgive me, but I think you should hear this.'

She folded her arms. 'Talk, then.'

'When you told me the other day about your mystery man, and how you were obviously spending a bit of time together, something didn't feel quite right.'

'What do you mean?'

'All the questions you said he wouldn't answer. Why not? I mean, he was obviously attracted to you from day one. Now, a measure of enigma is no bad thing, and we all have our revolting pasts to cover up while wooing. But – I mean, come on. He won't tell you who the old lady is. Where he used to live. What he really does for a living. He says he used to live by the sea, but won't say where. He—'

'Stop, stop. Pete – where is all this heading? I mean, come on. The guy is *shy*. He makes no bones about that. Not everybody is a mad self-publicist, you know.'

'Point. But not everybody uses a name that isn't theirs, either.'

'What do you mean?'

'Not everybody lives in a house registered in the name of a charity that, as far as I can see, doesn't exist.'

'What are you talking about?'

'There is no Sean Meadows registered as living at number twenty-six. I checked the electoral register, council tax, utilities, phone, banks, everything. He just doesn't exist.'

'How? One of your bent coppers give you all that, did he?'

'Don't change the subject, Ginny. And don't get all holy on me, either. You need to hear this. So I checked on the house. Does he say it's his?'

She said nothing.

'Well, if it is – look, the house is registered in the name of something called the Francisco Charity. But I can't find any other reference to such a charity.'

'It's Goya,' she said.

'What?'

'He loves Goya. Copies his paintings. Goya's first name was Francisco. Maybe it's a trust. Maybe it's how he keeps all his money for some tax break. Who knows? Who cares?' Her voice rose in frustration. 'Why are you doing this? Why are you trying to ruin this new thing in my life?'

He reacted fiercely. 'I am absolutely *not*. But look at it from my perspective. I have been doing this a long time. And I have a good nose for bullshit. And – I'm really sorry – but something about this guy stinks. He may be a great bloke, but he is hiding something. Nobody is that invisible.

It's just absurd. I'm sorry, Ginny. I don't mean to upset you. But you are my best friend, and as difficult as it may be, I do have a responsibility to protect you if I think you're being led up the garden path.'

'Are you saying Sean is a bad man? On top of everything else I have been through?'

Peter considered this. 'No. I don't know. What do you think?'

'I think he's a lovely man. And I wish I didn't know any of this.'

'I'm glad. Look, maybe there's a simple explanation but if there is I can't see it. All I am saying is: just be careful, okay? It's your life, and you're right, it's none of my business what you do. But it is my business if somebody gets close to you and isn't playing it straight. Can't you see the difference?'

Some of her initial anger had faded, but she was still resentful of his presumption.

'Yes. Well, I suppose I can. Can you see how violated people feel by what you do?'

He drained his glass. 'Yes, but they don't mind people like me doing their dirty work for them. Look: let me put it to you as bluntly as I dare. You have feelings for this man. Yes?'

'Yes. Yes, I do.'

'That's great. But there is something odd about all this, too, isn't there? I mean, grant me that, won't you?'

She relented. 'Well, unexplained, anyway.'

'Fine, call it what you like. Now, would you rather find that out now, or a year down the line? If there is something iffy about him – let's say he's an identity thief, or a common-or-garden charlatan, or maybe just an incredibly secretive trustafarian – I bet, however much you're cursing me now, that you'd rather find out today than later.'

'You can't expect people to thank you for making them anxious.'

'I don't expect any thanks. I just expect you to take on board what I've told you, and to be careful. Act on it, make sure he's kosher. You've only just walked out of a horrible divorce, Gin. I don't want to see you get hurt again.'

She sighed. 'Okay. Okay. Look, I really am having the day from Hell and you haven't made it any easier, I promise. Do you mind if we just draw a line under this conversation and I go home now? I badly need to sleep.'

'Of course.' He stood up, and she motioned for him to sit. She did not want him to come out with her. She wanted to walk on her own for a while, like a cat.

The bell awoke her. It was already 6:30. She went downstairs and opened the door. He stood before her, laden down with shopping bags and a box: an angel of mercy from Waitrose.

'I have everything we need to cheer you up,' Sean said. 'Food, drink, flowers. I even bought a new music machine, so you won't feel that you have gone back in time when you come next door. On which note, come next door.'

She threw her arms round his neck. She held on to him tightly and waited for him to drop the bags and put his arms round her. However private this man might be, whatever he preferred to keep to himself, she was learning to adore his touch and the warmth of his presence. He withheld nothing that mattered to her.

Peter's digging proved – proved what? That Sean did not meet the ruthless criteria that journalists applied to people in their daily trawls. But why should she care about that sort of thing? Whoever, exactly, owned his house, or paid his phone bill – the man holding her in his arms, with his kind, expectant eyes, was a friend. She could not, would not, let go of that conviction. Whatever she needed to know about him, she would find out in good time. If he chose to keep some of his past, or even his present, to himself, then who was she to judge? Her own past was nothing to boast about. Why should it matter if they enjoyed each other so much? Trust did not require full disclosure. That was the point of trust. And even as she thought all this, she remembered how she had felt on the landing as their bodies had mingled frantically, the sensation on her skin and in her belly and the heat of it all. Damn Peter.

'That's nice,' he said, drawing apart slightly. 'What did I do?'

'Nothing,' she said. 'Nothing really. Just – you're here.'

He laughed. 'Of course. How has your day been? Grim, I guess.'

'Had better,' she said. 'But it's done. Gave him a good send-off, the little brute.'

'Come on. Let's go and toast his memory.'

He cooked salmon which they ate sitting on the floor in his drawing room, listening to a new CD of the Schubert

Octet. The strings spoke to the wind instruments in a dialogue that mesmerised her. She had not heard the piece for many years, and as the light began to fade outside and the candles flickered to the beautiful phrases of the Menuetto: Allegretto, she felt the sadness within her settle. It would take time to fade, but here was a setting in which such feelings, such misfortunes, need not be all-consuming: where the care of another person could cushion her against horror, and permit her to heal. She laid her head on his lap and closed her eyes as he stroked her forehead. The music transported her to a place that she could imagine describing, with practice, as tranquillity.

'You're falling asleep,' he said lightly.

'What's that?' she replied. 'Christ. What time is it?'

'Don't worry. Go up. I'll tidy up and follow you in a little while.'

She sat up and looked at him. He touched her face and kissed her tenderly. 'Come on,' he said. 'You must be exhausted.'

'You don't need any help?'

'Leave it to me. Go on. I'll be up in a minute.'

'Okay.' She yawned. 'Okay. I will. Thanks.'

She made her way upstairs, past the gallery and then, as she ascended the next flight, she looked down at the locked door beside it. For a moment, she considered shouting out a question to him but then thought better of it. What, really, was the point? In any case, he was in the kitchen clearing up. He would not hear her.

Sean was right about the depth of her fatigue. A day

that should have been spent savouring the memory of a first night with a new lover had been devoted to revenge, the burial of one old friend and the unwelcome meddling of another. She washed her face and used his toothbrush to clean her teeth. Then she undressed and got into bed. She looked at the clock on the table beside her. It was not yet ten. She drifted off again.

He awoke her, stumbling into the room. She was about to speak his name, but then heard the pace of his breathing, his apparent distress. She watched him sit down at the little desk and could see the silhouette of his shoulders, rising and falling. He stood up and his face was briefly illuminated by the light from the street. It was a portrait of – of what? Despair, and panic. His eyes moved from side to side, and a sheen of sweat covered his forehead. He was thinking of something terrible, and thinking deeply. He mopped his brow quickly with his sleeve and then began to pluck at his temple with his other hand, absorbed by his thoughts and utterly alone with them. His mouth opened and closed fractionally, as if he were uttering a private mantra. He held up something and looked at it. Even from the bed, she could see what it was: an old-fashioned key. He grimaced, closed his eyes and shook his head. Then he put the key in the drawer of the desk. It was three o'clock.

She was full of pity for him, and for his inexplicable suffering. But she did not want him to know that she had seen him like this, and that she knew how long he had stayed up after she had gone to bed – doing what? As much as she wanted to comfort him, she could see that he would be horrified if she intervened now, if she approached his pain directly. That would not work for Sean. He would recoil, clam up. Because she cared about him, because she wanted to be with him, and because, if she was honest, she was still a little wary, she would have to learn about him first, at his own pace.

The key.

No, it was out of the question. There was nothing to be gained from prying. Nothing to be gained, and plenty to be lost. Did she really want to jeopardise what she already had with him? She closed her eyes as he drew the curtains and the room fell dark. She listened to him as he prepared for bed. She heard him hang up his trousers, throw his shirt into the laundry basket and quickly brush his teeth. He came to the side of the bed and sat down. She thought she could hear a single stifled sob. Then, without reaching over to touch or kiss her, he lay down very quietly, as if in disgrace in the dead of night.

She could not get back to sleep. Sean's breathing became soft and even, more quickly than she expected. She turned on to her back and looked over. He was already in a deep sleep, one hand behind his head, the other on his chest. What had so disturbed him? Five hours ago, he had been relaxed and attentive. Now he was consumed by some pain, present or remembered, that was so deep that he had waited until she was asleep to acknowledge it. She wanted to wake him, embrace him and ask him to let her help him. But she knew how futile that would be. Sean would not respond to the outstretched hand. He needed to clasp it in his own time.

And then there was the key. The key. Was it really so monstrous to want to know what was in the room? She scrutinised her motives as she lay in the dark. Wouldn't it be sensible if she understood what was making him so wretched? Couldn't she then help him properly, even if she did not mention the cause, whatever it was, directly?

Yes, that was it. And – in truth – if her lover could be reduced to this state, did she not have a right herself to know what was going on? She did not want to betray his trust. But, suddenly wide awake, she realised that she could not brush the matter aside. Too much was at stake: about that, at least, Peter was right. She could not afford to be hurt again.

She looked across at Sean, slipped out of bed and put on a T-shirt. She crept over to the desk and, with as much care as she could muster, opened the drawer. She foraged inside and, to her relief, found the key quickly. Then she shut the drawer and walked softly over to the door, testing the handle before she opened it. It creaked a little, and she winced. But Sean did not stir. She scuttled out of the room and shut the door behind her.

Only a flight of stairs and a few paces separated her from the second door. She could be back quickly. She would go down, have a look and come back. Then, whatever it was, she would be better placed to deal with it, to help him. Still, she was shivering. She could only begin to imagine how he would react, how betrayed he would feel, if he found her creeping around his house at three in the morning, clutching the key. Well: she must make sure that he did not find her, then.

Aided by the skylight, she made her way downstairs and on to the landing. Now she was in front of the door. She looked back once more. What, after all, could there be in the room that was so bad? No, it was time to put an end to the evasion and find out for herself.

She slipped the key into the lock. It opened remarkably easily.

Part Two

Alex

IX

The first two nights at Peter's flat were the worst. She found it all but impossible to sleep, miserable on his sofa bed and tossed around, in any case, by her new fears and imaginings. In its favour, his home was a long way from her own, on the other side of London. But it lacked any sense of comfort or domesticity. There were expensive appliances in the kitchen and a large plasma screen in the sitting room. The furniture was modern and new, but it had not been chosen with any method. This was unmistakably a place where an affluent bachelor came to sleep, and nothing more. Plates piled up in the sink until the cleaner came to deal with them. There were books, papers and CDs everywhere. Dry-cleaning hung in odd places. Files of cuttings perched where there should be pictures of family and friends. Peter had made no effort to impose order on his living space, to give it a personality or to make it welcoming. It was bleakly functional, no more than a bolt-hole for her that served its immediate purpose while Ginny decided what to do.

She tried to rest as much as she could, to read and watch television or DVDs: anything to distract her. But it was impossible to think of anything else. She paced a lot, lay in the bath, tried forlornly to exercise. But the walls closed in very quickly and she wondered how long she could truly last in this makeshift sanctuary. For now, she was safe enough, but none of the questions that had to be resolved had even been addressed. And the security of the flat – the double-lock and the video entry phone – could not stop her from being scared. She saw him everywhere, and not only in the shadows. She looked down the steep stairwell that led to the front door, expecting to see his apparition.

Peter himself was seldom there, often breaking her sleep at two in the morning as he arrived back, climbing up the stairs, tiptoeing past her, bashful and drunk. He arose early to surf the web, showered, changed and offered her a cup of coffee before he left by 7:30 at the latest. He was solicitous enough when he was around, but his work and the social life that spilled out of it absorbed most of his time. She was grateful to him for offering her a place to stay without probing her distress too deeply. She told him the bare facts and left it at that.

He called her once or twice a day from the office or from whatever job he was working on to check that she was okay, and to ask if she needed anything. She insisted that he phone her on his own home landline, as she did not want to answer her mobile, scanning the text messages to see if there was anyone who needed to speak to her urgently. There was only one such message – or rather, many from the same person – and to answer them was out of the question.

A small part of her regretted getting up from the bed,

taking out the key and opening the door. But only because her ignorance would have been so much simpler than the terrible, dark waters into which she had hurled herself. Such a small thing: to turn a key in a door, open it, and see what lies inside. With the best of intentions, to help a suffering lover.

After the baroque clutter of the rest of the house, she was shocked by the room's emptiness. The plain, perfectly white walls and the single light bulb. If the gallery was a celebration of Sean's unfocused but joyful creativity what was this blank space a shrine to? Except it wasn't quite blank. She shut the door behind her and switched on the light, screwing up her eyes against the brightness. In the middle of the room there was a wooden chair and a table on which were stacked three large albums. Nothing more. She sat down and began to read.

She read, and read, and read. Newspaper cuttings and magazine articles and captions and jottings. There were fifteen years' worth of carefully preserved reports of a single story, a story that had made a nation examine its conscience and horrified the rest of the world. It had made a boy famous: famous, notorious, vilified and feared. A boy called Alex.

Even at the distance of a decade and a half, the story of Alex Blakeley still cropped up in conversation, as a benchmark of the twisted and unimaginable. This was to be expected. After all, Blakeley was one of the few cases on record of a child serial-killer. At the tender age of ten, he had killed seven other boys of his own age and younger, all living near him in the Kentish coastal town of Herne Bay. As she read it all again, she remembered the impromptu crowds of local people searching the scrub and the fields. The horrific trawls of what quickly became known as 'Bluebeard's Cove'. She even recalled that initial suspicion had turned to a local man on the sex offenders' register. There was no evidence of sexual trauma on the body of the first dead boy, but the violence with which he had been killed suggested a physically strong adult, perhaps panicking. Only subsequently when Alex killed two children in the same family was he caught out. His trial ten months later became a horrific international circus, with politicians, churchmen and pundits jostling to pass judgment on what it all meant.

Did it mean anything? She remembered, even at the time, thinking that it was nothing more than a demented spree of savagery and sadness. Let others delve for generalisations and deeper lessons. But now that spree was spread before her in three immaculately organized albums: an archive of the investigation, the case, the sentencing of Alex to fifteen years, his release after ten, and the acrimonious aftermath. The coverage had tailed off in the years that followed. But there was a magazine article on the 'New Life' of the sister of one of the dead boys from a Sunday supplement, dated two weeks previously and newly pasted in. The story slumbered, but it was not dead. Like a weevil burrowing through a plant, its head curled and twitched out into the open air from time to time.

It is possible for someone to become so famous, or

notorious, that their continued existence as a flesh-and-blood human being ceases to be plausible. They exist only in the two dimensions of television or photographs, in the sensational prose of the press, in the pursuit of the paparazzi. School photographs taken against a nondescript backdrop, the tie askew, the smile forced. Alex Blakeley was one such person: a boy turned bogeyman who had vanished from the face of the earth even as he was taken down from the dock. Rumours of sightings, of his whereabouts, of his rehabilitation, failed or otherwise, surfaced from time to time. But he had entered the ether of folklore, of monstrous possibility. Nobody truly believed, in their hearts, that somebody so wicked, so deformed of soul, could have carried on living, growing up, passing exams, playing football, learning to shave, assuming a new identity, starting to work, perhaps even forming relationships. It was impossible to conceive of such a thing. Alex Blakeley would forever be frozen in time, aged ten: the appalling pictures that were beamed around the world, of the grinning, dark-haired boy holding a football. Pictures that were printed a thousand times alongside photos of his victims, and the blotched, wrecked faces of their families as they hurried into or out of court. No, such a boy could not possibly grow up, or grow old. Part of his punishment was to be suspended in time, in the collective imagination, as a child denied growth and adulthood, as were his victims.

And yet now, in this bare room, Ginny found that, only an hour ago, she had been lying next to him. That the day before, he had been inside her. That she had shared caresses and intimacies with this man, who had once been a boy, whose evasiveness was, it turned out, no mystery at all, but the necessary deception of a convicted killer living out the rest of his days as someone else. Except that, as Peter had warned her, that someone else did not really exist. Alex was Sean was Alex. On the inside cover of the third volume was a faded colour picture of the young boy and a photo, no more than a few years old of Sean, glued close to one another so that he could remind himself in the long watches of the night where he had come from. Did he shudder as he thought of his terrible crimes? Did his legs become leaden with the guilt of the survivor? Or did he sometimes hug himself with glee at the trick he had played on them all: to escape the circus and end up in a comfortable house, on a respectable street, utterly secure even as the victims' families struggled to build 'New Lives'? Did he see Ginny as just another trophy in his mocking conquest? Or did his misery that night betoken some half-understood sense of impropriety, that in deceiving her he was cheating everyone, that he was mocking God? Did he feel something approaching guilt, or merely the familiar terror that he might be unmasked once more?

She closed the book, turned off the light and shut the door. Then she grabbed her things, ran out of the house and was packed and out in the street in five minutes, heading to the nearest junction where black cabs passed even in the darkest moments of the night. She ran faster than she would have thought possible.

On the third evening of her stay, Peter came home early with a takeaway and sat down with her. He sensed, correctly, that she was ready to talk about it, though he did not press her to do so. In tracksuit bottoms and an old T-shirt, she helped him share out the chow mein and pancake rolls, and crunched on prawn crackers as he poured glasses of champagne.

'Christ. Not much to celebrate, is there?' she said.

'I don't know, Gin,' he said. 'You're still alive. Aren't you?'

'Yes. Well, there is that, I suppose. But – my God – how can this be? I still can't – is it really him?'

Peter put down his chopsticks. 'Well, you have no actual proof. He could just be a nutter obsessed with the Blakeley case. There are plenty of them. Look on the web. There are people who've been following it for fifteen years, since the first body was found. Religious maniacs who think Alex Blakeley was the Antichrist. Conspiracy theorists who think he was fitted up by MI6 and that one of the boys was actually the love-child of a member of the Royal Family, murdered by the Establishment to prevent a great scandal. You name it. There are plenty of people with cuttings files like that. Plenty of hacks, for a start.'

'But Sean isn't a hack. Is he?'

'No. And more to the point, he just doesn't exist as far as the system is concerned. All the stuff I told you before.'

'Explain it to me. Properly, I mean.'

'Simple, really. When a child murderer finally leaves custody, what do you do with him? There's a lynch mob waiting, right? Not to mention people like me looking for a story. So the Home Office has strict rules: Mary Bell, the Bulger killers, cases we don't even hear about, all these precedents. They have got rather good at it.'

She emptied her glass and gestured for more. 'How? How does it work?'

'Alex Blakeley got a lifetime injunction protecting him when he was released five years ago – only on life licence, mind you, with all the parole board supervision. But free, to all intents and purposes. One of the families appealed. I remember that – don't know how far the case got. As far as Strasbourg, maybe. Anyway, the family lost and Blakeley got to keep his new identity.'

'But why not just play it straight with a new name? Why all the tricksy stuff with the Franscisco Charity, and staying off the electoral register?'

'Because, my love, that's the way the game is played. Alex's lawyers got him a serious upgrade with that injunction – a real guarantee of protection. The Home Office is obliged to do all in its power to protect him from the vigilantes and the hacks. Well, you saw how easy it is for us to find out stuff about people. How long do you think a fake ID lasts with people like me on the case? Not long. But if the fake ID barely exists – well, that's a different matter. The point is: nobody would know Sean Meadows existed if you hadn't met him.'

'That's true, I suppose.'

'Imagine he hadn't come across you. He gets his visits – from his parole lady or shrink, I'd guess. His mum died years ago, that's known. He holds down a job, with Whitehall help over references, academic qualifications, his past and so on. No records to speak of. So he's next to impossible to track down. And – best of all from Alex's point of view – he's got an injunction in the bag if we get within a mile of him.'

'So you couldn't put this in the paper.'

Peter laughed. 'Christ, no. I'd receive a written warning if I even tried, maybe get sacked. The paper would be held in serious contempt if it ran anything like that. The PCC would issue public condemnations. If they found out I was planning such a story, we'd be injuncted. It doesn't even arise. And if your friend thinks his cover is blown, my guess is he'll already have squealed to his probation people and his lawyer. I wouldn't be surprised if we get an all-round scary letter this weekend warning all media not to go within a million miles of any tips as to his whereabouts. Sean will be thinking about the *News of the World* as much as he's thinking about you, believe me. But the law is most definitely on his side my love, I'm afraid.'

'And what about me? Who protects me?'

'What about you? He's paid his debt to society, officially anyway. He's done you no harm. His panel obviously believe that he no longer represents a threat to anyone. So what's he done wrong?'

She remembered the powerful hand that had smashed Harry's head into the wall of her hallway and then scooped her up like a ragdoll when they made love on the landing. She said nothing.

'Has he tried to call you today?' Peter asked.

'Christ, yes. About fifty times. He keeps send me these pleading texts.'

'I see. Does he mention the books and his little museum?'

'No. Not at all. Just says that whatever it is, we can talk it through and that he misses me.'

'And how do you feel about that?'

'How do you think I feel?'

'I really have no idea, if I'm honest. You're in uncharted waters. I imagine it's complicated – more complicated than you think. I mean, you have to decide for youself if he is a monster or not.'

She looked at Peter. 'I would have thought it's bloody simple. You were the person who first warned me about him. You were right. I have to get out of his life. Completely, and as soon as possible.' She hugged her knees to her chest. 'I'll sell up and move on. This is madness. I refuse to live with this in my life.'

'I can see that, and you're right: all that I care about is your welfare. But don't do anything hasty. Think it through. Remember, you don't have a new identity like he does. If you move house, what do you really achieve? If you genuinely believe he'll come after you, that won't solve much. If he's a risk, then we can get help. But – I'm just asking – do you really think he's dangerous? Remember that you *did* have feelings for Sean even if you hate the idea of Alex. You've got to think about all that. See it through. Let him know you want no more contact, if that's what you decide. You can stay here as long as you like. But don't be panicked into anything.'

'I can't have Alex Blakeley as my neighbour.'

'No, I understand,' he said. 'Listen. Let me make a few calls and see what I can find out. There's someone who owes me a favour. They might be able to give me a steer.'

'A steer on what?'

'Who Sean really is.'

Those words echoed in her mind the next morning as, for the first time since she had hurried up Peter's stairs with her hastily-packed holdall, she ventured out into the street. She needed fresh air and to shed the skin of captivity. She told Peter that she was going to the London Library, happy for him to think that she was resuming her studies of Bluebeard and Bettelheim. 'Do you good to get back into the book,' he said as he left for work. But the world of folklore and fairy tales would have to wait for another day.

She wanted to share Peter's rational approach to her predicament. But she could not. All she could think of as she walked down the street, past the mothers and fathers taking their children to school, was of her own fragility, the infantile vulnerability that had not been scorched out of her by adulthood. At that second, beneath trees rustling in the breeze, she felt completely helpless. How had she allowed a man of this kind to get so close to her heart? To cook for her, undress her, soothe her, make love to her? Those very hands had beaten the life out of children, waited till the last breath had been shaken from their bodies, tossed them aside contemptuously, before disposing of them like a butcher getting rid of unsold stock. Those hands had touched her skin in a pretence of love as fake as his paintings.

She had seen him pummel Harry into the ground. And yet her deceived heart had made allowances, had allowed him to continue his charade. She had handed him a victory of sorts, this boy who had cheated the system. And now she walked down the street, looking over her shoulder, quickening her pace, nervous of every shadow, or every bird's sudden flight, of every distant siren. He – this man, who was not really there – had turned everything into a threat. From her stupid, misplaced trust, he had woven a great net of fear and cast it over her, to watch her struggle, to watch her weep.

She took the Piccadilly Line from South Kensington to Green Park and walked across the road, past the Ritz, and turned right into the warren of art galleries and cafes around St James's. In the square, she dodged the cabs and couriers and made her way to the door of the library, this inconspicuous portal in the corner, and showed her card.

The librarian smiled at her, peering over his glasses, and asked if she needed any help. She thanked him, but shook her head. A man in an ancient check suit with a buzzard's shock of grey hair was tapping furiously into one of the catalogue keyboards, his eyes wild with scholarly intensity and his hand full of scraps of paper covered in spidery writing: the demented bibliography of a one-man crusade. She slipped beside him at the next terminal and clicked on to the catalogue search. In the space for keywords, she tapped in 'Blakeley'.

Five titles flashed up. There was *Walthamstow Marshes and Lammas Rights*, by G.A. Blakeley; *The Colonial Office 1868–1892*, by Brian L. Blakeley; and *The Mystical Tower of the Tarot*, by John Dyson Blakeley. All useless. But the other two were promising: *Lad of the Flies: the Untold Story of Alex Blakeley* by Derek Staples, and *My Name is Alex* by Meredith Lincoln. Neither book was on loan, according to the screen. She made a note of their references and set off into the stack to find them.

At a tiny desk at the back of the third floor, Ginny opened up *Lad of the Flies*: it had never been borrowed from the library, and, to judge by the stiffness of the binding, had never been read. Derek Staples, according to the author's note, was a 'very experienced reporter with extensive knowledge of Kent, its environs and its history. He followed the Alex Blakeley case from its very beginning, and continues to follow it to this day.' The book had obviously been written by a local reporter with half-decent contacts – probably a copper or two – very quickly, and for a pile of cash. The prose was execrable and the use of hyperbole shockingly tasteless. If Derek Staples had any capacity for empathy, he kept it to himself. But as a primer the book was useful. In amongst its mixed metaphors, gumshoe prose and semi-literate crime scene forensics, were most of the facts of the case.

Alex Blakeley grew up on a hill overlooking Herne Bay in what amounted to a castle where he lived with his father, a defeated artist drinking his way through inherited wealth. The court-appointed psychiatrist had concluded that there was substantial evidence of physical abuse at this stage of Alex's life, though he had been unable to establish whether this had been sexual. Whatever the truth of the matter, the ménage at Belial Hall – thus renamed in the Twenties by the Hon Oscar Blakeley, a dilettante of the dark arts – was indeed a vision of Hell. Alex's mother, a daughter of the Sussex gentry, died when he was three, perhaps of drug abuse, perhaps of starvation, and his father had not even pretended to fill the gap. Instead, he had left every detail of his only child's upbringing to an aged and complicit housekeeper, kept Alex out of the local school with spurious promises of home tuition, and instructed his son that all he could possibly want was there in the long, stinking corridors of his home, with its scores of unused rooms, perilous attics and pantries of rotting food.

Duncan Blakeley, when he was not drinking alone or screaming at another canvas of failure, hosted parties of legendary depravity for his old Oxford contemporaries, most of whom had proceeded to success in London. They were, of course, more than happy to use his home for such purposes, confident of discretion. Alex was witness in these years to most of the debauched and twisted behaviour of which human beings are capable. When his father grew bored of his presence, as he frequently did, he would lock him in one of the cellar rooms: a part of the Hall that had no heat or electricity. According to the court papers, he had done so on one occasion when badly drunk and stoned, and forgotten all about it the following morning. Alex languished in his cell for several days before the housekeeper discovered him, starving and frozen, his clothes soiled and his fingernails broken from his attempts to claw his way out. Many times, he ran away. But Duncan Blakeley was always able to track him down, often with the help of the local police who regarded him as a harmless bohemian toff who might throw the occasional dodgy party, and certainly liked a bit of wacky baccy but always found it in his heart to chuck a few grand into the station benevolent fund at Christmas. Alex would return, sometimes in a police car, wondering only how severe his beating would be once the officers had waved him goodbye.

From an early age, Alex developed a taste for hurting animals. He started with insects then graduated to birds and rabbits, once, by his own later admission, coaxing someone's pet dog into a rabbit snare. He liked to hurt things that could not hurt him back. 'My God,' Ginny whispered to herself. 'Winston. Poor Winston. It was *him* all along. My poor darling cat.' She felt herself choke in anger and misery.

Soon enough, however, such sport was not enough to slake his ghastly thirst. In the past 250 years, Derek Staples noted, there had been twenty-seven recorded cases in Britain of children under fourteen killing other children. In the summer of 1992 Alex Blakeley became the twenty-eighth, killing seven children in the space of a few weeks, all boys: Hugh Barlow; Henry and Robert Warren; Marcus Steeples; Joseph Groom; Stevie Baldwin; Sam Tucker. Those whose bodies were found had been beaten to death or strangled, and with such ferocity that the killer was initially assumed to be an adult. He was caught out only when he made the mistake of pursuing a vendetta against a particular family. Alex had already killed seven-year-old Henry Warren, but became greedy and set his sights on the dead boy's older brothers. The ten-year-old, William, saw his nine-year-old brother, Robert, being beaten to a pulp by Blakeley, and dragged off for the kill. William testified against Alex at the trial, sealing his fate and, in his fearless act of witness, captured the essence of the case for the world, the loss of innocence that it dramatized. Even the conviction of Alex Blakeley came at a terrible cost.

Only three of the dead boys were found. Alex indicated in one of his first police interviews that he had disposed of the rest in the waters of 'Bluebeard's Cove', although the extent of his psychotic denial was so great that investigating officers were unable to state with confidence that this was so. All trawling of the water near where the killings had taken place and excavation of the beach itself had been in vain. After intermittent digging in the years that followed, the police finally admitted defeat, to the disgust of the families denied the chance to bury their loved ones. There was a picture of the beach and the ruined Roman fort and the two towers that overlooked it. Again, she felt a chill of recognition. There, before her, was the scene Sean had described: his beloved beach and the 'black pillars stretching all the way up to the sky'.

Transcripts of the Blakeley police interviews took up most of the middle section of the book – easy copy, no doubt. But they were compelling, the black ice of the boy-murderer awful to behold.

DI UPTON: So, son, do you know why you're here?

ALEX BLAKELEY: You're angry with me.

UPTON: We just want the truth, Alex.

BLAKELEY: I didn't do anything.

UPTON: How did you kill Hughie Barlow?

BLAKELEY: I didn't kill anyone. We were only playing.

UPTON: Playing? Playing what?

BLAKELEY: Hide and seek. Near the beach. Near the towers.

UPTON: Did you see Hughie when he was hurt?

BLAKELEY: No.

UPTON: Alex – you need to tell me the truth. When he was hurt –

BLAKELEY: He had blood on his face. And his arms. But I didn't see who had done it to him. He was lying on the beach. Like an old toy.

Again and again, they asked him the same questions. Sometimes he would become distressed, usually when his father was mentioned or his life at the Hall. He would discuss killing only in hypothesis, but when he did, he was expansive on the subject:

DCI SPENCER: You've never killed anything? Nothing at all?

BLAKELEY: Only bugs. And spiders, I suppose.

SPENCER: What do you think of killing, Alex? You're a bright lad. Is it wrong?

BLAKELEY: Killing?

SPENCER: Yes. Is it wrong?

BLAKELEY: Depends on who you kill. They used to hang really bad men.

SPENCER: That's true. I can remember when they still did. I'm glad they don't nowadays. What do you think, Alex?

BLAKELEY: I think killing is right sometimes, yeah. Sometimes you can get really cross with someone, you know, so cross – that, then they –

SPENCER: They should be dead?

[Blakeley's solicitor intervenes]

SPENCER: Sorry, Alex. Use your own words. What did you mean?

BLAKELEY: All I meant is that some people deserve to die.

SPENCER: Ah, well. But who decides that?

BLAKELEY: I don't know. I suppose it just happens. Like some people die in car accidents. Some people die in stories.

SPENCER: But Henry, and Hughie and Marcus. They weren't in stories. Or in accidents. Someone killed them with their bare hands. For nothing.

BLAKELEY: Well, it wasn't me. But if they got killed, there must be a reason.

What reason? Reason, as a thousand pundits had observed, seemed to be sleeping when Alex Blakeley turned his hands on these and the other boys. Derek Staples concluded: 'When we look into the face of Alex Blakeley what do we see? Ourselves, of course.'

Meredith Lincoln's prose was better but her cod psychology was, if anything, even more grating. The author was a self-styled laureate of human affliction, paid exorbitant sums by distinguished journals to cover trials which addressed 'the heart of darkness' and then even more by publishers to turn her despatches into frequently-updated books. Though Ginny intended to take out the books, she transcribed some passages out of habit:

It is all a matter of the question we ask. If we ask 'why?' we shall quickly resort to the Manichean dualisms of our ancient forebears. We shall look into Alex Blakeley's dark heart and see only evil, a feast of sadism, an apparition of the Beast. These were acts of unparalleled wickedness. When we ask 'why?' we see the fires of Inferno, the Fall of Man and the incursions of Lucifer. Yet I do not think this is the right question.

Ginny put down her pen but continued to read:

We must ask instead: *whom*? Whom was Alex Blakeley trying to kill? Hugh Barlow; Henry and Robert Warren; Marcus Steeples; Joseph Groom; Stevie Baldwin; Sam Tucker: all were ordinary boys, from ordinary homes. When he took their lives, he infected those same homes with the insanity that had always permeated his own. He exported the pain that was the principal product of his twisted family. Was it revenge upon the parents of these boys, and thus upon his own? Perhaps. But there is a more simple explanation for his acts. Alex Blakeley wanted to kill the boy he could not be. He wanted to kill the intolerable incarnation of the boy he believed he was capable of becoming, in a different, gentler world. As he rained blows on these defenceless children, he was murdering not only them, but his better self, the self that his wretched circumstances had stolen from him. In the end, Alex Blakeley was unique in yet another way: he was the first serial suicide.

What, Ginny wondered, made people want to write such things? Why did they believe that significance could invariably be squeezed from horror? To seek meaning only in badness – it was a peculiarly modern disease.

Eventually, Meredith Lincoln relented and resumed the narrative. The legal doctrine of *doli incapax* – 'incapable of crime' – had been artfully invoked in defence of the young Alex, and the original recommended minimum sentence of fifteen years was quickly commuted to ten by the Chief Justice. Eleanor Warren campaigned vigorously against the release of Alex Blakeley. 'I have lost two sons to this monster,' she told the *Daily Telegraph* in 2002. 'I do not wish to see another mother go through the torment which continues to afflict every day of my life.' But her campaign failed. Alex Blakeley walked free in the same year, in time to celebrate Christmas at an undisclosed location. Since then he had eluded those whose lives he destroyed, as well as the journalists and biographers. Meredith Lincoln at least had the decency to conclude with an admission of the dead end she had reached:

Almost nothing of Alex Blakeley's life after his conviction has been disclosed to the public. It is known that he developed well academically whilst in detention, obtaining high grades in examinations and correspondence courses. He was said to have revealed a talent for drawing and art, although a picture depicting the murder of a boy that was printed in the press was shown not to have been by Blakeley, but a forgery sold by a corrupt member of the probation service for a five-figure sum. The mothers of Hugh Barlow and Marcus Steeples fought a long and unsuccessful legal campaign to ensure that he remained incarcerated and, when that failed, to disclose his new location. Again, the Barlow–Steeples campaign was thwarted: Mr Justice Bowdley said that the unique character of the case required stringent measures. He granted Blakeley a lifelong injunction against disclosure. Occasional sightings of the now-adult Alex Blakeley have never been verified. At the time of writing, he is twenty years old and living somewhere in England.

After all the banalities and pseudo-intellectualism, here was the most important fact of all: that Alex had survived ten years of custody, prospered during that time, and emerged more or less intact to resume his life with the System as his impersonal but mighty protector. He had fooled them all, just as he had, in his new guise, fooled her. Had she been in danger in his bed, in her garden, as their fingers intertwined? As Meredith Lincoln would have said, that was the wrong question. What mattered was that she *might* have been in peril. It was for him to decide. It was his choice whether he stroked her face with the kindness of Sean or dashed Harry's head against the wall with the remembered ferocity of Alex. The power had always been in his hands. He had forced her surrender without her even knowing it. His weeping on the night she discovered the albums was all the more egregious because it was so self-indulgent. She grasped, at last, that his had been the tears of self-pity – the memory, probably, of his own comparatively minor ordeal as the captured killer – not the true misery of remorse.

Stiff now from hours of reading, she stood up, stretched and went downstairs to get the books stamped out. The catalogue area was deserted and silent but for the tapping of the librarians at their keyboards behind the desk. She took back the books, put them in her bag, and stepped out into St James's Square. It was still hot, the breeze having subsided. She hailed a taxi and gave the driver Peter's address.

She dug her mobile out of her bag: thirty-six missed calls. Christ. Then she saw that twenty of them were from Peter. She called his number and assumed that it would click, as it invariably did, on to his message service. Instead, he answered after the second ring.

'Ginny?' he said.

'Yes, of course it is. Where are you?'

'I've been out of town. But – look – I spoke to my source. It's definitely him.' There was a silence. 'Ginny: Sean Meadows is definitely Alex Blakeley.'

X

There were, at least, no further text messages from Sean.
Her father, with his endearingly perfect punctuation and
spelt-out words, inquired after her well-being. Harry, to
her surprise, left a voice message in which he said, hesitantly
and awkwardly, he had located a book she had been looking
for and, then, as if reading out a weather forecast, that he
had not a drink for a whole week. There was a text from
Julie: 'Supah idea, luv! Can't wait to see you jxxxxx'. What
was she on about? It would have to wait. They would all
have to wait.

'Ladies you should never pry, You'll repent it by and by!'
That was the moral Charles Perrault had distilled from the
legend of Bluebeard. 'I might do anything.' Bluebeard
warned his young wife of the anger she would provoke in
him if she used the little key to open up the forbidden
room. But of course she could not resist the temptation,
and found inside the room the carrion of Bluebeard's brides.
The key was smeared with blood – and could not be wiped
clean. Only the arrival of her brothers saved her from the
wrath of Bluebeard and certain death.

Well, maybe she would repent. But prying was better
than ignorance. Prying was better than dancing on the

puppet-strings of a retired murderer with time on his hands. As horrific as his crimes were, it was difficult to read the deadened words of the transcripts and not to feel a measure of pity for Alex Blakeley. He was not a whole human being: more of a rejected experiment in flesh and blood, discarded by his unspeakable father and left to exact vengeance wherever he could. He had found meaning in nihilism, in violent extremity. But one could not feel pity for Sean, the human being he now pretended to be. In adulthood, Alex Blakeley had become the manipulator, playing with her heart and doubtless the hearts of others who wandered into his path. In his penal limbo, he had at last discovered his own, twisted form of freedom.

Later, she sat with Peter on the sofa and told him what she had been doing. He nodded. 'Well, I can understand your curiosity. But – listen – I checked this out with a source who has never let me down. Very high up and he didn't want to talk about it at all. I had to plead.'

'A politician?'

'It doesn't matter. The point is I went on and on about it, said I had very good reason to believe that Alex Blakeley was now resident at number twenty-six. And then I said all I needed was a steer, I wasn't going to print anything, I understood the injunction. You know, the whole nine yards.'

'What happened?' she asked.

'Well, like I say, I have known this guy for years, and I could tell he was doing me a favour by even speaking to me about this. I could feel him squirming down the line.

He kept making me promise that I wasn't taping it, which I wasn't. He just didn't want the conversation to be happening at all. But after a while, he told me to shut up and said he would say one thing to me as long as I promised not to ask anything more. So I said, fine. You know, what else could I do?'

'That was the deal.'

'That was the deal. Correct. So I said: tell me then. And there was a bit of a pause. And he said: "Peter, listen: don't go anywhere near number twenty-six. Okay?" Just that. Nothing more. And then he put the phone down.'

'Christ. He didn't have to say any more, did he?'

'Not really. That's as good a confirmation as I could have expected, I reckon. So: we know for certain who Sean Meadows is, at least.'

She leant back on the cushion. 'What do I do, Pete? What am I supposed to *do*?'

He took his jacket off and threw it on an armchair. There were sweat patches under his arms. 'Let's be as calm about it as we can be. Point one: we know he is Alex. We know Alex is a high-profile serial murderer out on life licence. We know that he is considered to be no danger to society. Point two: do we share that opinion about him? Very important.'

She closed her eyes. 'Is he dangerous? I don't know. To me, no. Not yet, anyway. Was I ever scared of him? The night he attacked Harry — yes, I was, if I'm honest. But I was attracted to him by then, so I pushed it to one side. I pushed it to one side, and decided that it was chivalry rather than bloodlust. But then — then, there's Winston,

187

isn't there? I mean, the *bastard*. He knew how much I loved that poor cat. And he knew I would blame Roger Benson. That was why he did it. For fun. Just to fuck with my mind. This wasn't some damaged kid experimenting with animal torture. It was an adult using all the tricks of his trade to amuse himself.'

'When did he do it, though?' said Peter.

'Oh, I think we know from his record that he's pretty good at nocturnal manoeuvres. Must have waited till I'd gone to sleep. I don't think he would have given it a second thought.'

'Yes,' said Peter, 'and look at what he did to Winston, after all.'

'Crushed him into bits, poor little thing. The act of a maniac. Sorry, a *rehabilitated* maniac.'

Peter patted her knee and fixed her with sombre eyes. 'But do you think – do you reckon he could ever hurt you? Do you think he *is* still a threat? Because – if you do – well, that might change everything.'

'What do you mean?'

'Listen. If there is one thing politicians fear more than vigilante justice, it's letting out someone who goes on to reoffend – a serious offence, I mean. Look at all the scandals over the courts and early release. Look at all the calls for a Megan's Law here because they put a paedophile on the streets, or in some bail hostel, and, before you know it, he's arrested outside a school. Now, if Alex Blakeley is living out his days, minding his own business – even, I'm afraid, getting himself a girlfriend – well, nobody can touch him, not the police, not the press, politicians, nobody. But if we could show that he is still a menace, that he is still capable of violence, and that the release was a bad decision – well, that would be a very different matter.'

'So we go to the police, then.'

'I wouldn't advise it, not at first. Never go to the cops with anything half-finished. Only the most senior officers will know anything at all about his relocation to their area, and they'll be reluctant to cause a fuss. If he goes back inside, or even if he has to be moved, there'll be a huge drama, and that's the last thing any copper wants in his backyard. As things stand, they'd be defensive. Mr Meadows hit your ex-husband, you say? Defending you, I gather. He killed your cat? Do you have proof, madam? I understand there are urban foxes in this area which attack cats quite regularly. Were you romantically involved with Mr Meadows? Oh, I see . . .'

'Enough,' she said. 'I get the picture.'

'I'm just saying what I said yesterday. Don't rush into anything. We can sort this if we don't lose it.'

'So what, then?' Her voice was barely a whisper. 'Look, Pete – I'm really scared.'

'Don't be. Listen, my guess is he'll be back in touch very soon. He needs to be. He's been trying to call you ever since you left. Worried sick for himself, no doubt. Worried that he's gone too far. Probably looks out the window every morning and expects to see a thousand photographers, or a lynch mob. Remember, however protected he is, he only has to slip up once. Can you imagine how many death threats Alex Blakeley must have received over the past fifteen years? Look at it from his point of view: you could send one email to the right website and he would be running from every have-a-go hero in Britain. So he'll want to end this, is my guess. When he does call, fix up to meet him.'

'No way. No bloody way. I'm not going near that psychopath.'

'I'll come with you. Goes without saying. And I'll get some muscle along in the background, just in case. He won't be the first dangerous man I've had to meet, believe me. We can tell him what we know – he'll have worked that out, anyway – and then I think we tell him to move on somewhere else. The deal is: he gets out of your life forever, and we save him a whole load of fuss. What do you think?'

'I'm not sure,' she said. 'Most of me thinks he belongs behind bars right now. Wants him there. In a dark cell he can never escape from.'

'Maybe. But you know that isn't on offer yet. It might be eventually if he steps out of line and we can prove it. But right now this is the least worst option. Will you consider it?'

She looked at him but did not answer. She did not have an answer to give.

Peter went back to the office, warning her that he would be working very late on a big exclusive – he couldn't say what, not just yet. But it was taking up most of his time, and would be a massive story when it broke. She wondered how, even now, after all these years, he managed to keep his emotions so successfully at bay. How he managed to be such a loyal and efficient friend and yet to set those feelings aside without hesitation so he could concentrate on his reporting. No wonder he was so good at what he did and so feted. While most people stumbled through life, always a few beats behind the score, Peter managed to glide from one challenge to another without apparent strain. No matter: he had come to her aid and she needed him more than ever.

She looked out of the window at the scene below, the fading of Friday work and the blooming of the weekend spirit. A group of kids played football in the communal gardens at the centre of the square, their holdalls acting as goalposts. At the bus stop, a Filipina she recognised as a cleaner in Peter's building sat wearily, every puff on her cigarette signalling fatigue and irritation. What sort of home would she be going to, wondered Ginny? Would she step into ease as the door opened, or into even greater friction, greater demands upon her than she faced in her daily work? Beside her stood a young couple, twitching with anticipation at the evening ahead. The boy pranced in front of the girl, mobile in hand, telling a story with dramatic gestures. She laughed out loud, the piercings in her face suddenly mobilised. They would go out and drink heavily, Ginny thought, before going to a party, taking drugs and having sex in somebody else's bedroom. In the morning, he would be as morose as she was needy. For now, they stood in the shadow of the bus shelter, and awaited the varieties of oblivion the evening had to offer.

Ginny stepped back from the window. She wondered if she would be permitted such mundane pleasures again or whether, hand in hand with Alex Blakeley, she had passed a point of no return. This artificial man, a construct of the legal system, his own intellect, and the human capacity for survival, had presented himself to her as a normal person. But he was no such thing. He was a visitor from the books she carried in her bag, a caricature of the media and pop psychology, a bloody footnote in social history. Alex Blakeley could never re-enter the world of Friday night dates, and ordinary work, and half-happy lives. He could only drag other people into his own private no-man's-land. That was where she had ended up. Following Sean credulously into what seemed a safe haven she had woken up on the scorched earth of Alex's world. She wanted to find the thread that would take her back. But it was not to be found. She had not known of the dangers when she set out. She had not protected herself or her heart. And now she sat in a silent room: at his mercy, at his disposal. No more the killer, he had found new ways to claim victims. That, in the end, was his genius.

Peter left very early, as he had said he would. When his phone rang at eight, she stirred herself from the sofa to answer it, in case he had news.

'Hello,' she said. 'Peter? What's – how's it going?'

'It isn't Peter,' he said.

She slammed the phone down. It rang again. She was about to push it on to the floor when it clicked on to answerphone. 'Ginny, it's me,' the same voice said. 'Why don't you just pick up and talk to me? I'm here with Julie.'

She lifted the receiver. 'Julie? You mad bastard. What are you doing?' Finally, she screamed at him: 'Don't you dare fucking hurt her! I'll *kill* you!' Her fists clenched and unclenched in powerless fury.

'Don't talk like that. Don't. Why didn't you answer my messages? I left so many. All I wanted was for you to call. Is that so much to ask? I need to talk to you, I really do. Can't you see that? I know what happened. I know what you think.'

'You have no idea what I think.'

'I told you not to go in there. I asked you not to. It was important to me that you didn't.'

'I'm *glad* I did. I found out what sort of a man you are, at least. What sort of a monster.'

'I'm not a monster,' he said. 'That's such a terrible misunderstanding. I want to explain. Everything. Just let me.'

'Go to hell,' she said. Then she remembered: 'What are you doing with Julie?'

'Oh, I invited her here so we could all have a picnic. I said that you still needed cheering up after Winston. I knew that she would come, and that that would make you come, too. I gather that she texted you.'

'Yes.'

'Don't try and get her on her mobile, by the way. I got rid of that this morning, when I discovered she'd contacted you. She didn't notice at first. I imagine she's furiously trying to get a new handset now, although it won't be easy round here. I said it was a secret, meant to be a nice surprise for you, but I think she assumed I was kidding and that you were bound to know.' He paused, as if reflecting on human frailty. 'Why can't people keep secrets when they're asked to? Anyhow, if she calls again – I did ask her not to – don't answer the phone. I need her here till you arrive.'

The import of his threat dawned on her fully, and she began to plead. 'Don't hurt her. Please. You know how much I love her. Please. Don't take her away from me, too. She is like a sister to me. Just let her go.'

He sighed. 'I'm not keeping her captive. She's going shopping later on. And I don't want to take anything from you, Ginny. I never did. Only to *give*. This has all been forced upon me by your breach of trust. Why couldn't you just respect my wishes? We could have been happy. I really believe that.'

'Happy?' she said, doing her best to conceal the scorn she felt, if only for Julie's sake. 'How could I possibly be happy with you? What sort of a person do you think I am?'

'Just a normal person, like me. You have needs, so do I. You were starting to be content. You said so yourself. What has actually changed? You think you know all about me now. Do you? What makes you an expert on me all of a sudden?'

'I know enough.'

'Nowhere near enough. That's the problem. Nowhere near. You were in my home, in my bed. Now you think you are entitled to call me a monster.' His voice changed, dangerously bitter now. 'How do you think that makes me feel?'

'I don't know. Listen, where is she? Julie.'

'Oh. At her little hotel, I think. She decided to come down yesterday before you arrived. In fact, I gave her a lift. She's marvellous, fantastic value. We laughed all the way down on the motorway. I can see why you're so fond of her. Very clever. She's looking forward to seeing you later. Well, so am I.'

She sat down, her legs weak and her head pounding. 'What is it that you want, Sean?'

'I just want you to hear my side of the story. I want *justice*.'

She considered this. What could he mean? Justice: what did Alex Blakeley mean when he used this word? But, then, what choice did she have? 'I won't come alone. I'm sorry.'

'Don't even think of bringing your journalist friend,' he said. 'That would be a *very* bad idea.'

Something occurred to her. 'Sean, how did you get this number? Peter's ex-directory. Has been for years.'

He laughed. 'You're not the only one who's resourceful, you know. Help comes from the most unexpected quarters, I find.'

'You can't seriously expect me to meet you on my own.'

'You can't seriously expect me to do anything else. Do you honestly think I'm going to meet you with a reporter? Do you really think that?'

Of course he wouldn't. And what, in the end, had Peter been thinking? Sean Meadows – Alex Blakeley – was not going to stand by meekly while a journalist with a bodyguard in the car dictated terms to him. That was never going to happen. And, in her heart, she had always known that the conversation would have to be between the two of them. Whatever union they had formed on the landing of his house could only be sundered properly in person. She would have to look him in the eye. And she needed him to know that, as frightened as she was, she would not let him win, or threaten her friends. It all had to stop, and only she could make sure that it did. She bit her lip. 'All right, then.'

'Good,' he said. 'Good. I am sure we can bring this all to a good conclusion.'

'Just don't hurt Julie. Or I'll hurt you.'

'Don't worry. You're doing the right thing.'

'Where are you, Sean?'

He laughed again. 'Oh, you know where I am.' The line went dead.

Of course she knew. The place where he told her he would go if something bad happened. The place with the two black pillars stretching to the sky. Bluebeard's Cove.

XI

'I watched a programme about volcanoes last night,' the old man said to the woman – apparently his daughter – as she pushed him past the little pavilion towards the pier. A mechanical plastic penguin by the railings chirped inanities at them. The promenade was not busy: only a few stray families braved the strong breeze.

'That's nice,' the woman said. 'Did you take your pills?'

He ignored the question. 'They never know when they're going to erupt.' He shook his head, held on to his cap which had become dislodged by his disapproval. 'Well, you would have thought.'

'Yes,' the woman agreed, revealing snaggled teeth. 'You would have thought.'

Ginny watched them pass and considered sitting down on the bench, or by the clock tower. Built by a wealthy widow called Mrs Ann Thwaytes in 1837 – driven, according to the noticeboard, by the conviction that she was in communion with the Holy Ghost – it was supposed to be the oldest free-standing clock tower in the world. Could that possibly be right? The Victorian structure, with its dilapidated scaffold and chipped paint, looked like a minaret calling the lonely to desolate prayer, howling back at the sea. It made small claims for itself now.

She knew where she was heading and that she must make the journey on foot. You could take a cab or the bus, the lady in the fish and chip shop said, but if you want to see the cove you'd best walk. An hour and a half she said – adding, with something approaching disapproval: *if you're a good walker*. What did that mean? Anyway, she could not afford to take chances. He would not be by the ruins themselves. He would be lurking somewhere, among the rocks, by the sea wall, back on his own bloody terrain, waiting for her with his next surprise. She turned and surveyed the broken facades of the boarding houses and B&Bs, light years from the middle class chic of Whitstable a few miles away. 'Open all hours!' declared the hoarding on a store that had evidently been closed for months, perhaps years. The lights in the pie and eel shop flickered unsteadily. Outside, a lone smoker coughed loudly, hopping from foot to foot in the chill as he inhaled desperately between gasps.

She wondered where Julie was, and whether she was truly safe. No, she could not waste energy on such awful speculation now. Julie's best chance – her only chance, perhaps – was for Ginny to remain focused and to give Sean, or at least to promise Sean, the demented sense of 'justice' that he demanded. There could be no witnesses, no police, no Peter, no 'muscle' waiting in a car to spring out and run to her aid if Sean pulled off his mask and became Alex once more. She could not risk her friend's life, even if it meant endangering her own: this was her mess, her own bespoke disaster of the heart. This was between the two of them now: Ginny and the man she had embraced, not knowing he was a murderer of children. He would wait for her, of that she was certain. He sought a reckoning, whatever it entailed.

Giving Peter the slip had made her feel mildly guilty, necessary though it was. She had called him immediately and left a message on his mobile: she was going to the library again, she said, and then to see Julie: she would be back later that night or first thing in the morning. That gave her a window of time in which to settle her business with Sean, if such a thing were possible. And what she said was half-true. She was indeed going to see Julie, which would dissuade Peter from getting involved. He steered clear of her outings with Julie. He would not bother her today – not yet, anyway.

The train from Victoria took an hour and a half, and she sat opposite a disapproving man in a suit who watched her fidget and squirm, breaking off occasionally to take a call noisily on his mobile. After a while, he moved to another carriage. She was relieved.

Now she stood on the shore of dying England. The beach stretched as far as the eye could see in either direction, the unseasonally cold weather having driven the swimmers off the sand and the shingle. She wore a fleece and hugged it to herself. Out at sea was a handful of fishing boats, an old barge long relieved of cargo, a deserted jet ski lashed to a dinghy, and, much further out, the strange two-legged remains of a naval sea fort, squat, obsolete and solitary in the water. Whatever acts of courage had been committed on its huge pillars were long forgotten. The fort had been left behind by the waves, by history, by everything.

On the eastern horizon, she could see the two towers of the church rising above the undulations of the sand, a forbidding sentinel on the prow of the hill. Everywhere – in shop windows, on the seafront, in the cafes – there were black and white pictures of the town's gleeful holiday history. Men and women with parasols and prams enjoying a morning constitutional on the promenade, decked out in the starched uniform of the Edwardian seaside; a shopkeeper with Victorian bowler standing in the forecourt of a splendid ironmongers; a steamer departing the pier in the 1890s; a regatta before the Second World War, with hundreds of boats and thousands of spectators. These images were impossible to miss: they were a desperate offering to the newcomer, a plea for respect and affection. And yet all this was long, long gone. The town was little more than a shrine to its past now.

It was one o'clock already and she was more than an hour away from the cove. Some boys sped past on bikes and she wondered how often Hughie, Henry, Robert, Marcus, Joseph, Stevie and Sam had done the same, and whether Alex had seen them smiling and shouting as they pedalled off into the distance. Was that the provocation? Was their laughter how he excused his savagery, or did he need no excuse? The books said that he had roamed the town with ever greater boldness as he grew older, still terrified of his father, but no longer as easy to incarcerate as he had been. One thing was certain about Duncan

Blakeley, who had taken his life before the trial, and that was his cowardice. As Alex grew up, he became stronger and angrier, a little less likely to flinch and a little more likely to strike back. Duncan knew that he could still beat a ten year old into submission, threaten him with a spoon dipped in a boiled kettle and brandished before his son's eyes. But for how much longer?

She was, she knew, retracing Alex's steps. At dusk, as the drinkers shouted the odds outside the seafront pubs and the holidaymakers went for pie and mash, the boy had often made his way from the pier and the promenade across the dunes and towards the towers, around which caravans huddled in the summer months. It was ten minutes in a car, much longer by foot. Alex did not care. He was hardy by temperament or because of the horrific circumstances of his upbringing: perhaps both. He told the police that he liked to walk, and that he hated to go back to Belial Hall before it was absolutely necessary: if he waited until after nine, he risked a beating but he also knew that his father might already have passed out, on a sofa or at the kitchen table, a tumbler full of brandy in front of him. It was a gamble worth taking, he told them in the shabby interview rooms.

So this long stretch of sand and stone, along which the proud promenaders had strolled more than a century ago, down which the tourists in their kagoules still beat a less stately path, had been Alex's avenue of fear and anger. What thoughts had passed through his mind as he made his way to the cove? How much he hated his father? How he longed for a mother? How much he envied the boys: the dead boys and those he had not yet slaughtered? Was there a pinch of guilt, or shame, as he walked towards the next victim, bracing himself, his hands shaking, preparing his body for the task in hand? Or perhaps none of these things. Perhaps his mind had been a blank, a blank canvas of banal amorality. Perhaps he had not thought at all, as he rained down blows on those young faces, smashed bones, throttled and tortured; as his hands ran red. Perhaps that was the terrible secret at the heart of the great riddle of Alex Blakeley, the riddle that so many had presumed to solve: not a warning to humanity – take care, take care, this is what can happen unless you take care – but a dark, meaningless nothingness. Nothing will come of nothing. The reason is there is no reason. And the horrible possibility that such a universe might exist – in spite of Felicity, Julie, her father, and all the love she had known – stretched before her now like the pebbles and the shells towards a rendezvous beneath the two towers.

She wiped her eyes, stinging from the sea wind. There was sand in her shoes. She stopped to empty them and looked out to where a lone windsurfer was struggling against the tide and the unpredictable gusts. With rather abject merriness he waved to her, and she instinctively waved back. The last human being, stranded amid the grey waves, smiling helplessly at the lonely woman marching on. Ahead, there was not a soul to be seen.

She pushed on, pausing occasionally to steady herself, to seek some sort of poise. Hills, dunes, pathways: all merged into one, one long walk towards something very bad, a memory that was not meant to be exhumed. And then, at last, there they were.

The towers stood before her, the silent witness to all that had happened before, the terrible acts that had led her here. More tired than she had expected, she scaled the path to the church, past the signs warning visitors of the treacherous waves and rocks, up to the crest of the hill where the ruins stood, hemmed in by wire fences. Her heart raced, and she looked around. Apart from a man dressed in oilskins making a sketch, and a dog she assumed must be his, the site was deserted: in spite of the month, it was now bitterly cold, the winds blowing sharply through the spires and biting at her face. The holidaymakers had retreated to their caravans, or to the pub at the bottom of the hill. But she knew he would be here, near here, somewhere.

She walked up to the peak and past the tombstones with their illegible, wind-burnt runes. The towers loomed above her now, imperious and indifferent. The paths around them made no sense: they were like half a labyrinth left behind by absent-minded masons. Beneath the spires was a tablet with the inscription:

THESE TOWERS THE REMAINS OF THE ONCE
VENERABLE CHURCH OF RECULVERS WERE
PURCHASED OF THE PARISH BY THE CORPORATION OF
TRINITY HOUSE OF DEPTFORD STROND IN THE YEAR
1810 AND GROINS LAID DOWN AT THEIR EXPENCE

TO PROTECT THE CLIFF ON WHICH THE CHURCH HAD
STOOD. WHEN THE ANCIENT SPIRES WERE
AFTERWARDS BLOWN DOWN, THE PRESENT
SUBSTITUTES WERE ERECTED TO RENDER THE
TOWERS STILL SUFFICIENTLY CONSPICUOUS TO BE
USEFUL TO NAVIGATION. CAPTN. JOSEPH COTTON
DEPUTY MASTER IN THE YEAR 1819.

This was a holy place but it was also a place at the mercy of the elements from which sailors were warned. The spires had been rebuilt, not out of piety, but terror of the rocks. And the church itself was built on the ruins of a Roman fort where Germanic legionaries, hundreds of miles from their Rhineland home, shivering on the Kentish plain, had fought off pirates and shed blood on land not yet consecrated. The hill was soaked in blood.

Battling against the wind, she stumbled through the stone pillars and walls towards the prow of the hill. Immediately beneath her was the path leading to the northern sea wall and a maze of tiny canals and bubbling vats where, according to a warning sign, shellfish were being processed. Beneath the wall was the cove.

It was not as she had imagined. Not a silent lagoon, and a stretch of sand where children could play, but a small inlet in the cliff, with a sharp drop to a pebbled shore and a wall of rock. It was hidden, that was its magic: now she understood. Even from the towers, you could not see it properly, would not be able to make out the figure of a ten-year-old boy dragging something. It was a secret garden of the sea, a place of retreat or savagery. Alex had chosen well. The cove was ideal for his purposes.

There seemed to be no direct access – that had been cut off after the murders, she remembered reading – but she climbed over the fence, through a forest of chicken wire and edged her way towards a rusty ladder built into the cliff-face. It stretched down only ten rungs and then there was a drop of eight or nine feet. She looked down, and considered turning back. The cold was dreadful, the walls of the cove swirling with the sea winds. She could see nothing beneath her, other than a length of old rope and rocks thrown up by the surf. It was madness to be here: to follow a murderer to his lair, to play his game, to tell no one. Yet she had no choice. She thought of Julie, and remembered watching Sean smash Harry's head against the wall, and jumped.

Her fall was awkward and she thought at first that she had twisted her ankle. But as she stood up, dusting herself off, she realised that it was only a bruise. How, it suddenly occurred to her, would she get back up? She looked around. Beneath the ladder the cliff face turned sharply inwards: there was a small cave, perfect for a hiding boy, though too small for a man. She thought she could make out markings on the rock, chalk lines and deeper carvings. Were they warnings, too, like the rebuilt towers?

Most of the cove was scarcely visible from the hill. Behind her, it stretched beneath the sea wall, mostly in shaded darkness, a tiny pebbled beach enclosed by a cliff-face pock-marked with holes, some much bigger than others. The sea rushed in and out, made mud of the sand beneath the rock. The smell of seaweed and perhaps worse was overpowering. She dug her hands into her fleece and, holding on to the rocks, made her way into the cove. She thought, again, of the story.

'Open them all,' said Bluebeard, 'go into each and every one of them, except that little closet, which I forbid you.'

At what appeared at first to be the innermost point, there was an unexpected kink in the rock which concealed a further recess, dark and cold. Without a torch, it was impossible to see within, or even to guess how far it stretched. It was no wider than the span of her arms: she shuffled in. The water gushed into the cove and soaked her feet. She grimaced. If he was here, he could do anything: the wind would carry away her cries for help. Nobody would see her. Nobody would notice the slender figure clambering out later on, brushing off his hands, and loping back towards the spires. That's what he would do. Wait till nightfall, leave her there, and then walk calmly back to the town, his head down, barely noticed by the passers-by who would be asked, in the days that followed, if they had seen anything, heard about the woman found in the cove.

. . . she went down a little back staircase, and with such excessive haste that she nearly fell and broke her neck.

Now there was only the roughness of the rock to guide her and the strip of white light from above. The wind roared in her eardrums and the water lapped a little higher with each wave. Did she hear the snap of something behind her?

The impatient breaking of driftwood under foot, or something else? So hard to be sure.

Then she was face to face with rock on all sides but one. She had reached the innermost point of the cove. Fumbling, she ran her hands over the icy surface of the wall: at this point, it was smooth as bone from the dashing of the waves and the mossy seaweed. But there – there was something, not a cave, but something much smaller: a tiny ledge on which she felt a small and gnarled object. A candle. She felt her legs buckle. Of course: a candle. That was how he lit his home, and how, when he came here, he would light the cove, as he carried out his muttering rituals of remembrance. She shuddered again, felt a stab of anguish pass through her. Then she held up the candle in her trembling hand, sniffed it and wondered if she could indeed smell recent burning, or if her mind was now deceiving her. Edging round, she turned back, slowly, deliberately. He was here, all right.

She tried two or three times to wipe the key off; but the blood would not come out; in vain did she wash it, and even rub it with soap and sand.

The main part of the cove seemed a liberation after the constricting rock passage. She breathed deeply, gulping in the sea air. A wave of nausea coursed through her and she crouched for a few seconds. The foulness of the cove filled her: people were not meant to come here, to this desecrated place. She was an impostor: the ghosts of the children, left behind, deserted so many years before, howled anger at her intrusion. Too late, too late: why were you not here before? She looked up to the sky, now clouding over. Should she wait? Should she call out for him? This was his domain, after all. He had come back here because it was the only place where he had ever truly been master, because he felt safe. At Belial Hall, he had been subject to abomination. In prison and then in hiding, he had been at the mercy of his keepers. But in the cove he had ruled all that he surveyed: a watery abattoir in which he had dumped his prey, looking out to sea before he began the long trek home. Now, years later, he could light his candles and consider what he had done here, how he had once seized the world's attention by his deeds. This, too, was the very place where little William Warren had seen his brother Robert bludgeoned to death by Alex. The place that had sealed Alex's fate. So what satisfaction he would derive in returning here: ambling into his old kingdom with impunity, returning as a man, this time with a woman he surely despised for the weakness of her heart. That was the symmetry, wasn't it? That, with her, he would, at last, win,

She slumped against the rock, her aching body conspiring with her shattered nerves. She had nothing left to give. She had come to the place, as instructed, alone and unprotected. What more could he ask? What more did he want from her?

'*You do not know!*' replied Bluebeard. '*I very well know. You went into the closet did you not?*'

She looked up at the ladder and wondered once more how she was going to climb back up. The rope, perhaps. Yes, the rope. If she could throw it around the lower rung and tie it down on the shore ... but where was it? She looked around. Where had it gone? The tide. The tide had swept it back.

'Are you looking for this?'

She turned. And there he was, the rope in his hand.

XII

'Well, I knew I could rely on you to come,' Sean said.

'Did I have a choice?' she hissed. 'Where's Julie?'

'No – and don't worry about her.'

'Fuck you, Sean,' she said – then took a step back as she saw the look on his face.

'So much anger,' he said. 'Where does it all come from?' He shook his head and tossed the rope aside. 'Anyway, I knew you would come here – we would come here – eventually. It was inevitable.'

'Look, you're scaring me. God, what more do you want? I'm here. There's nobody with me, though Christ knows I wish there was. Now you've had your fun, so let her go.'

He turned out to sea. 'I knew you would come because you would want to imagine it. Because you would think that it might make you understand. That's your vanity. That's your *sin,* Ginny. You think you can conquer us all with your intellect.' He laughed.

'Is this where you killed them, Sean? Is it?'

He turned back to her, looking over her shoulder to the inner part of the cove. 'Try to imagine what it was like, then. That's what you want, isn't it? A blow-by-blow account.'

'I just want to go, Sean. I want to get Julie and *go*.'

He ignored her. 'Well, it was at night, for a start, not like now. The night of the second Warren, I mean, the one that brought it all to a head. First question: what were those two boys doing out, for a start? Well may you ask. With their brother Henry dead and the town full of lynch mobs looking for the killer, or any poor bastard who looked a bit odd, for that matter. I mean, what were they doing out in the first place? That's a good question. Well, they had slipped out, it turns out, because their Mum and Dad were so distraught that they had locked the other two boys in their room, and then forgotten how easy it was to open a window and sneak out. And they did. Which was very, very stupid.'

'Why?'

'Alex had already killed five kids, one of them their own little brother. How stupid was it to go out? But they were stir crazy, the two boys, unable to take the rows and the tears and the drinking a second longer. So I imagine. They wanted a breath of fresh air, and to remind themselves that they were still children. Mad with grief in their own way, too. Children respond differently.'

'Weren't they scared?'

'Maybe. But they were young, too. Robert was less keen than William, I think. He was reluctant. But it never occurred to them, you see, that Alex hated the Warrens *specially*. That he wanted them *all*. There was something about those three boys that maddened his blood. And – well – he simply couldn't believe his luck when the remaining two scuttled out across the garage roof, down into the lane and towards the shore.'

'He had planned it.'

'Oh, worse than that. Much worse. He had *hoped* for it. *Longed* for it. But he assumed he would be thwarted. I mean, five was a pretty good tally. More seemed greedy. And now these two Warren boys were presenting themselves on a plate. How could he resist? His triumph: three in one family.'

'Didn't somebody see the boys? Didn't anybody think of stopping them?'

'An old man tried to stop them, and a woman called out from her car. But you'd be surprised, Ginny. Do you know how many people saw Jamie Bulger being taken to his death? *Thirty-eight*. Thirty-eight people saw and did nothing. That's the ones that *admitted* it. Once these things start, it's as if they are unstoppable. It's the strangest thing As if they were meant to be. I mean, in all honesty, how many people do you think will remember seeing you make your way here?'

She looked at her feet. She was trembling again. 'I don't know,' she whispered.

'Can't hear. Speak up.'

'I *don't know*. Very few, I'm sure.'

'Exactly so. We imagine we're surrounded by safety, and help, and so on. But all these nasty things go on right under our noses. And mostly we don't even notice.'

'So you were waiting for them.'

'The boys went to the shore – here – and threw pebbles into the sea. They were nervous, of course, but they talked, and after a while they even laughed a little. They were just happy to be out of the house.'

'What did you do?'

He turned back to sea, seemed to falter and then regained his composure. His profile formed a vivid silhouette. 'Alex hit William first, very, very hard, with a rock. William fell to the sand immediately, and Robert didn't stand a chance, then. Blakeley brought the stone down on his temple too, and dragged him – I mean, the strength of this boy! – dragged him a few feet away from his brother. And then he went to work on him. Oh, he really went to work.'

She put her hand to her mouth, stifling her tears. 'Why, Sean? Why did you want to hurt them so badly? They were *children*.'

He ignored her, his eyes awful and translucent with memory. 'And that was the first and only mistake, and the only one that was necessary. Because William came to, you see, and saw Alex pounding at his brother. By then Robert was already like a rag doll, limp and lifeless. And he screamed like the Lord God Almighty – William, I mean. And for the first time, Alex – I mean, he had always been so cool, so unmoved – this time, even Alex did, at last, panic. He tried to drag Robert off, into that little space there.' He pointed at the hidden recess where she had found the candle. 'Eventually, people came and managed to get in there. And they saw the state of William – my God, he was in a mess – but he was able to tell them what had happened, quite quickly, and then it was all over, once they absorbed what he was telling them. Alex had tried to run, across the marshes and the flatlands, but it didn't take the villagers and the police long to find him. And then – as I'm sure you know – William was the key prosecution witness. It was an open and shut case.'

Silence hung between them like incense at a funeral mass.

'Do you often come back here, then?' she said. 'To think about what you did? Seek inspiration for your paintings?'

'No,' he said quietly. 'I don't like it here. It's the last place on earth I want to be.'

'Then why are you here?'

'I needed to see you.'

'Are you going to kill me too?'

'Why would I kill you?'

Through the fog of fear and despair, she felt a stab of irrepressible anger. 'Don't you kill *girls*, then? Am I too old? Is that it?'

'I don't want to kill you. I never hurt anyone.'

'*Christ*. Even *now*. Can't you at least admit it? Can't you even show that decency?' She was yelling now, out of control. 'William Warren *saw* you killing his brother. Don't you realize how disgusting it is that you can't say that you did that? That you can't pay those boys even *that* respect. Even *now*. You live in a nice house, hold down a job, you have the freedom to – to try and be close to someone, to me, and to lead a halfway ordinary life. You have had the freedom to *grow*, you bastard. And all those boys are *dead*. Everyone calls you Sean, protects you from the mob that would tear your eyes out of your face in a second if they knew where you were. And you can't even bring yourself to utter that single, small sentence. You can't even say that you did it. *That*'s your greatest shame. *That's* what will be unforgiven.'

He sat down on the sand. She wondered if she had gone too far, if his legendary temper would now emerge from its enforced hibernation. She looked at his twitching hands, hands that might be convulsing with nerves or might be scrabbling in the sand for a rock.

He exhaled: much more than a sigh. It was the sound of the deepest weariness, of horrors too tightly knotted ever to be disentangled. The sigh of a frightened child. When he spoke, his words were barely audible: 'I am not Alex.'

'Of course not. You're Sean Meadows. You are someone else now. You escaped what you did by becoming someone else. So easy. We made it so easy for you, didn't we? All of us. So fucking easy.'

He stood up, trembling suddenly with outrage. 'No! Not *easy*. Never that. Never *that*.'

'Damn you, Alex. You are a coward.'

And then he was upon her, the same man who had bashed Harry's head against a wall, the same man who had taken her up against the wall. He seized her jaw, not hard enough to hurt her but hard enough to fill her with fear beyond anything she had believed possible. His face was pressed against hers now, as he bellowed. 'I – am – not – Alex!'

She dared not speak, dared not take the next step. She

knew that, now, he was capable of anything, that he might dash her head against the crag, that he might pull her into dark inlet and finish her off by candlelight. She was silenced by his towering rage and by a fear that the clock might move a second further and reveal her awful fate.

And then she felt herself released, spun round by his hands to face out to sea.

'I'm going now, Ginny,' he said. 'I've told you everything you need to know.' Still she stayed silent.

'Don't turn round. Don't even think of it. Count to a thousand – yes, a thousand, slowly, and when you're finished, the rope will be waiting for you and you can climb back up. No – don't say a word – don't say another word. Don't look back.'

She looked out at the grey, bleeding at the horizon into the dull tones of the late afternoon sky. A gull swooped close to them, pecked something from the rock, and resumed its flight.

Now, his voice was more distant, as though he were already scaling the wall. 'By the way, she's at the Belvedere. You'll find her there. But not until you've finished counting.'

The Belvedere. She wanted to bolt, call for help, protect her friend. There must be someone on the sea wall, walking a dog or braving the elements, who would hear her, who would bring help. But then – she could not be sure where he was, what he would do if she disobeyed him. If she sounded the alarm, or even clambered out too soon, who was to say what might befall Julie? Was he, even now, lurking behind the medieval towers, waiting for the game to finish, just as Alex had watched the desperate locals and policemen follow false trail after false trail? No: she could not take the risk. Not with a mind as monstrous as this. She must finish the game and then rush to her friend's side.

One, two . . . One, two . . . One, two, buckle my shoe, three, four, lock the door, five, six, pick up sticks.

One, two, three, four, five, once I caught a fish alive, six, seven, eight, nine, ten, then I let it go again.

One, two, three – Clap! Clap! Clap! – Look at me – Clap! Clap! Clap! – Being the sea!

One potato, two potato . . .

One for the master, and one for the dame . . .

By the pricking of my thumbs . . .

The wind rushed through her, seized her, so strong it seemed that she might be swept away, a small, helpless mannequin, mouthing numbers to herself.

'Ginny!'

The voice was sharp, urgent: not Sean's, she realised immediately, even in the depths of her frozen reverie of counting and rhymes.

'Ginny! It's me! What the fuck are you doing down there? For Christ's sake . . . Let me help you.'

She turned round, and the world did not end. She saw instead the distinctive crumpled grey of Peter's coat as he climbed down the ladder towards her.

XIII

'You look terrible,' he said, as they sat in the car park by the pub. 'Here, have a nip of this.' He pulled a half-bottle of brandy from the glove compartment. 'Medicinal purposes.'

She shook her head. She could not stop rubbing her hands together, as if trying to cleanse herself of what had just happened.

'Please yourself. You should, though. You've been in shock, or something not far off, I think. You were howling and whimpering like – like some trapped animal when I got to you, you know? Now, I know you've been through Hell. But Ginny – you need to calm down a bit if you want me to help you. What is this about Julie? Just take your time and tell me.'

She closed her eyes and took deep breaths. She could still feel his hand on her jaw, the intimations of savagery. Never had she felt death to be closer, not even at her mother's side in the last days. And yet he had not harmed her. Was that the point? To parade his power and then – for whatever twisted reason – to hold back. To relish the sadism of arbitrary mercy. Was that the new thrill that Alex had discovered in cosseted adulthood?

'Julie,' she whispered finally. 'He took her.'

'Yes,' said Peter. 'That's what you said. Is she with him?'

'I don't think so. He said – the Belvedere. That's where she is. That's what he said. Sean – Alex.'

'Why is she there?'

'He tricked her into thinking that he was treating me to a break by the seaside, and bringing her along. He drove her down. Then he hid her phone after she sent me a message, she was – she was alive then, at least.'

Peter tapped into his phone keyboard. 'The Belvedere . . . Yes, it's on Central Parade, past the pier. We can be there in ten minutes.'

He turned the key, reversed the car, and turned left into the winding lane that would take them back to town.

'Can you talk?' he said as they passed another little church and a row of bungalows.

'Yes – I – yes. Sorry, I'm not good for much, Peter. Not yet. Thank you for coming.'

'You're a bloody idiot, you know, lying to me like that.'

'Had to. He said nobody was to come with me, and he meant it.'

'Yes, but you must be mad going to the cove where – you know, the scene of the crime. With Alex Blakeley, for Christ's sake.'

'I had no choice. It was that – or well, God help Julie.'

'I could have hung back. I know what I'm doing, you know.'

'Sorry, Pete. It wasn't worth the risk. This was my problem. He knew what he was doing, too.'

'Well, you're a fool. He could have killed you. If I'd been there, we could have the whole thing on tape, and nail the bastard once and for all. I told you, if he's threatened you, or anybody else, he's toast. He did threaten you, didn't he?'

'Yes – and, well, he made it clear what would happen to me, to Julie – I mean, he's mad, delusional.'

Peter frowned. 'Your word against his. But in this case, I think – well, I think the court would see it from my, from our point of view.'

She sat up. 'What do you mean?'

'Time to put this maniac behind bars, Gin. He shouldn't be out at all. Now we know that for sure.'

'I don't want this to be public.'

He turned to her. 'Okay, okay – first things first, let's find Julie.'

They turned into a steep hill leading to the seafront. 'How did you know where to find me?'

He grunted grimly. 'I didn't, did I? But I remember the case.' He nodded to the back seat. On top of a pile of papers was a book with a lurid red cover entitled *Britain's Deadliest Killers*. 'There's a chapter in there about him – dreadful book, but it has all the key facts. Idiot's guide, you know. Sutcliffe, Fred West, Shipman, Crippen, Alex – they're all in there. These madmen have a weird sense of theatre. If he was going to entice you anywhere out of London, it was likely to be here. He'd want you to himself on his stamping ground.' He turned to her again. 'I thought I might never see you again, to be honest.'

'Well.' She managed a weak smile. 'Well, I'm still here.' She put her hand on his arm. 'Thank you, Peter.'

'Don't mention it. Ah, here we are.' They pulled in by the Belvedere Boarding House: it was spruce, well-kept and advertised wi-fi connection, a cocktail bar in its cellar, and mini-spa. Yes, this is where Julie would be staying.

She pulled on the door handle to get out. He stopped her. 'No, Ginny. Let me. Just in case – you know.' Their eyes met. 'Look, I'm sure she's fine. But on the off-chance – you have had one encounter with Alex Blakeley today. That's enough. Let me.'

She slumped back, and nodded. He was right. She was not equal to another confrontation with Alex today, or with his handiwork. Peter would have to do it.

'Just stay here. Sit tight. Okay?' She nodded and he got out of the car.

She closed her eyes and tried not to dwell on where Julie was and what state she might be in. She turned around and looked at the debris in Peter's car: newspapers, crisp packets, an old blanket. There was the book that had reminded him of the details of the case. She picked it up, and looked for the chapter on the cove killings: 'Alex Blakeley: the Devil's apprentice'. Where did they find the people to write this rubbish? Still, she flicked through the well-thumbed pages to the section on the murders and scanned it. It was familiar stuff: the death of the mother, Duncan, the parties at Belial Hall, Alex's incarcerations as a child, the first murder, the cove, the trial. A cuttings job. Nothing new. She was distracted by a child on the promenade calling for her father to push her on a swing.

Then her eye lit upon something on the page. She looked again. She gasped quietly, closed her eyes, as what she had seen, and what it meant, sunk in.

The knocking on the window startled her. She dropped the book, blinked and saw that it was Peter, his face frozen in alarm, pointing at the window. She opened it.

'What?' she said. 'What? What's the matter?'

'She's not there. Manager says she hasn't checked out but that she left at lunchtime and hasn't been back.'

Her heart pounded. No, not Jules. Please. 'Was she alone when she left?'

'Yes,' he said. 'Definitely. They said that she checked in alone, hasn't had company as far as they know. Wanted to know if I was the law.'

'What did you say?'

'I told them the truth – that I was a reporter. They got quite helpful on condition that the place wasn't mentioned.'

'But not helpful enough,' she said, an edge of contempt creeping into her voice.

'Okay, take it easy, Gin. We'll find her. I promise.'

'So you keep saying. But how do we know he hasn't moved her already to some – some godforsaken place? How do we know he didn't see you and panic?' She was crying again.

He took her hand. 'Stop it, Gin. Stop it. We'll find her. Okay?'

She pulled herself together. Now was not the moment. She had to concentrate on her friend. 'Okay.'

Ginny got out of the car. 'Where?'

'It's a small town. The High Street is back there, everything forks off that. It won't take us long.'

They headed down a cobbled path, past a pub called the Admiral Benbow and a boarded-up dry-cleaners.

'Where are we going? Christ, wait, I'm trying to keep up.'

'We'll go everywhere until we find her,' he said.

They were, she realised, retracing the desperate steps that the Grooms, the Baldwins and the Tuckers had taken as they searched madly, forlornly, refusing to give up hope for the children who were already dead. Without method or logic, looking down alleys, into shop windows, in restaurants and cafes, in the post office, as if that were where their loved one would seek refuge. There was no sense or system in what they did, only the absolute refusal to acknowledge the grim compass of probability and the terrible direction in which its needle was swinging. He had gone back and taken her, hadn't he? Drawn her out. More lies, more charm, more promises. Where was Ginny? Julie would have asked that, and he would have said: Why, this way. And smiled, and smiled, and been a villain. Then taken her God knows where to do God knows what.

Was that what Alex had learned in adulthood? That if you really want to hurt someone it is better to kill the person they love. The pain lasts longer. Was this to be Alex's 'justice'? If he could not lead a life of freedom, then neither should she. He would flee, go back on the run. And she would be burdened forever by the fate towards which she had led her beloved friend. Yes, she could see the insane logic in that. All those years had not been wasted. Alex had watched and painted and programmed computers and, with infinite patience, devised new ways to cause pain. And she, God forgive her, had helped him find a way of trying out his new methods: here, where it had all started. Fool, Ginny, fool.

'Oh God,' she said. 'You're not shagging *him*, are you? Please tell me you're not.' Julie had emerged from a chic cafe, loaded down with shopping. Her Prada coat and her heels made her absurdly conspicuous.

Ginny rushed up to her friend and embraced her with the ferocity of a parent. Her tears flowed recklessly now. He had not won.

'Bloody hell,' said Julie. 'It's not that bad. Even if you had. I mean,' she said, 'I did once. Didn't I, Pete? Our night of shame.'

Peter smiled sheepishly and looked at the pavement.

'Anyway,' Julie continued. 'Now you're here at last, let's go for a drink. And does anyone know where I can get a new Nokia handset in this appalling place? Taken me hours to get this shopping. What? Why are you both laughing?' She lit up a cigarette. 'And, anyway, Miss Elusive – where's your dreamboat boyfriend? Where's Sean?'

XIV

It was nine by the time they dropped off Julie at her flat. She was subdued and bewildered, still absorbing what had happened, and how close she had danced to the lip of the abyss. At first, she would not believe them as they laid out the facts, laughed at them as was her way. And then, her hand to her mouth, thinking of the car journey down, the disappearance of her mobile, the silken charm of Sean, she had realised the truth of it. He had been going, he said, for a walk, leaving her to spend the afternoon in the town before Ginny's arrival. The plan, he told her, was for the three of them to go for oysters and champagne in Whitstable when she arrived: why not meet at the Belvedere for a drink at six? She thought this an excellent plan, and had done her best with the highly unsatisfactory selection of shops, looking for a present for Ginny.

And all that time, Julie now realised, she had been at the mercy of Alex Blakeley, a name forgotten only because so many years had passed. And she had *believed* him: believed him when he told her that he had fallen in love with Ginny, believed him when he said that it would be fun if they all went to the seaside, believed him when he revealed his plans for celebration. All that time, she had been a helpless plaything of this monster, bait to draw Ginny into his unfathomable game. What had he achieved by manipulating the three of them so successfully? No blood had been spilt, no bodies pushed into the surf. Power. Power: that's what he had asserted, yet again. The power of Alex, in the face of an unbearable world, to bend people to his will.

Well, Peter said in the car, they would stop all that now. Alex had gone too far, overstepped the mark, and it was time to run him to ground. The question was: how best to do it so there were no loopholes, no chance of him slipping the net? He would make some calls in the morning. They would go to the police together, make statements, end this once and for all. He said that Julie could stay at his place if she wanted, if she was frightened. He would put up the camp bed in the main bedroom, and he would sleep on the sofa. Julie said she preferred to be in her own home, with her own security system and neighbours she knew. She would feel safe there. They should pick her up in the morning. Peter urged her once more to get some sleep, leave it all to him.

Ginny looked at her watch as he put the key into the lock of his front door and ushered her in. Past ten: where was Alex now? Still by the sea? Or already moving on, preparing a fresh identity, a new legend? Even now, she thought, Sean Meadows is probably fading from history, to be replaced by another alter ego, another convenient life. The Francisco Trust will be putting the house on the market and looking for another, somewhere far away.

'Christ, I need a drink,' Peter said. 'Join me?'

She shook her head.

'Sure? I'd have thought you could use one.' He shrugged. 'Well, I am having a large vodka. Because that was the kind of day I don't want to have again in a hurry. Like bloody Bosnia.'

She sat down on the sofa and waited for him to turn on all the lights. 'Peter,' she said, 'why are we here?'

'What do you mean?'

'I mean, given that I was more or less held captive this afternoon by one of the most notorious serial killers of all time, don't you think we should be at the police station right now? I mean, if a murderer like that is on the loose again, don't you think it would be sort of a good idea to tell somebody immediately?'

'Well, I told you. I think we should wait until I have made a few calls in the morning. Spoken to a few of my people. I mean, you know how delicate Alex's situation is. He is still a protected man, insane as that may seem. I just want to check what the best way to go about this is. I thought you and Julie agreed.'

'Julie agreed. She was in such a state that she would have agreed to anything.'

'And you?'

'I wanted to speak to you on my own before deciding.'

He lifted his glass in her direction. 'So. Speak away. If you don't agree, we can do it your way.'

'I am just confused by your lack of urgency. I would have thought that you, of all people, would have a sense of what Alex is capable of. You know how quickly he used to work.'

He was very still. 'What is this? What do you mean me "of all people"?'

'Well, you know all about this case.'

'Of course, I told you about it. That's my job.'

'That's not what I meant.' She paused. 'Why didn't you tell me that you'd covered the Blakeley case at the time?'

He was silent for a moment. 'What makes you think I did?'

'The book you had in the car. There was a footnote. Only saw it by chance. And you know what it said?'

He did not reply.

'It said: "Private interview by the author with Peter Byrne." You reported the case, didn't you? You've been chasing Alex for years.'

'For Christ's sake, Ginny. I – I didn't want to get into all that.'

'What do you mean? What *can* you mean?'

'Well, it was a horrible business, easily the nastiest story I have ever had to cover. Gave me nightmares. I didn't want you to get even more obsessed by the case. And I suppose, selfishly, I didn't really want to relive it.'

'That's a bunch of crap. I don't believe you.'

His voice betrayed irritation. 'Well, that's too bad, Ginny. Because it's the truth.'

'Is it? Is it, really? It strikes me as very odd that I tell you, supposedly one of my dearest friends, that the reason I have moved out is that my next door neighbour is Alex

Blakeley, and you omit to mention that you spent a year of your life writing about him.'

'I don't have time for this, Ginny.'

'Really? Is that because you planned it all along?'

'What are you talking about?'

'On the way back, when you were doing your "leave it to me" number on Julie, I thought it all through. And I realised two things, Peter, that struck me as very odd. The first is that I would never have moved into that house if you hadn't steered me towards it in the first place. Oh, you played me very cleverly. Pretending you weren't sure. But you knew I'd go for it. Or at least you hoped I would – and you were right. I did. The second is that you came back so quickly with the information from your contact, about Sean being Alex. It was all so very fast, so convenient.'

'So what?'

'So – what I was wondering is whether you had that information all along. I wonder whether you had a tip a while ago about Alex Blakeley's whereabouts, and just needed confirmation. Needed someone very close, someone you could rely on to find out.'

'You're tired, Ginny, and you're talking rubbish. Alex Blakeley has a lifetime injunction. I told you. No journalist would dare to break it. No newspaper would print it. Even if I had a lead as to where he was, it would be useless to me.'

'Yes, I thought about that, too. And I remembered what else you said: what if there was an overwhelming public interest defence for disclosure? What if – say – a vulnerable woman had become friends with Blakeley and inadvertently discovered who he was? Even better: he hurt her in some way? What then? I can see the headline: "The Serial Killer, the Divorcee – and the scandal of a neighbour with a terrible secret."'

Peter looked at her and this time he spoke quietly. 'Well. You have to admit, it would have made a good headline.'

She sprang up and slapped him hard. 'You – you are – *beyond unspeakable. Shame – shame on you*.' She collected herself a little. 'Damn you. Damn you forever, Peter. You let me buy a house next door to a murderer. All so you could get your precious scoop. You risked my life and Julie's, you *bastard*. No wonder you panicked when I went missing. And no wonder you don't want to go straight to the police. You want to square your contact first, don't you? Break the news to your paper and think about how to do the story up? No wonder you wanted to be there with your "muscle" in the passenger seat. What you really wanted was photographs of me with Alex Blakeley's fingers round my throat. Didn't you? That would be – what? A world exclusive? The serial killer, let out, grown up and back to his old tricks with a poor little woman this time. You follow him, intervene at exactly the right moment, and become the most famous reporter in the world overnight. A regular hero. And what – ministers resign? How could this have happened? Thank God for brave have-a-go reporter Peter Byrne, saving the day. What a celebrity. Imagine the interviews, the fees.'

'I—'

She slapped him again. 'Shut up, you pathetic excuse for a man. I'm not finished yet. Not by a mile. But it didn't go to plan? Did it? At the last moment, I gave you the slip and you were worried that you'd have no pictures and maybe a dead body on your hands. Maybe two, if he'd got Julie, too. And then someone would have made the connection between you and me, and your contact might just have blown the whistle on you. Christ, no wonder you were scared.'

'You're hysterical. Don't rush to conclusions.'

'I'm not. I'm simply seeing what I should have seen ages ago. You put me in harm's way, Peter. And I trusted you. Just like I trusted Sean. What a fool I am. What a bloody fool.'

He put his hand on her shoulder and she brushed it away. 'Look, I know how angry you must be. I realise that. I probably do seem a complete scumbag to you. From your perspective, after what you've just been through. But – look, you're right. There are *millions* to be made from this story. I can go it alone, write books, do television. You can clean up, too. "Alex Blakeley was my lover": do you know how much you could make for that sort of story, a woman with your looks? It'll be syndicated around the world. Exclusive interviews, magazine rights. Whatever you want.'

'Are you totally deranged, Peter? Do you really think I care about the money I could make from this? It's not worth a penny to me, believe me.' She felt her gorge rise, tried to compose herself. 'Do you know how *broken* I feel? You can have no concept, I think. It's just another story to you, another sales opportunity. I let this man into my life, thought I cared for him, and – and it was all for nothing. Your game, his game. Evil bastards, both of you.'

Peter snorted. 'Are you really comparing me to Blakeley? Only a *woman* could say something so stupid.'

'Is that it, Peter? Do you hate women? Is that why you never married, why you treat them the way you do?'

He shook his head. 'You're no advert for marriage. Don't preach at me, Ginny. I helped you. I have always helped you.'

'You helped yourself. It had nothing to do with me. It was always for your own purposes. Don't insult me by pretending otherwise.'

'Look, Ginny. I understand how furious you are. This isn't how I wanted you to find out.'

'You were going to tell me?'

He turned away from her. 'Yes – well, not all of it.'

'Any of it?'

'Yes – listen, if you would only get off your high horse you would see how we can turn this to our advantage – both of us.'

She shook her head. 'You are a sick, sick fuck, Peter. The saddest part is that you really do think that I should go along with this. With your plan. You don't really know me at all, do you? After all these years.'

'Oh, come on, Ginny. You're not telling me that, after

all you've been through, you're not going to squeeze it for all it's worth. Please. Take a deep breath and be reasonable. For Christ's sake.'

She turned and looked in the mirror. A further, horrible truth gripped her like a sickness. It was probably no more than a detail to Peter, but it had broken her heart – and made her behave like a madwoman. That part of her that remained rational could not help but be struck by how thorough he was.

Finally, she whispered: 'Winston.'

'What?' he shot back,

She faced him. 'Winston. That was you too, wasn't it?'

'You're – ridiculous. Get some sleep. For God's sake.'

'I don't think so, Peter. You killed Winston, didn't you? Just to be on the safe side. The thing with Harry – that was great stuff, blood on the walls and so on. And you have your final scene with me on the cove now and Julie an unwitting hostage. But Winston was just a bit of garnish, wasn't it? Or maybe a bit of insurance. Alex hurt animals – ergo Sean would kill his lover's cat. That would get all the animal lovers reading. Wouldn't it?'

Peter smiled and shook his head. 'Prove it.'

'I can't, of course. But it makes a lot more sense now than Sean getting up in the middle of the night or Roger Benson turning into a psychopath because of his rose beds. Poor bastard. No, you did that and I'll bet you took a few pictures too for your portfolio.'

'A couple,' said Peter. 'We don't have to use them if you feel strongly. Look, Ginny—' He was starting to whine.

'The only thing I feel strongly about is going to the police right now, Peter. I am going to tell them the whole story, including and especially your part in it. And all I hope is that they get to Alex before he does something awful and that they tell your newspaper how you operate and make sure you never work again. That's what I'm going to do,'

'Christ, you are so *naïve*,' he said, his face reddening. 'How do you think the world works? You sit in your ivory tower writing what you want, living in a house bought by someone else. And you dare to judge the rest of us?'

'No,' said Ginny. 'Only you.' She picked up her bag. 'Bye Peter.'

'Don't you *dare*. Do you think I'm going to let you ruin everything I have worked for all these years just because you have one of your moral fits? Calm down and think before you do anything – anything you'll regret.'

'I regret it all,' she said, and walked towards the top of the stairs. He chased after her, grabbed her wrists, but she was too fast and slipped his grip. She made it to the top of the stairs, but now he was upon her once more, flailing in his fury, out of control. She stood at the top of the steep stairwell, clutching the banister.

'I'm going,' she said. 'Let me go.'

'You're not going anywhere,' he said. She turned, and he tried to grab her, but as she stepped aside, shouting out his name, trying desperately to avoid his clumsy hands, he tripped on the top step, and then, crashing against her, he was falling, falling fast, his hands grabbing for something, anything, his cry a cry of sudden helplessness, his angle awkward because of the force with which he had lunged, his legs useless as he tumbled, his head hitting the doorframe first, so that the sound of it splitting open was sharp and clear, and the silence that followed no less piercing.

XV

'Is that it?' said Daniels.

'Isn't that enough?' she said.

'Ample,' he replied. 'Of course, we'll need a formal statement. But there's plenty here for me to be getting on with.'

'What will you do first?'

'Have a chat with Mr Meadows, I should think.'

'A chat? Shouldn't you just lock him up? What more do you need?'

DI Daniels looked at her sympathetically. 'Miss Clark, I can see you've been through a terrible episode. But what you say is – well, it doesn't match my experience.'

'What experience? How could you have experience of this unless you'd been through it?'

'No, that's not what I mean. You say that Mr Meadows is Alex Blakeley. What I am saying is that, were that the case, I would already have been contacted by my superiors with very clear instructions. And I haven't been.'

'What does that have to do with your own experience?'

'Miss – a high-profile case like Blakeley would not be living in a big house, and he wouldn't be living in London.'

'Why ever not? He might have made his own money or inherited some. And why not London?'

'It – well, it's not a good place to put people like him. Crawling with journalists and nosey people. It's not standard procedure. Quite the opposite, in fact.'

She snorted. 'How can you have standard procedure with a man like that?'

He smiled bleakly. 'I take your point. But – well, we need to chat to this person and see what his game really is. He sounds disturbed and there may be a case for sectioning. Or at least a restraining order.'

'A *restraining order*? He killed seven boys. He needs to be locked up, not told off.'

'Miss – I do understand your position, I really do. But unless I hear otherwise I can't just throw him in a cell. He didn't take your friend against her will, did he? Or hold her hostage?'

'No – but he used deception to make me do what he wanted. He put her life at risk.'

'Did he say he would kill her, or anything like that?'

'No, not in as many words. But it was clear he meant her harm. It was mind-fucking. Manipulation. He wanted to get me on the cove.'

'He sounds very unpleasant, I agree. But that's not the same as kidnapping, I'm afraid. Emotional manipulation is not a criminal offence. Perhaps it should be.'

She could no longer contain her exasperation. 'Inspector. For Christ's sake. This man is a murderer and he is playing with lives. You need to do something.' Her tone was growing shrill. 'Jesus – when will you start listening? When you find a body? Is that what it takes?'

DI Daniels closed his notebook. 'I have been listening, Miss Clark. And I assure you that we will take all necessary and possible measures to prevent a recurrence. He isn't at his house, but we've got a squad car there. You're perfectly safe.'

A uniformed officer approached and whispered something into his ear. He frowned and nodded.

'Will you excuse me?' Daniels said. 'I am wanted outside. I'll leave WPC Atkins here.'

Ginny nodded. The woman police officer, chubby and beaming, sat down opposite her.

'Do you want me to make some tea, Miss Clark?' she said.

'No, no thank you.'

'Right. Well, I'm sure he won't be long. Probably the Yard wanting an update.'

'Yes. Yes, maybe. Look, where is Peter?'

'Oh, he's at St Michael's having stitches put in. He's a lucky sod. Could have fractured his skull or broken his neck with that fall, that angle. Seen it before, especially when they've had a few drinks. He'll be cleaned up and then charged.'

'What with?'

'Attempted assault, I would guess. His actions with you and your friend are more a matter of gross professional misconduct. Depends on how much harm he believed you might be subject to. Tricky one, that. Bit hazy, the law is, on that sort of thing. But he'll struggle to keep his job, I'm sure. Bloody menace, these reporters.'

Ginny nodded and saw Daniels coming back up the stairs. He looked pale, as if somebody had given him a dressing down, or put him in his place. His manner was chastened.

'Miss Clark: we are more or less done here. Can one of my officers give you a lift somewhere? You can't stay here, I'm afraid, as it is a crime scene, and not your home in any case. Would you like us to drop you off at your house?'

I would rather die, she thought to herself. 'No. No, thank you. I'll stay – I'll go to Julie's place, if that's okay.'

'Of course. Just give my officer the address and we can get you there immediately. The statement can wait till tomorrow. We'll call you and fix that. I have your mobile—' he flicked through his notes '—yes, I do. I do.'

'That message you had to take just now was about Alex – about Sean Meadows. Wasn't it?' What had the voice on the other end of the radio or phone told him? Lay off, this is above your pay grade. This goes all the way to the top, don't get involved: just keep the woman under control. Or something else?

Daniels scrutinised her with something approaching pity. 'Leave the details to me, Miss Clark. You're perfectly safe. I assure you of that.'

You poor man, she thought: you couldn't keep me safe from Alex Blakeley even if you wanted to.

Julie woke her with breakfast in bed: warm croissants, apple juice and a pot of tea. The spare room was also her study: a laptop, printer and bound legal files sat on the desk, below an array of framed holiday photographs, pictures of godchildren and a photographic portrait of Julie taken by Stephen that showed her posing as Audrey Hepburn with cigarette holder, evening gown, tiara and up-do. He was away for the week, she'd explained. Typical Stephen: a full-blooded crisis and he's in Chicago for a conference.

'I always find,' said Julie, 'that a good breakfast is essential the morning after you've spent the day at the seaside with a serial killer.'

Ginny laughed weakly. 'You can say that again.'

'Did you sleep?'

'I did. I did. Surprisingly well. I think I just caved into exhaustion.'

'Didn't sleep a fucking wink,' said Julie, tightening her bathrobe. 'It's all a bit new to me, this dicing with death stuff. And I didn't even have to do the bit on the beach.' She paused. 'What are you going to do now?'

Ginny turned on to her side, rested her head in her hand. 'Make a statement, I suppose. Go through it all again. Get what I need to exist out of the house. Put it on the market tomorrow. Never look back.'

Julie nodded. 'And what are you thinking?'

'I'm thinking that he won – again. I'm thinking that someone, somewhere, would prefer this was all hushed up and Alex moved on rather than that there was a huge scandal. He's smart, isn't he? He knew exactly how far he could push it. Did he attack me? No, he didn't. Did he kidnap you? No, not literally. And Peter played into his hands. Stupid bastard. He'll be out of hospital and pleading for his life at work. But they won't want a convicted woman-beater on the staff, however much they wish he'd kept his cool and brought in the prize.'

'Won't they just put someone else on Alex?'

Ginny shook her head. 'No point. Peter just put the investigation back ten years. Alex will get a new identity and a new home, and probably a new injunction. The papers will be told to steer clear, and they will. What's in it for them? Another decade chasing the case to Strasbourg? No, Peter has well and truly fouled this pitch. Alex can enjoy himself again now. He's free.'

'Do you really think so?' asked Julie. 'He doesn't sound free to me – from what you say.'

'I think he defines his freedom by deceiving other people – by defeating them. We were just the latest chapter in this story he's writing for himself. There will be others, further down the line. And all the time, he knows his protectors want nothing more than a quiet life. Smooth surfaces, calm exteriors. It's unthinkable that Alex Blakeley should be on the loose, up to his old tricks. So – as far as humanly possible – they keep it all quiet. If he had been the one pushing me downstairs, that would be different. But it wasn't. It was Peter. Mad bastard. Alex has led them all a dance, and he will again.'

Julie's voice was softer now. 'And how do you feel?'

Ginny gave the question some thought. 'I feel – I feel blank, really. As if another period in my life has just been erased, like my time with Harry. Either I'm finished, or

I'm starting over from scratch – again. I'm not sure which. Ask me in a year or so.'

'I will,' said Julie, leaning over to kiss her friend on the forehead. 'And you're not finished.'

XVI

A week passed before she felt able to return to her own home. DI Daniels took her statement and called her twice with what he described as 'updates'. Meadows had not surfaced, and there was good reason to suppose that he would not. He could not elaborate, for operational reasons, but she was not to worry. In his professional opinion, and that of his superiors, she could go back to her house safely whenever she wished. She declined his offer of a squad car to accompany her – simply to put her at ease, he assured her. No, she said, that would not be necessary. As much as she dreaded going back to the house where she had embraced Alex and whispered intimacies to him, she knew he would not be there. If he decided to find her again, he would pick another, more imaginative venue. That was the game, always the game.

Julie drove her over early on a bright Sunday morning, making small talk to distract her friend and changing radio stations in search of music that would kill the time. In the boot, Ginny had packed suitcases, bags and a few boxes: she would clear out everything essential, lock the place up and send a removal company to pick up the rest for storage. For now, all she needed was to *absent* herself from the house: to make it possible for her to live somewhere else and to begin the painfully slow process of purging the sickening memories that it had spawned. All that she had hoped for when she moved in had died, swept away by a foul and scheming mind that had chosen her for its plaything.

They drew up to the house. It was only a fortnight since she had fled to Peter's flat, and yet it seemed like years. Already, the windows looked smeared, the garden a little more disorderly, the cans and wrappers thrown from the pavement on to the path a sign of desertion: the warmth of occupation had already drained from her home. It had shrugged her off.

Julie turned to her: 'You okay?'

She nodded. 'I'll be fine.'

'Do you want me to help? Or just come in and keep you company? I won't get in the way.'

'That's all right, thanks. I'd rather just storm through the place like a swarm of locusts and be out of here as soon as humanly possible. I really don't ever want to come back.'

'I don't blame you. Well, I'll be here. Shout if you need anything.'

'I will.' She got out of the car, her legs leaden with reluctance. She opened the boot and pulled out two large shoulder-bags packed with smaller holdalls that would do for her clothes. She noticed that the Bensons' car was not in its usual spot: good, she would not be disturbed. Then she turned and walked towards the gate, averting her eyes from number twenty-six, its drawn curtains and its three locks.

An hour and a half later, she had most of what she needed. Ten bags full of her belongings, stuffed in hastily, and three boxes packed with books, computer equipment and papers: enough to be getting on with. The furniture, pictures, and everything else could wait. This would do for now.

In the kitchen, she found what she was looking for: the drawing by Sean. It was, considered objectively, a fine and loving study, executed by someone with talent. What, she wondered, had gone through Alex's head as he sketched from memory, drawing his next door neighbour as if already half in love with her? Had any of that emotion been real, or was it all just calculation – a means to ensnare her? Was it possible for a mind as wrecked as Alex's to be both sincere and calculating: to feel the stirrings of a normal human emotion and then to twist it to his own ends? Well, it didn't matter now. All that mattered was to be rid of it all, to cut out the poisoned heart and throw it away forever. She took the picture into the back garden and added it to the pile marked 'For Disposal'. Let the removal men put it on a skip and consign it to the oblivion it deserved.

At first, she thought the noise was coming from the street, but then recognised it for what it was: a slow, insistent knock on the door. Her first instinct was to flee, as fast and as far as she could. But to where? And why? No, this could not be him. Not even Alex would be so bold as to seek her out here. And Julie would have warned her. She went up the stairs, across the hall and saw through the frosted glass that it was a woman. Ginny opened the door.

The unexpected visitor was elegant: that was her first thought. Mid sixties, perhaps, certainly no older: grey hair neatly cut into a bob with a shawl over a grey suit and mauve turtle neck. She wore a string of pearls and carried an expensive handbag. She might have been a magistrate or a lawyer. But Ginny knew instinctively and instantly who she was: the woman who had summoned Sean from her kitchen, to whom he had rushed so obediently, as if the future of the world depended on it.

The visitor spoke first, in tones both clipped and polite. 'Excuse me. I'm sorry to bother you.'

'What do you want?'

'My goodness, that's not very welcoming.'

'I suppose you're his case officer,' Ginny said. 'The one who visited him. Well, you did a great job. I hope you're all happy, whoever you are.'

'I'm not his case officer, young lady. I am his aunt.'

'I didn't know Alex Blakeley had an aunt.'

The woman blinked with vexed incomprehension. '*Alex Blakeley* doesn't have an aunt. Not as far as I know. My nephew, on the other hand, has two. Of whom I am one.'

'I don't understand,' Ginny said.

'That's the first vaguely civilized thing you've said to me. Now – why don't you let me in and we can have a chat? I'd really rather not have this conversation in your porch if I can help it.'

Ginny was too exhausted to resist a request that had

been made to sound so reasonable: so neighbourly. The woman sensed her acquiescence and walked past her into the sitting room.

Ginny followed her in. She was already seated, poised and dignified on the old armchair.

'I don't want a cup of tea, in case you were thinking of asking.'

'Who are you? And what exactly do you want?'

'Well, the second question is the easier one to answer. I am looking for – for Sean, and wondered if you knew where he was.'

Ginny laughed bleakly. 'You are asking me where Sean is? Surely I should ask you. You're the one who looks after him.'

'Well, ask away, I have no idea where he is. I'm a little concerned. That's why I'm here.'

Ginny sat down. 'Look, I'm sure the police have told you everything. Is this really necessary? I understand how complicated it all is, and that you have to pretend to be his aunt and—'

'I *am* his aunt. No pretence at all. And I haven't spoken to the police about anything. I have very infrequent contact with the authorities, for whom I think I am something of a nuisance, or an embarrassment. I am worried about my nephew. That is all there is to it.'

'Well, you bloody well should be worried about him,' Ginny said. 'If you really don't know: the last time I saw Alex – Sean – was at Herne Bay. He scared me half to death, and a friend of mine. He played some sort of sick game to get us down there, said he needed to talk to me. I found him at the cove – I knew it would be round there – and he talked about the night of William and Robert. Replayed it all, sick bastard, as if he could relive it, even now. Then said he wasn't Alex, he wasn't Alex, he was Sean. And then told me to count to a thousand and ran off.' Her eyes met those of her visitor: a clear, unflinching blue. 'Happy now?' said Ginny.

The woman frowned. 'Ah. I see. Herne Bay. What an interesting choice of location. Tell me: did he actually hurt you?'

She paused. 'No.'

'Did he threaten you?'

'Not in as many words. I've seen his temper, though. I know what he's capable of.'

'Do you, indeed? And, tell me, when you saw his temper, was he in the wrong?'

She thought back to the night of Harry's invasion. 'No. It was simply . . .'

'. . . because he is so gentle normally. Yes, well, let's just say the poor boy has good reason to fly off the handle once in a while. God knows. I'd be inclined to be a bit tetchy from time to time. The wonder is that he is the way he is.'

'Meaning what?'

'How rude of me – I forgot to answer your first question. I'm Helena Warren. Sean is my nephew.'

'Warren? That was—'

'Yes, that's right. *Those* Warrens. Alex Blakeley killed

darling Henry. He'd be twenty-two now, poor boy. And a beautiful young man he'd be, too. That's what makes me cry these days: not his death so much – not like in the early years – but the life he never enjoyed. Thinking of all the lost promise. Well, Blakeley tried to kill William, and failed, as you know. And he near as God killed Robert.' She clenched her fist. 'But he *didn't*.'

Ginny wondered if she had misheard. 'I don't understand.'

'Well, of course you don't. You weren't meant to, and I suppose it's not really your fault that this has happened. Still, forgive me for wishing that you had never moved next door.'

'What difference did it make me moving in?' Ginny asked.

'Well, only that the poor boy fell for you, dear. And you for him, apparently. Bound to happen sooner or later, I suppose. He is a loving boy. But I wish – I *wish* it had been a bit later. Or, frankly, never. You see, you think you've stumbled on something horrible, when what you've stumbled on is a miracle. The fact is – Blakeley did not finish off Robert that night. So nearly. *So* nearly. Robert was in a coma for quite a while, it was touch and go. The injuries were severe, internal some of them. And when he finally came through it, he was so, so, so scared. *Mortally* scared. Of course, we all were, and William, too. But Robert. Well, it was of a different order, his fear.'

'I don't – so Robert survived?'

'Yes. Very few people in the world know that: close family, a few suits in Whitehall, a lawyer or two. I think the police are told to steer clear, or something similar: very unofficial, I imagine. By telling you, I might add, I am taking a great risk with the fate of someone who is more dear to me than words can say.'

'But how could he possibly have survived Alex's attack?'

'Through *will*, dear. Through *love of life*. You see, Robert's desire to keep hold of life was stronger even than Alex Blakeley's desire to take it away. Which is saying quite a lot, it really is. And when Robert awoke, he had no more courage left. It had all gone on this great, titanic effort to stay alive. He had no fight left in him, and I can quite see why.' She paused. 'He was very, very fragile. For quite a while. And it was clear that the one thing that would certainly kill him was the knowledge that Alex Blakeley knew he was alive, and would come and get him sooner or later. To finish the job. Robert's gift to us all was to stay alive. The price was that we didn't tell. The price was that Alex must never know that Robert had survived.'

'How has this not come out? It is – it's extraordinary.'

'It nearly has, once or twice. It has been a close run thing. A few have asked uncomfortable questions. But people are so *obsessed* with tracking down Blakeley himself that they aren't on the look-out for a survivor. Nobody is interested in the dead, even when they are alive.'

'But William testified—'

'No, William told the truth. William is a very honest boy. He said that he saw his brother being savagely beaten and dragged away, which is absolutely true. Remember: Blakeley was not charged with Robert's death, although the papers reported the trial as though he was. He was convicted for the deaths of Henry, Hughie Barlow and Marcus Steeples. The others were missing. If you were to check, you would find that, officially at least, Robert is still listed as missing. Of course, Blakeley thought he was dead, and so, more importantly, does everybody else.'

'My God. My God.' Ginny felt her stomach turn. 'But why – why didn't he – Robert, I mean – just carry on with his life? Blakeley was behind bars.'

Helena bridled. 'Well, why have you got a friend with you here? Why did you hesitate to answer the door? Do you think it's that easy? Robert's last act of will was to make a request: more of a final offer, really. He was wise, in a way. What Robert had realized was that Blakeley's attacks on him and his brothers were different from the others. Blakeley wished to destroy all three Warren boys, and he succeeded with dear little Henry. Robert believed that Blakeley would get out one day – quite true. And that Blakeley would come for him – quite wrong. I don't know where Blakeley is – I am not allowed to know, even though I am the relative of a victim. *Especially* because I am a relative, I imagine. But I am reliably told by the friends I have made in this wretched business that he is about as likely to resume his killing spree today as he is to become President of Venezuela. He apparently leads a very diminished life somewhere up north. He lives in a flat in great squalor, tends to his budgies, and rattles with pills. He has grown obese, so they say – wrapping himself in fat, I suppose, like a womb or something. The only person he is likely to kill is himself, I'm told. But none of that is any consolation to Robert. He remembers Alex Blakeley as he was fifteen years ago: that face in the papers, that amazing strength, those eyes. That's what he paints, sometimes. The Goya pictures, you know. That's what he flees from. And now he's fled again. Sad. Very, very sad.'

'Why did the courts let the world think Robert was dead?'

'Because in the end, we pleaded with the prosecution, threatened them I suppose. Let Robert disappear, and William will testify. And they needed William to say what he had seen, they really did. The jury needed to hear his testimony, because, for all the forensic evidence they had, they knew what a good witness Blakeley might be. And he would have been, if William hadn't been there. It was a small price to pay for them. The authorities just didn't answer questions about Robert. They hedged, they evaded. They told no outright lies. They helped to give him an identity so that he could, if he wanted, resettle. Everyone assumed he was dead. People lost interest. They stopped asking questions. In fact, he was with me.'

'What about his parents?'

'Well, clearly, he couldn't stay with them. Or his brother. So I took him abroad for a while. I thought he would change his mind, want to go back to his mother and father, and his surviving brother, and his real life. But he didn't, you know. And so Robert really rather faded, and, before too long, he became Sean. And we came back when he was a little older, and he drifted in and out of schools, and I taught him as best I could and he did the best that he could. He has talents, he thinks very deeply. The world still scares him, and he fears he can never escape what happened, though I believe he could, given time and care. He lives day to day. He loves me, and I think he thought he could love you, too. I still think of him as much the most remarkable person I have known in my life. He is very special.'

Ginny stared ahead of herself, absorbing all that Helena had told her. 'Yes. I know.'

'Do you? I wonder. He came back from the dead, you see. Almost literally. And when he came back he was not willing to be the person he had been.'

Ginny looked at the picture above the mantelpiece: of a shore, and a dog, lost by its owner, looking out at the crusty carpet of blue paint. 'What will become of him?'

'Of Robert? Oh, I suppose he'll contact me sooner or later. We have our codes, he and I, that make him feel safe. He can tell me where he is without anyone else knowing. This is not the first time that he has disappeared, you know. He'll turn up in a hostel somewhere, or a seaside town, in a bit of a state, and finally call me, and I'll go and pick him up and we'll see what we can do. This time, he lasted for several years. Perhaps he will again.'

Ginny did not know how to respond. This was a gift she had been given, the gift of a great secret. 'What should I do?'

Helena seemed genuinely surprised. 'Do? Nothing you can do. No, I can see you are moving on. Well, you don't have to. He won't come back here, if that's what you're worried about.'

'No, I meant – I'm not sure. I mean . . . why did you tell me? You didn't have to. But you chose to.'

Helena nodded. 'Yes, that's true. I am taking what I suppose is a fairly colossal risk. But I have to trust you, as he trusted you. In his own way, that is. And I owe it to Robert, I think. He is incapable of saying these things himself. It's like an autism born of savagery. But it would cause him great pain, I know, if he thought that you were out there, still believing that he was Alex Blakeley. You of all people confusing him with his tormentor, the man who killed his brother and nearly killed him. I think it may give him some comfort, one day, to know that you knew the truth.'

'Yes,' Ginny said. 'I can see that.'

'He loved you, you see. You know that, don't you?'

She nodded. Yes, she knew that. She knew that now.

Helena gathered her things. 'Well, I should leave you to finish your packing.'

Ginny stood up. 'Thank you. Thank you for telling me.'

'I did it for him. Please remember that. Don't betray his trust. He has so little, you see.'

'No. I do see. I do.' Ginny looked up. 'Will I see you again?'

'I very much doubt it, dear,' said Helena.

She smiled and stretched out her hand. Her grip was light, feminine. Ginny took it and said goodbye.

Then Helena Warren was gone, swift and methodical in

her movements, venturing forth once more into the world from which she would now, once again, seek to protect her beloved nephew, Robert.

Part Three

Wiltshire

XVII

Winter had come early, and with it the sudden frosts that made the grass crunch under foot when she went out into the orchard in the mornings to see how the apple trees were faring. She loved the cottage especially at this time of year, when all was crisp and clear: much better than the drear and drizzle of October or the moody heat of August. From her study, she could see into the next field and watch the farmer inspecting the soil, shaking his head, absent-mindedly pulling at the fingers of his gloves.

She tended her vegetable garden, folded over the leaves of the cauliflower curds, picked sprouts and carrots, staked the taller plants to protect them from the wind. She cleared up the remains and added them to the compost trench, cleaned the seed trays and pots, covered the bare soil with a winter mulch. She put out food for the birds, hoping they would come and feast on the aphids, slugs and snails. Such work filled hours of her time and made her deeply content.

Her father had feared that she would become a recluse in the country, but the opposite had happened. She ran errands for her elderly neighbour, Jim, knew all the shopkeepers in town and always went into the Lazy Eye when she was there to pass the time of day over a half of bitter with the landlady, Billy. The pace of life was slower than Ginny had ever experienced, a change to which she quickly adapted and came to relish. The demands made of her were connected to her home and the seasons. She enjoyed true neighbourliness for the first time.

Julie had promised to come and stay before Christmas, and, to Ginny's surprise, proved true to her word. 'Darling,' she said on the phone. 'I'm going to Harvey Nicks to buy wellies and a pitchfork. If you can manage this countryside nonsense, so can I.' She said she would be arriving on the 11:43 on Saturday at Porters Newton, and so she did. Ginny drove to the station to pick her up and the two women embraced like long lost sisters, talking over one another excitedly as they drove back to the cottage.

It was a Victorian structure, some of its masonry much older, sprawling across two storeys that lurked beneath thickets of wisteria and honeysuckle. Its oak doors and joinery spoke of warmth and generations-old solidity, and she loved the wood-burning stove, the exposed beams, the inglenook fireplace. All the bloody clichés, as Julie put it when she told her friend that she had bought a place outside London and that she wanted to give the rural life a try. But they were clichés for a reason. For the first time in her life, she began to experience something approaching tranquillity: the madness of the city and the sea were, for now at least, banished from her life.

'It's a bit bloody old, isn't it?' said Julie, setting her overnight bag down in the hall. 'Won't it all fall down when you're asleep?'

She smiled. 'Do you feel threatened by old things, Jules? Is that why you won't shag that QC who's been pestering you?'

'Bits falling off him for years, definitely. He's a lot older than this bloody house. And I think if I ever leave Stephen, I owe it to him to do so for a younger man. Anything else would be insulting. No, I just wondered whether you have to call the V&A when the plumbing goes. Presumably they haven't made pipes like this since the Armistice?'

'Why don't you fuck off and help me in here?' called Ginny from the kitchen. 'I have some rural farmhouse tasks for you.'

'You must be joking,' said Julie. 'I didn't come into the wilderness to chop things up. There'll be snails and bugs and dead sheep hiding in the vegetables. I don't trust vegetables that don't come from Waitrose.'

'Fine,' said Ginny. 'Just sit down, for Christ's sake, before you faint. Here—' she handed her a glass of champagne '—that should help you recover from the culture shock.'

'What culture? Where is the nearest theatre, or cinema? Where do you go to buy clothes? What about *Vogue*? Is there a Space NK?'

'No,' said Ginny. 'The only entertainment is the Friday night pub quiz. Oh, and we burn a wicker man every Wednesday. But obviously only virgins are at risk, so you can relax.'

'Cheers,' said Julie. They clinked their glasses, and toasted the life of the accidental bumpkin.

Over coffee, Julie told her what she had not wanted to say over the phone. 'I saw Peter, you know.'

'Oh,' said Ginny, taking a sip from her mug. She reached over and stirred the fire with the poker. 'No, I didn't know.'

'He's working again, only on a local paper in south London somewhere.'

'I see. How did you run into him?'

'On the street, would you believe. In Covent Garden. Don't know what he was doing there. He looked the same, bit ragged at the edges. I thought he would blank me but he didn't. Came up and said hello, so I couldn't really avoid him.'

'Did you reciprocate his greeting?'

'No. He tried to make small talk, told me he was back in work, in spite of the conviction. Then started ranting on about the Blakeley case and how he wanted to write a book about it all, how he had come so close to smoking him out.'

'He hasn't learned, has he? And he'll never know how far he was from the truth.'

'No. I got the feeling that nobody takes him seriously now. He said there was a conspiracy in the intelligence community to keep him down, to prevent his book from being published. More like a conspiracy of sane people. I don't think that particular masterwork will ever see the light of day.'

'Poor bastard. It's pathetic, really. And of course he can't write about it, precisely because of what he did.'

'Yes, there was a lot of defensiveness, I thought, but he

looked ashamed. I think it was a condition of his prompt resignation that his paper not reveal why he had gone – why he had really gone, I mean. Your letter to his editor made quite an impression, but the official line was that it was because of the criminal charges.'

'Well, I figured as much. Nobody beat a path to my door afterwards, thank God. That was my one worry. That Peter's downfall would make the whole thing a story anyway.'

'Your one worry?' said Julie, as gently as she could.

'Well, not my only worry, of course. But let's say my most pressing one. I think, subconsciously, it was one of the reasons I decided to get out of London. I know it makes no sense – I mean, if the media want to find you, they'll find you, right? Harry did, after all.'

'Yes,' said Julie. 'And look how that turned out.'

Harry had tracked her down, doubtless using one of the shady investigative contacts his profession depended upon from time to time. She had seen the handwriting on the envelope, and felt sick. But the long letter within was as touching as it was unexpected. Harry began by saying that his only real purpose in writing was to apologise to her for his unforgivable behaviour, not only on the night when he had pushed her to the ground and Sean had intervened, but on all the nights before, when, drunk or sober, he had mistreated her. Now he was trying to change. He had stopped drinking, he said, but more importantly, he had stopped lying to himself. He was in therapy, and he hoped, one day, to say sorry to her in person: though he understood that day might never come and would respect her decision either way. His humble tone had a new dignity, drained of all sarcasm, that delighted her: in spite of everything, she did not want Harry to be miserable. She knew, better than anyone, that he had suffered, perhaps for many years. She wrote back, noncommittally, a brief letter of thanks, and wished him well. She had no idea whether they would ever speak again. But there was a sort of peace between them now, and that was a blessing to be cherished.

'Anyway,' Ginny continued, 'I wanted to be away from the centre of it all. I didn't want the whole Peter thing to be hanging over me. As it turned out, I needn't have worried. And I ended up loving it here, anyway. Funny how things turn out.'

'I'll say,' said Julie, with a sniff. 'I had you down as a perfectly sensible urban woman. Not one of those nutters who moves out to weave their own yoghurt and till the soil. I remember you quite clearly saying: moving out is giving in.'

'Well,' said Ginny. 'I meant it. And, you know, I did give in. I was done fighting. I just wanted a break from – from whatever it was that happened. Still not sure what did happen, really.'

'And the rest of it?'

She sighed. 'Well, the rest of it – it's over, I think. He won't be back, I'm sure of that. And I don't think his aunt will either. God knows where they will have pitched up now. But what happened between him and me – it nearly unravelled their whole story, didn't it? And that was the last thing he wanted. He didn't want to live in the light at all, and that's where he was heading. So he'll have scurried back to safety, as far as that's possible.'

'Do you think he wanted a normal life with you?'

Ginny shrugged. 'I think about that every day, if I'm honest. I am not sure he really knew what "normal" was. I think Alex Blakeley beat that out of him. But he wanted more than he had got, that's for sure. I was a sort of halfway house between absolute solitude and the world out there. That's what I was. But his past was everywhere, he wrapped himself in it. Even if I hadn't found his scrapbooks that night, I would have found out sooner or later. He didn't like revealing the whole truth, but he was a bad liar. If I had got much closer to him, it would have all come out – and then what?'

Julie poured herself more champagne. 'Do you think things could have worked out differently?'

'I can't dwell on that. Does that make sense? What happened, happened. Too traumatic and horrible to be anything but the end of – of whatever it was. I can't see beyond that to other possible outcomes. And, really, there's no point. I could spend a thousand years trying to work this one out.'

Silence enveloped them like a blanket. Finally, Julie asked: 'Did you love him?'

Ginny drew her knees up to her chest protectively. She ran her hand through her hair.

'I wouldn't know how to start answering that. You're the only person I could even try with.'

'So try.'

'The problem is the word "him". Everything happened the wrong way round. I only found out who "he" really was after he'd vanished. Which "him" do you mean? You see, there were three of them. There was Sean, then there was Alex – and only afterwards, when he'd gone, the real person.'

The two women were awoken from their reverie by a sharp, piercing cry.

'Oh my God, what time is it?' said Ginny.

'Um, half three.'

'Christ, poor thing. She must be starving. When did we put her down? Oh well, there goes the sleep routine thing, again. Really, I'm not very good at this.'

'Oh, I don't know,' said Julie. 'You're learning. We all are.'

'Come on then, Godmother. Let's go and get her. Poor hungry girl.'

When the baby was satisfied, Julie took her off Ginny's hands and cradled her on the rug. 'She is a beauty, Gin. Such a beauty, aren't you? My little Flick. Seven months old. That's a *very* fine age for a young lady.'

Flick looked up at her with the luminous eyes of the very young, wide and welcoming: the eyes of the child for whom life itself is still a matter of astonishment, for whom the memory of absolute nothingness is still real and vivid. Her arms wriggled appreciatively as Julie tickled her and pressed a squeaky dog to her tummy.

'Set her on her front, Jules. She's crawling now, you know.'

Gently, Julie turned Flick over and encouraged her to

crawl for her Godmother. The child sprung into whirring action, scrabbling on the rug for all she was worth. 'That's good, darling, keep going!' cried Julie. But Flick remained where she was, not quite managing the promised crawl. She began to cry and her mother came over, scooped her up and nuzzled her for comfort.

'There's my Flick, my little angel,' said Ginny, stroking her daughter's brow. 'We'll get there. Don't you worry. We'll get there.'

Nobody was more amazed by the arrival of Felicity Clark than her own mother. She had not believed it possible that she was pregnant until she was more than four months gone, and she had visited her GP, seeking confirmation that her bump was the result of overeating and that acute stress explained the long wait for her period. Not at all, said Dr Russell: congratulations are in order, not to say offerings to the heavens. He had steered her through her unhappy years with Harry, when all she had wanted to know was why this – this very thing – had not happened. And now, as if in one of her fairy tales, it had. No, he could not explain why she had conceived now rather than then. There were limits to science, he confessed, especially on the spectacularly unpredictable matter of fertility. He had seen it before, more than once. A woman tries and tries for years, despairs, and then finds herself, quite against expectation and logic, changing nappies and bathing a newborn. Such things were not to be probed too deeply: in these cases, doctor and patient were equals, both supplicants to the gods.

He would sacrifice a rooster, he said with a chuckle – or whatever one was supposed to do in such joyful circumstances.

She was born in April, the labour taking less than two hours. There was not even time for an epidural by the time Ginny was admitted to St Bede's: she had to make do with gas and air and the ministrations of a Vietnamese midwife. The doctor was summoned when it seemed, from the monitor, that the baby might be in distress, perhaps that the umbilical cord was wrapped round its neck: a false alarm. Her daughter was born at 9:15 on a bright Spring morning, weighing seven pounds and six ounces. Ginny's father came to visit her later that day, weeping for the first time in years when he saw his granddaughter sleeping peacefully in her cot. He held Ginny even more tightly when she told him that the child would be named Felicity, to be called Flick, in honour of her grandmother.

She did not tell her father why she chose Roberta as the child's second name. That would have been to burden him with knowledge that he did not need, that he would find hard, perhaps impossible to handle. It would also be a grave breach of trust. She had sworn not to break a confidence and – apart from telling Julie, who had been involved and had a right to know – she kept her promise. Roberta was as good a name as any, said Geoffrey, beaming as he sat in the little ward she shared with three other new mothers. That's right, thought Ginny: as good a name as any. No need for him to know why she had chosen it. He knew she had been briefly involved with her neighbour Sean, that he had disappeared, would not be back. He was sad that she would have to raise Flick on her own. But not that sad.

Geoffrey looked more complete than he had since his wife died. He visited his daughter and grandchild often in Wiltshire, and interpreted Ginny's move to the countryside as final proof that she was a 'spinster doomed to write books in a crumbling cottage'. He thoroughly approved, he added. Though he missed her in London, he had found himself, much to his surprise, squiring a fellow librarian, ten years his junior, called Elspeth. They went to the theatre, cooked together, discussed books. He was bashful when talking about this unexpected reprieve from solitude: but his eyes sparkled eloquently.

Ginny and Julie bathed Flick together, playing a game with bubbles that made the baby laugh so much she started to hiccup. They dried her off, got her ready for bed and lay together in Ginny's room reading a picture book with bright colours and mirror pages. As Flick became drowsy, Ginny took her next door to the nursery and whispered her child slowly to sleep.

When she emerged after half an hour, she could hear Julie downstairs speaking to Stephen, telling some raucous story that involved 'Christmas' and 'drunken'. She would leave her to it, let her friend enjoy chatting to the partner for whom she affected disdain but whom she truly cherished. Ginny smiled and went into her study, turning on the desk-light.

There it was: the completed manuscript, copy-edited and ready to go to the printers. The words had come easily to her in the end, the glacier of her prose finally melting in the heat of all her emotions. She wrote many thousands of words a day, tore up whole chapters, revised, rewrote, kept at it, working longer hours than she had believed possible. Her writing was no longer so dry: it became more confident, often too enthusiastic so that she had to revisit a passage and restore order to it. But the ideas flowed easily, the footnotes becoming less important than the drive of the argument, the presence of her personality and of her convictions in the pages. It was what she thought, what she believed, and if others disagreed – well, so be it. This was from the heart, as well as the head. The book would be published by an academic imprint in hardback and then – if it prospered – by one of the larger London houses in paperback. After much pacing, some inner turmoil and a few exasperated phone calls from her editor, she had finally settled on the title she now read on the typescript's cover: *Bluebeard's Child: the Meaning of Fairy Tales and the Conquest of Fear*.

She sat in the deep leather armchair, and looked around the room. Well, it was a start. She could do more here, write more, read in the hours that motherhood left to her, and perhaps make something approaching a living. All that, so much of it, lay in the future. A future no longer defined by her own anxieties and hopes, but by her dreams for the child sleeping next door.

On the wall above the little mantelpiece was the picture: a pencil drawing of a woman reading, one hand under her chin, absorbed by her book and deep in thought. The picture of herself that she had thrown on to the rubbish pile in the garden more than a year ago. And then, one summer morning, as she went out to remove a jammed envelope from the letter box, there it was: wrapped in clear plastic, laid quietly against the door of the cottage during the night. No letter, or note: none needed. She knew what the return of the gift meant. It was its own message.

At first, she was full of dread. With a feeling of hollowness in her stomach, she remembered, with shocking clarity, another picture: the oil painting in his drawing room that showed a man in a cape seizing a small child and whisking her away from her garden. On the frame written in a hasty black brush-stroke had been the title: *Grand Meaulnes*. That night, in her panic, she took down her battered copy of Alain-Fournier's novel from the shelf, and read the half-remembered passage:

'I could see that the child had at last found the companion she had been unconsciously waiting for . . . I could see that *le grand Meaulnes* had come to take back the one joy he had left me. And already I pictured him, in the night, wrapping his daughter in a cloak, to carry her off with him on some new adventure.'

She had slept on the floor of the nursery, sobbing silently, filled with terror that his return could mean only one thing.

And yet in the pale light of dawn she had realised that she was wrong. That she had mistaken the return of Sean for the return of Alex. And she had never known Alex. Nor, in truth, Sean, for there was no Sean. The man next door had been someone else: the ghost of a frightened child, an adult living behind a mask, drawn out by a longing for love and sent back into hiding by the demons of a terrible past. But Helena Warren was right. Her nephew was a gentle man. It was not in his character, or his power, to take the child away from its mother, or to hurt either of them in any way. The return of the picture was not a warning but an offering: the best he could do. This is the best I can do, what I drew for you. I survived again, I still exist. Do not forget. Remember me by this.

There was a kink in the rug: it looked like the swell of the sea, lapping against the pebbled shore. She thought of the rocky cove, the water rushing into its depths, as if to retrieve its dark secrets or to bury them more deeply. The voices of sorrowful children and those they had left behind, consumed by the wretched roar of the wind and the cry of the gulls. The blackness of blood. A figure, dark and trembling, looking out to the distant silhouette of a deserted sea fort, then above to the looming presence of two ancient towers. Keep away, the spires said, hour after hour, day after day, year after year. Stay away from this place, stay away from these desecrated rocks.

After a while, she glanced at her watch and thought it was time to make a light supper. There was washing to be done, and some preparations for the morning. What should they do tomorrow, though? She must ask Julie. She put the typescript into its folder, picked up a book that was lying on the floor, and, looking back one last time, as if to check on something, turned off the light.

ACKNOWLEDGEMENTS

I would like to thank the Warden and Fellows of All Souls College for their generous hospitality when I was writing sections of this novel.

Warmest thanks as ever to my agent, Peter Robinson. At Hodder, the wonderful Sue Fletcher was more patient and supportive than I deserved: thanks, too, to her colleagues Karen Geary, Swati Gamble and Sarah Christie.

I owe a great debt to a number of friends who helped in different ways: Johnnie and Sarah Standing, Dylan Jones, Neil Midgley, Deb Khan, John and Louise Patten, Tamzin Lightwater and all my *Spectator* colleagues, and – for light and laughter – Nikki Bedi.

I send my love to the growing d'Ancona clan. Most of all, I want to thank my beloved sons who make everything possible: Teddy, to whom this novel is dedicated, and Zac, who has already booked up the next one.

The Old Forge
Victoria Park
August 2008